Locked Up

GB Williams

To Lowri

Enjoy. & Thanks.

Gail
Williams.

For Jonathan, Conner and Tyrell
For putting up with, joining in with
and encouraging the crazy

Chapter 1

Every breath felt like scorched iron. His heart fluttered, defibrillated. Hot urine flooded his groin.

Tommy knew fear, having spent most of his life afraid. Oddly, prison was the one place he usually felt secure. Until now. Never much good in a fight, he made himself useful to those who were. He wasn't the smartest man on the block, but he could tell who was. His allies kept him safe.

Now weak and fallen, he watched the sharp thing thrust into his belly, and the flow of blood he couldn't stop. As the light darkened, he looked up at the figure looming over him.

His murderer.

With the blood, all aggression, anger, and fear poured out of him. In that last second of life, Tommy experienced the only moment of peace on earth he had ever known.

Chapter 2

The lockdown began shortly after breakfast. Charlie lay on the top bunk staring at the ceiling with only the weak illumination of a waning sun for company. Strips of light from the barred window crawled slowly across the room. In a different world, he might have reached up and made shadow faces for his son, but not today, not with Oscar so far away. *That's how I want it*, Charlie lied to himself.

The sharp, metallic retort of the viewing panel in the cell door being pulled back announced the guards were checking on him, probably checking on everyone. Even though the prison was full to bursting, and this cell could hold two, for the last four days Charlie had enjoyed being the only occupant, the other inmates having little desire to share with someone they still considered the enemy. The view cover slammed shut, metal scraped against metal, and the sound of the key in the lock filled the cell.

Frowning, wondering what he'd done to deserve such attention, Charlie raised his head to watch the door open, but otherwise remained still. The door swung in to reveal Officer Robbins. Bulked up from too much gym time, the ape-like man nearly filled the doorway. *Looks like a real knuckle dragger*, Charlie thought, except he knew Robbins wasn't as dumb as he liked people to think.

Behind him, almost hidden by the man's greater width, stood Officer Teddington. At five-seven, the quality of her figure was hard to determine beneath the unflattering uniform. Her dark hair was always pinned back, and her face free of make-up. No muscle-woman, she looked more like a negotiator than a fighter, but she was more than capable of handling herself. Just two weeks ago a new arrival had tried manhandling her. Charlie had watched, ready to spring into action if necessary, but a swift defensive elbow jab to the nose had her attacker's eyes watering, his head down, and his respect levels way up.

Every time Charlie looked at Teddington, he saw a puzzle. She talked to him like he was human. Not only him to be honest, she treated everyone fairly. She understood prison wasn't about being punished inside, but that being inside was the punishment. She knew where to draw the line.

Charlie didn't know why any woman would want to be a prison officer, or why the Ministry of Justice thought female officers in a male prison were a good idea, but he was hardly in a position to influence the decision, or, at this point, even disagree with it. Not to mention she was easier on the eye than any of her colleagues, even the other female ones. Or perhaps that was just Charlie's view; there'd been something about her from the start. When she processed him into Whitewalk, she was the first person to treat him with some common courtesy after his arrest.

Of course, generally, he had the same problem with the screws as he did with the inmates; in a world of 'them' and 'us,' both sides considered him 'them.'

'Stay put, Bell,' Robbins commanded.

Charlie was about to point out he wasn't moving, when Teddington's hard look and small head shake stopped him.

'We need to search your cell,' Teddington added in monotone. 'Don't move. Don't get in the way.'

Why? It had to be related to the lockdown. He didn't know what had caused it. Being an outsider on the inside, few would talk to him so he expected to be the last to find out, but whatever was going on, it wasn't sounding good so far.

Teddington stayed by the door and Robbins began the search. Not that there was much to go through. The room was roughly eleven feet by six, door at the narrow end, window opposite. The bunk beds took up most of the floor space, although there was a small table, a chair and two lockers – all in regulation boring grey, stainless steel sink and toilet unit in the back corner. Given the lack of space, it was little surprise Robbins wanted him to stay put. The two of them would pretty much have filled the room. It was only a cursory search, and when he was done, Robbins stood against the outer wall beneath the window and shook his head. Teddington held her silence, but her gaze switched to Charlie. He saw nothing in her eyes, nothing. No warmth, no coldness. No hate, no affection. Absolute indifference. It was chilling.

'Down.'

Frowning at the single word command, Charlie unlinked his hands from behind his head and carefully twisted his body until he was sitting on the edge of the top bunk. With slow control, he used his arms to lower his feet to the floor. Standing facing the long wall, the officers either side of him, Charlie glanced from one to the other.

'Legs spread, arms wide.' The order came from Robbins.

There was no obvious reason for a pat down, so Charlie faced Teddington before he complied, outstretched his hands easily touched each side of the cell, so he had to keep his elbows bent as he offered her the option to run her hands over him. He smiled, part invitation, part dare, all mockery. Certain she had a wry sense of humour, he wondered how far could he push her.

He'd served three years and he'd only known her to pat down five men - all complete queens – men who didn't care for a woman's touch. She or Robbins would tell him to turn around any second now. In the second surprise of the day, Teddington stepped forward, running her hands down each of his arms in turn and down his sides, over his chest. Then her hands smoothed around his waist, checking for anything hidden in the waistband of his jeans. Her touch moved up his back, bringing her up close and personal. She tipped her chin up to look at him; the coldness of her eyes took away any potential invitation. As she reached his shoulder blades, he recognised the scent she carried: Fresh apples. *Yum.*

Then she crouched, checking he had no weaponry in his trousers. The sight of her kneeling before him assaulted his imagination with ideas he had forced aside for years. Images crowded his head, and heat pooled in the most inconvenient way. Then her hands were running down his legs, first one, then the other.

He was feeling at a distinct disadvantage, and he didn't like that. Time to see how far he could push her. 'Wanna feel the crown jewels, babe?'

She was standing now, though at six-four he easily overshadowed her. Her eyes shifted over his shoulder, but he knew she wouldn't be able to see Robbins, nor would Robbins see her, Charlie stood taller than both. Her eyes shifted back to his, not that there was anything there to see. Whatever she was thinking, she was hiding it well. With the same steady look, she grabbed his crotch. His eyes widened and his breath caught. The grip eased, turned more intimate, teasing as she ran her hand slowly over his hardening length. Oh, dear God, he was in trouble.

'I've had better.'

Behind him, Robbins sniggered, and for the first time, Charlie wondered if Robbins was the 'better' Teddington had had. He just as quickly dismissed that idea.

Robbins grabbed his still outstretched arm and forced him back, spine against the bunks then down to sitting, pushing past him to get out of the cell. Teddington flattened her chest against the top bunk, pushing her hips into the gap between the beds to give Robbins room to pass. As soon as he did, Charlie stood.

Robbins stood at the door, but Charlie concentrated on Teddington.

'You, Bell,' she spoke carefully, 'are scum.'

He heard no inflection in her voice; she was simply stating a fact. That she called him Bell was a worry, since she usually addressed him as Charlie. They weren't friends – they couldn't be – but right now there was a wall between them he didn't understand.

'Not because you're in here. Not because you killed a man. Not even because you're a bent copper. You're scum because you refuse to see your own son.' She withdrew something from her pocket, threw it on his bunk. The folded papers automatically opened up a little and he could see bright crayon images as drawn by a five-year-old. He kept his eyes on the papers, but his heart and mind were rebelling. This didn't make sense.

'Bleeding heart.' The scoff was from Robbins.

'No, just a mother.'

Teddington was focused on Charlie. Robbins couldn't see her face, and now, her expression was less glare, more hesitation, nervousness even. He frowned, his look questioning. Swallowing, she composed herself and turned smartly on her heel. Then, the officers were gone. The door slammed, like a coffin lid. He was alone. Again.

Teddington was wrong. He wasn't refusing to see his own son. True, he didn't want the boy to see the inside of a jail – not for any reason, not even as a visitor. However, the real reason Oscar couldn't come was because his mother wouldn't bring him. Cathy had never offered. She wouldn't ever apply for a visitor pass. Hell, she wouldn't even write and let him know Oscar was okay. His letters out were returned as 'addressee unknown.' Their three-month relationship had been flawed from the get-go. If it weren't for Oscar he would happily forget that whole period in his life. Having met when she was working at a drug rehab facility, they'd both been trying to help the same kid. Being together had felt good at the start. But, he'd kept secrets, and was too late in finding out she had too.

Whatever Cathy might once have felt for him had turned to hate, so much so, she'd kept her pregnancy from him. When he found out, she tried to keep the baby from him, too. He had had to go to court for the right to see his own son. For a little over a year, he had enjoyed those visitation rights just as often as she would let him, which wasn't often enough. Then, another court case had put an end to that by sending him here.

Charlie's frown deepened.

He glanced to the closed door. Never mind past problems, it seemed there were present problems to deal with. Something was wrong. Teddington wasn't acting like Teddington.

Carefully, he reached for the papers. Dragging them with him as he sank to the lower bunk, he opened up the quarter folds. The top picture near broke his heart. A line of green at the bottom, a line of blue at the top, a yellow disk in the top right. Standing on the green band were two stick figures, one labelled *Daddy*, and one, *Me*. He didn't know Oscar could write. A lump lodged in his dry throat.

He moved to the next picture. *Daddy and Me*, and a house. He turned to the next, but this time, it wasn't a drawing that caught his attention. It was the small ripped scrap of paper folded into the centre of it.

'Something's rotten in the state of Denmark. Need your help.'

Chapter 3

Teddington bit down on the inside of her lips to keep them compressed. Embarrassment and confusion warred through her. *What is wrong with me?* Grabbing a man's crotch was something she'd never done in her private life. At work, it was an act so unprofessional if Charlie or Robbins reported her, she would be on a warning, possibly lose her job. She was already on thin ice for elbowing that scrote a couple of weeks ago.

Her insides were knotting and quaking. She dragged in a deep breath and let reality overtake her. The scent of battery-farmed men really wasn't pleasant. She controlled her features. *Carry on. Business as usual.*

'What was that?' Robbins demanded as he locked Charlie inside again.

'Pat down,' *Be calm.* 'As ordered.' *Business as usual.*

Only business wasn't as usual, no matter the veneer they were trying to put on it. All the vague menace and lurking threats she had been trying to convince herself weren't real had stepped out of the shadows and killed a man. Killed a man. Right here. Inside HMP Blackmarch. That had never happened before.

According to the bosses it hadn't happened this time either.

'I meant whatever you gave Bell?' Robbins faced her, closer than she cared for, but she wasn't about to be cowed.

'Kid's drawings. There was a harassed young mother having to deal with a son who didn't want to leave without seeing his daddy. A man refusing to see him. To help calm the kid I said I'd pass the pictures to his father.' She shrugged. 'Meant to pass them on ages ago, but forgot.' She turned slightly, hoped her mask of calm was intact, and indicated the next cell. 'Shall we?'

As Robbins unlocked the door, she swallowed.

The menace was out of the shadows, but the killer had stepped straight back into them. Looking at her colleague's back, his bulk worried her. For the first time, she was seeing him as a threat. She glanced around – on the ground floor beneath them, the second floor above – she saw other pairs of officers searching those floors. None of them knew what they were looking for – scrub that – one of them might know what they were looking for and they'd therefore know where not to look.

Bile bubbled and burned through her. These were people she knew, the men and women she should trust, but she couldn't, not now.

She glanced at Charlie's cell door. Why did she instinctively trust him? She'd thought being able to fetch those drawings had been a bonus. Now, she chewed her lip. It could be the biggest mistake of her career. Robbins was telling the next lot they were to do a search. She stepped in behind him. *Business as usual.*

* * *

Charlie stared at the scrap in his hand. *What is with the Hamlet quote?* Like most people he knew it was a tale of murder and betrayal, but that was about all.

Stomach gurgling, he checked his watch. Lunch time. He stared to the door; it remained obstinately shut.

Why would Teddington send him such a message?

His mind and stomach still churned a couple of hours later when the door finally unlocked and Teddington said he could go to get food, as she moved to unlock the next cell.

'Tommy Walters.'

He heard the name whispered along the line. He knew Tommy, a skinny little runt in for possession with intent to supply. Tommy had managed to find ways to continue to supply inside; it was probably what saved him being beaten every night and used as a sucker to those who wanted to cop off. Until today, when he had caused the lock down.

''e used enough to top 'imself.'

Charlie frowned at that.

'Nah, he stuck himself with a screwdriver from the engineering workshop.'

'I 'eard it was a sharpened trowel from the gardens.'

It was impossible for Charlie to know which rumour was true; it literally depended on who he believed. Charlie based his belief on trust, and he didn't trust any of the men around him. He took the food tray and found an empty seat at a table. Most men chose to eat in their cells; for once, he made a different choice.

Charlie looked up and saw Teddington. She was walking the first-floor landing, making sure those coming from or going to their cells were aware of constant observation. He must have been watching her too long. She looked down and their eyes met. He nodded just once.

If she had any reaction to the acknowledgement, she didn't show it. She simply looked away and carried on her rounds; same old, same old. He, on the other hand, felt punched in the guts. With her brown hair always scraped back in an unflattering bun, Teddington's mouth looked too flat and unsmiling, her nose sharp, and her brown eyes had no distinction, except sometimes, they did. There was something about her. Something –

'You getting a boner for Teddington now?'

Charlie switched his attention from the guard to the gnarled man opposite. Baker was in for a five stretch; Charlie had known him for ten years.

'Hey Teddington!' Baker tipped his head up to call.

Now Charlie looked up too. Teddington had stopped, her ringless hands on the rail. She didn't say anything, but her attention was on Baker. Everyone else's attention was on the exchange.

'Charlie boy here was wondering if you would be his Teddy-bare tonight.'

This wasn't the first time someone had used sexual innuendo against Teddington, and she was both used to it and untouched by it.

'Sure, in his dreams.'

The crowd laughed.

She clasped her hands behind her back and continued her slow pace around the landing, as if the interruption had never happened.

Charlie bore the ribald exchange without comment, knowing full well Teddington would be putting up with just as much, both from inmates and her officer mates.

Turning, he looked at Baker. *49 going on 65*. Baker's love for the Costa Del Crime had resulted in skin like leather, and a near pathological hatred of dentists had left his teeth – what remained of them – crooked and yellow-brown. His old blue eyes laughed at Charlie. Charlie let his eyes wander up to the first floor. Teddington wasn't within view. His eyes drifted back to Baker. Some things didn't change. Baker's eyes were crinkled around his smile. Charlie knew that look. Baker had intel to hand across.

'Not now,' Charlie told the man.

Dumping his food, Charlie paced back to his cell, ensuring the journey took him past Teddington. Each maintained an indifferent manner; as they passed he said, 'I'm in.'

She didn't pause, didn't react.

Back in his cell, he checked the note. He *hadn't* imagined it, someone was asking for his help. It wasn't Robbins' hand writing; his was too blocky. It had to be Teddington. The delivery system, if nothing else, showed that.

His last cellmate had covered the wall between the bunks in pictures of topless women. Earlier Charlie had removed a few of those and used the sticky tack to put up the kid's drawings on the wall by his bunk. Standing beside the bed, elbows on the thin mattress, he looked at those images now. *Daddy and Me*. A family scene he would love to buy into, but things with Cathy were beyond repair and Oscar barely knew him. They were probably better off without him, but when he got out he was going to know his son whatever that woman thought of him.

He heard slow, measured footsteps on the landing. It was only ever the screws who walked like that.

'Teddington?' The call was soft as she walked past. Taking one step back to put her central to the doorway, she turned on her heel and stepped up to the door.

'Charlie.'

Now he had her attention, he wasn't sure what to say.

Her eyes darted nervously, checking the corridor.

'What's going on?'

Her breath was overly controlled, her stance full of stress rather than regimented posture. He knew uncertainty when he saw it.

He turned to her, stepped closer. 'You asked for my help.'

For a moment she closed her eyes, swallowing. When she looked up again, he saw the apprehension. She was stuck; he could see it. Between a cliff and a crag, and terrified it was all about to come crashing down on her. He knew that feeling.

'Forget it.'

'Not a chance,' the dark statement held her back when she shifted. 'Is this about Tommy?'

'Don't.'

This time her look was as dark as the warning.

'I'm not that easily put off.'

Her regard was steady, but the slight frown gave her concerns away. Her lips parted, and for a fleeting moment, he saw need. 'Tommy committed suicide.'

He didn't believe that statement any more than she did. 'Don't lie to me, Teddington. And don't think I can't spot a lie a mile off. I'm used to it. I was a cop, remember?'

'And now you're a murderer.' Her eyes widened, like she couldn't believe she'd said that. He wasn't sure he could believe she'd said it, either.

Her eyes dipped then slipped to the side. She froze; he suspected she saw something he couldn't. When she looked up again her eyes were clear, her posture altered, but it was just for show.

'What's wrong, Charlie boy?' This time, her voice was softer and lower, as she took a single step inside. Her voice wouldn't carry beyond the grey peeling walls of this one cell. If he was interpreting right, she was flirting. *What's going on?*

'Not sure how to ask to see Teddy-bare? You desperate to deliver that impressive package?'

It wasn't just what she said, or the way she said it. It was the way she looked. Her eyes had darkened, she had licked her lips, and she was smiling. God, she was actually sexy under all those masculine clothes. And she thought he had an impressive package, one which was busy crowding his jeans again. She lowered her lashes, blatantly staring at his groin. The murmur of appreciation was primal and suggestive, and hardened him to the point of pain.

Caught off-guard, his reaction was instant and insistent. In acting the siren, she had become one. *How sexy would she be if she really wanted it?* He'd not really thought of her that way, but now, he couldn't think of anything else. She thought he had an impressive package? She brought her eyes back up. The instinct to reach for her was almost too much.

She grabbed the door and pulled it shut as she stepped back out.

'What is up with you lately?'

The door clanged, the scrap of the key told him it was locked. That last harsh demand had been Robbins'. Whatever game Teddington was playing, it was a dangerous one. Locked up here, there was nothing he could do about her situation right now. He peered down at himself. Nothing he could do about her situation, but there was something he could do about his.

Chapter 4

Charlie contemplated the slop on his plate. *How does anyone make porridge even more uninteresting than porridge already is?* He was tempted to admire the kitchen's achievement. Instead, he sat at the grey table in his grey room and felt … grey.

Yesterday evening's physical relief had done nothing to ease his knotted thoughts. He did not consider himself very good at very much, but he knew people. He knew Teddington. Absently stirring the slop, he worried about her. For three years, she had been calm professionalism personified, but not yesterday.

'Still thinking about your Teddy-bare?'

Charlie focused on Baker, slouching in his doorway.

'Thinking about bacon and eggs,' he said the first thing that came to mind. 'Sausage and tomato.'

'Add black pudding and you might just have a decent breakfast,' Baker said, as he stepped inside, wincing disparagingly at the glutinous mass on the plate before he sat down. 'Which that is not. So,' he looked Charlie up and down, 'you interested in what's going on out there?' The too old head nodded towards the door. 'Or you keeping to your state of splendid isolation?'

Letting the plastic spoon fall into the bowl, Charlie sighed, sat back, and looked at Baker. 'Anything interesting enough to break isolation for?'

Baker's eyebrows rose in a quizzical, comic book expression. Inside his head, Charlie added the honker sound effect. 'Tommy Walters is dead. You don't think that's interesting?'

Of course, he did, but he knew better than to show his hand. 'Official word is, he topped himself.'

Baker huffed a sigh and stood, slouching back towards the door. There, he twisted back, almost sneering at Charlie. 'You know, I remember a time when you used to listen to the unofficial word and had the balls to make up your own mind. Prison hasn't changed you for the better.'

Staring at the now-empty doorway, Charlie had to agree. He had changed, and it wasn't an improvement. Some days, he couldn't even face himself in the mirror. Slowly, his eyes drifted down. He might be a mess, but not as much of a mess as the porridge. The chair scraped on the floor as he stood, returning the offering to the kitchen for washing. Let them deal with the concrete mess; his stomach couldn't.

The things Baker had said played on his mind. Remaining safe these last three years had meant staying out of trouble, keeping his nose clean by not inserting it into other people's business. The bowl clanged down with the others and Charlie drifted to the notice board. He had requested time in the gym, but didn't expect to get any. Running his eyes down the list, his own name jumped out at him – not on the gym list, but on gardening detail. Still, he had plenty of time before it started. In no particular hurry, he wandered back towards the stair, past Baker's ground floor cell. The man was leaning against the door jamb. As Charlie approached, he raised one eyebrow in query to the older man. That was enough. Baker shifted to step from his cell, and as they passed, the exchange was made as easily as ever.

It was probably stupid, but Charlie felt like something inside him had woken up. *Is it possible I've missed solving puzzles?* For the first time in a long time, Charlie felt the thrill of the chase. He quickly tamped it down.

Sitting on the chair in his own room, he grabbed a book from the shelf and opened it, using it as cover to unfold the note from Baker.

TW Hero OD. Belly stab. Unknown sharp.

Closing the book, the note inside, Charlie placed his elbows on the table, put his hands together and leaned on them. None of it made sense.

Deciding to let his unconscious mull it over, Charlie stripped off his shirt and swapped his jeans for joggers, then started exercising. Sit ups, dips, press ups, squats, the plank, T-stands. Sixteen reps, three repeats, three circuits. Concentrating on his workout allowed his mind to mull over what he knew about Tommy's death until the discrepancy was that last idea standing. Tommy had been a dealer and a stoner, but he didn't use heroin, didn't even like needles. *And what exactly was the sharp implement?* The lack of reference was strange. *How could they not know what the sharp was?* It didn't make sense.

Something was rotten in the state alright, but not Denmark, here, inside HMP Blackmarch – though everyone referred to it as Whitewalk. Was someone really trying to tell him one of the guards was corrupt? Why was he, of all people, struggling to believe that? He'd been a cop, for God's sake. That hadn't saved him from a downward slide.

He was on the last set of dips when footsteps stopped outside his door. His hands gripped the rounded bar of the lower bunk, as he controlled his triceps in the down stroke. So, someone had stopped; it would either be to mock or insult. He'd made it clear in the first week of being here he wasn't anyone's bitch or bodyguard. He was big enough not to need a gang and any that tried to impress him usually ended up pressing wounds to stem the blood flow. So, Charlie took no notice of the intruder, as he kept his gaze forward, watching the wall, and pushing through the muscle burn. His peripheral vision told him his visitor wore black trousers – a guard.

Sanchez, this time.

Charlie carried on. He'd never had trouble from Sanchez; there was no reason to expect any now. He was on the return lift when Sanchez's hand landed on his shoulder, keeping him at the painful halfway point. Sanchez was no roid head, but he was strong. Charlie had no option but to stay where he was. To go down would be submission, to fight would mean defeat and removal of privileges. So, he remained stationary, no matter how his triceps screamed.

'You were disrespectful to one of my colleagues yesterday.'

Listening to the East End accent, the clear pronunciation almost felt incongruent. Charlie grit his teeth. What was really incongruent though, was hearing London and seeing the Iberian Peninsula. He decided not to highlight it was actually Baker who'd been disrespectful; no point in prolonging this torture.

'It's not to happen again.' The words were intoned with quiet menace. 'Understand?'

His teeth clenched against the lactic acid burn. 'Yes.' Charlie kept as still as his twitching muscles would allow him. Sanchez didn't move. 'Sir.' Only once the uniform disappeared did Charlie allow himself to collapse to the floor.

Chapter 5

Charlie stood in line behind the eleven other men on gardening detail. As the others had before him, he passively spread for the pat down, before being allowed through the external door. The stench assaulted him before he'd even stepped through. Manure. Moving into the next queue, he quietly waited for Robbins to hand out his assignment. The twisted grin Robbins showed before he spoke confirmed the assumption of what Charlie was going to spend his time doing. Shit shovelling. Great.

From Robbins, he moved over to the tool shed, where he found Teddington handing out – and getting signatures for – their assigned equipment. Last in line, Charlie found himself alone inside with her. Like all the others, he told her his assignment, but before she turned, he added, 'What was the sharp?'

Fear flickered in Teddington's eyes, but she blinked, readjusted her jaw and it was gone.

'I told you to forget it,' she hissed.

'I told you I can't.'

Her lips compressed, but as she drew in a breath, he watched her brown eyes gather steel. 'Okay.'

He waited, sure that there was more to the simple response than just agreement with his statement.

'And I don't know.'

She picked up a spade and pointed to the page for him to sign it out. Leaning forward, he whispered, 'I got Sanchez's message.' As he took the spade, he was surprised by the confusion in Teddington's captivating eyes.

Outside, all he had to do was follow his nose. The fresh manure released new steaming wafts every time he thrust the spade in.

Already pumped from the earlier workout, his muscles started to strain to all the hard work of digging the fertiliser into the clay-based soil. While he found the work physically exhausting, sweat soon soaking his clothes, it gave him plenty of time to think.

Tommy was a supplier, working for Keen, the wing boss, Category B. Keen ran a lot on the wing, including who got on the cleaning detail and got to go to the gym. There was no official sanction for such controls, of course. Officially, all privileges were for each inmate to apply for and the screws to permit. What could be controlled was who applied, and a swift jab to the kidneys soon got the 'unwanted' message across. For Charlie, it had been the guy on the treadmill beside him constantly spitting in his direction. Now, Charlie and Keen had a standoff agreement. Keen didn't bother Charlie, Charlie didn't bother Keen. The garden duty, however, was the province of relative new boy – Winehouse, the Garden Godfather.

Winehouse had been in possession of the garden for pretty much as long as anyone could remember. When Keen had arrived, he had quickly taken over every other part of the community, but he had stopped at the garden and no one quite knew why. But Winehouse was ambitious; the garden wouldn't be enough much longer.

Pushing the spade into the worked soil, Charlie stood, as if trying to catch his breath, while taking in the people around him. Eleven other inmates surrounded him, but only nine were working. Robbins and Teddington were in different areas doing their work, watching the men and ensuring compliance. Neither did or said anything about Winehouse sitting, relaxing, lording over his estate as his bodyguard, Paul, stood at his shoulder. Everyone keeping the state of status quo. Taking up the spade again, he resumed digging. *Why am I here?* He was no more in Winehouse's camp than he was Keen's. He'd never expressed an interest in gardening, though he found even his assigned task a relief from the monotony of grey cell walls.

Charlie resumed his digging at he tried to envisage the bigger picture. Tommy was a supplier, but Keen controlled most of the drug supply inside, because Tommy worked for Keen. Not that it would stop Winehouse getting his hands-on drugs if he wanted them.

'You can stop now.'

Charlie dug the spade into the diminished heap, before he turned to face Teddington. Using the back of his wrist, he wiped sweat from his brow to stop it dripping into his eyes.

'Tommy was murdered.' Though breathing hard, he kept his voice down.

'Not according to official reports.'

An amoeba could see it, so why would they cover it up?

Reputations. Charlie couldn't remember the exact statistics, but he knew murder within the prison system was extremely rare, a handful at most; five in a year in the whole country was considered a bad show. No unit wanted that on their patch. It was obvious why the top dogs would want to cover it up. But, clearly, Teddington didn't feel the same. Now wasn't the time to call her on it.

'Tommy never worked in the garden.'

The smallest shake said no. 'Records disagree.'

Which meant one of the screws was covering up. That was the rotten thing about this state prison. He reasoned that was probably Teddington's motive, too. She was a good person; she wouldn't turn a blind eye to a murderer.

'How did you get garden detail?'

The question was completely out of left field, and Charlie blinked. 'You don't know?'

He watched the slight frown mar her forehead. The expression didn't last.

'You applied for gym yesterday, I booked in for the afternoon.'

'Never happened.' Even though the schedule would have been after the lockdown ended, his name hadn't been on the list.

'I'll look into that.' She paused, glancing around, but only her eyes moved.

Charlie gave a single, silent nod.

'What was Sanchez's message?'

An involuntary intake of breath revealed his surprise at that question. He had assumed she knew. 'That I'm to be more respectful to you.'

Her brow drew together. 'I wasn't aware of you being disrespectful.'

He moved closer. 'You don't know what I was thinking last night.'

Her eyes dilated, and she swallowed. That slight smile appeared again.

'Hate to tell you this, but sweat and manure do not make an enticing combination.' Then, she walked casually away.

Charlie watched her. She was trying not to swing her hips, but she couldn't stop it entirely. He hadn't noticed before what a good rear she had.

Feeling he was being watched, Charlie looked down the garden to Winehouse. *Talking of rear ends.* Charlie grabbed the spade and sauntered over to where Winehouse lounged in his chair, surveying his kingdom. As he unofficially ran the garden, he didn't do the hard graft, and at this time of year, it was pretty much all hard graft.

The older man watched Charlie approach, sending his bodyguard away when Charlie neared. He stopped two steps from Winehouse; it conveyed a level of respect he wasn't feeling, but he needed to avoid looking like a threat. This constituted sufficient distance that any attack would be seen coming, and, therefore, was the perfect compromise.

'Was there something you wanted?'

Winehouse shrugged. 'I needed a strong back, you wanted a workout you couldn't get. Much better out here in the fresh air, than that stuffy gym.'

'Not a permanent arrangement, then?'

'Could be.' Winehouse looked him up and down, a critical assessment.

Charlie fell back on his years in the force to remain impassive.

'Come closer.'

'I've been reliably informed I stink.'

This time, Winehouse smiled. 'The aroma of fertilizer surrounds us all. Come closer.' Over his shoulder, Winehouse instructed Paul to fetch another chair. What arrived was a folding stool of unknown origin.

Charlie decided to plant the spade into the nearest raised bed, before he moved closer to Winehouse. He squatted to the low stool, which creaked worryingly, and, of course, left his head much lower than Winehouse's.

'I believe you were a cop.'

Hearing nothing but a statement, Charlie did not respond.

'What was your rank?'

Charlie took his time answering. 'Detective Sergeant.'

'Were you any good?'

Charlie's gaze switched to the muscle man behind them. 'Good enough to put Paul there in here.'

Winehouse smiled, leaned slightly forward, and kept his voice low. 'Not the sharpest tool in the box, but he has his uses.' Then, he sat back. 'You heard what happened to Tommy? Of course, you heard,' Winehouse answered his own question. 'Everyone's talking about it.'

Charlie watched Winehouse silently.

'I want you to find out how he did it.'

'Tommy?'

'No.' Winehouse scowled. '*Keen.*' He looked up at one of the other men mixing the manure into the soil. 'That's Benny York,' Winehouse told him needlessly. 'He thinks I don't know he runs to Keen with every tidbit he gleans from me.'

Charlie had always considered York a weasel, knowing he was playing both sides. 'So, why keep him around?'

'Because he tells me anything he finds out from Keen. Naturally, most of what he passes on is misinformation, in both directions. Keen will know within five minutes you've been talking to me.' Winehouse refocused his attention on Charlie. 'You help me, and time in the garden is only one of the privileges I can bestow.'

Chapter 6

A quick shower later, Charlie stood quietly in the dinner line. Feet at shoulder width, knees unlocked, hands relaxed at his sides, he could stand like this for hours. As a young PC, he occasionally had. Now, he just waited and kept quiet, listening to the murmur of voices, wondering if anything would be said worth homing in on. The jungle drums were oddly silent on the matter of Tommy Walters. That silence was broken by the rhythmic thunder-falls of Richard Hightower's steps; Charlie couldn't miss that approaching lumber.

Ricky the Runt. The least appropriately named man Charlie had ever encountered. He was taller than Charlie, which was remarkable in itself. Charlie wasn't used to physically looking up at other people. The man stood tall, wide and scary, like a bouncer, though his actions tended more towards breaker. He approached and leaned towards Charlie.

'Keen's cell, soon as you're finished.'

Charlie didn't turn to face the big black man, nor verbally acknowledge the order. Without comment or inflection, he watched Runt move to the front on the line and barge in. No one was stupid enough to try stopping him. Charlie stood, waited, and when the line moved a step forward, he followed suit.

The chatter died down. He could feel each furtive glance shot his way. The line shuffled along; people watched him. He took his tray, got served and sat to eat; most people took their trays back to their cells. Usually that was his choice, too, but if the monkeys wanted to watch, he could bear that. The weight of their observation felt different. The distrust was still there, but it had an added piquancy of curiosity. Today's mystery meat was, well, a mystery. It swam in an inconsistent gravy that didn't taste of anything amongst slushy lumps that might once have been vegetables. He missed *al dente* vegetables. A rare steak. Hell, any steak. In no hurry to enjoy such delights, he took his time eating, the wary gaze of the general population began to smother him. There was a question that wasn't being whispered, but that he heard on every bated breath.

Which side will he choose?

He didn't want to choose a side. He wanted the maintain the status quo, to continue keeping his head down, to get through his time quietly and without incident. Uncertain if the meal was tasteless because it was tasteless, or because he couldn't taste it, he shifted it around, seeking inspiration. Six months. That was all he had to go. He sucked on a lump of something that disintegrated in his mouth. He was nearly halfway through his stretch. Reach that milestone, and he was eligible for parole. He could get out. Getting mixed up with prisoner politics was unlikely to bring freedom forward.

No matter his reluctance to engage with prison life, there was a limit to how long any meal could be dragged out, so eventually, Charlie had to return his plate, and head back to the landing. Inclining his head, he saw Teddington patrolling, but he didn't catch her eye. *Perhaps, it's for the best.* He paced between the tables, the watching eyes burning into his back. He stopped on the first landing, went to his cell. There was an almost audible intake of breath from the men below.

From the small cupboard, he withdrew his wash bag, noting with relief his hands were steady as a rock. The tap had its usual momentary pause on the first quarter turn, then, feebly spat a steady trickle. He squeezed a pea-sized lump of toothpaste on the brush bristles and ran it under the flow. Head down, he leaned over the sink and brushed.

'What's going on?'

Charlie forced himself not to react. Unlike Runt, Teddington had managed to creep up on him. She kept her tone low to keep their conversation private.

'Why's everyone watching your every move?'

'Keen wants to see me.' Charlie straightened, peering at her in the mirror as she stood at the cell door, and spoke around his toothbrush.

She considered his words, and gave the slightest of nods. 'Makes sense.'

'Really?' The word bubbled through a mouthful of foam.

'Winehouse spoke to you this afternoon,' she noted. 'Makes sense Keen wants your attention this evening.'

'Makes no sense to me.'

Again, he watched as Teddington broke one of her rules. Her breaths were too deep and slow to be normal. She was controlling her breathing, trying to make everything seem normal, when, clearly, it wasn't. She stepped into the cell alone. This, it wasn't just one of her rules. He was pretty sure it was a general regulation for all the guards not to enter a cell alone. He kept his eyes fixed on the mirror as she bridged the distance between them. If someone had been in the cell directly across from them, they would have seen everything.

She watched as he rinsed. 'The note?'

Charlie looked meaningfully at the basic metal toilet. 'Shredded first, of course.' Neither of them needed that kind of evidence laying around.

When she looked back, she gave a start, apparently surprised by just how close they were. Charlie had great peripheral vision, so he knew no one was outside. Close and unobserved. *How far can I push her?* A small dip of his head, and he planted a quick minty kiss on her lips. It was over so swiftly, it hardly started, and they were left staring at each other.

Teddington retreated from the cell.

Charlie couldn't define why he'd kissed her. He'd wanted to, so he had. Now, he wanted more. Taking a deep breath, he pushed such aberrations aside. Carefully, he expelled all the air from his lungs, steeled himself with another deep breath. *Time to make a house call.*

The weight of expectation wasn't just from the other prisoners. Charlie felt it in his gut. It dragged him down like concrete boots. He reached the second floor. *Was it too late to turn back? Why would he turn back?*

The Runt stood outside the open cell door.

'Let him in,' Keen's voice came from within.

Runt shifted aside and Charlie stepped in. Never having been in Keens cell before, he took a moment to catalogue the space. In construction, it was the same as his own cell, yet it was still a world away. Keen had a mattress; not like the ancient lumpy thing Charlie slept on, but a proper mattress, or at least a foam overlay. He had sheets of quality cotton and a proper wool blanket with wide ribbon edges.

Keen sat back in his padded leather chair, appraising Charlie. Charlie envied that; so much better than the rickety plastic thing he had to sit on. 'You don't look much like a cop.'

'It's the bars. We all look different behind them.' He stepped forward. The rug on the floor felt odd beneath his feet. He looked up at the window to underline his point and spotted the potted plants, each in a brightly coloured pot.

He watched Keen dab his mouth with a proper napkin. It matched the table cloth. Table linen. Until this moment, Charlie hadn't realised how much he missed that either.

'Indeed.'

With a click, Keen drew Runt's attention, pointing to the plate indicated to the big man to come and collect it, another flick of the wrist and he was dismissed. Outside Runt literally grabbed another inmate and jammed the tray in his hands, the smaller man slumped and headed away. Charlie concentrated on the real power of the play. Keen always dressed sharply. Even now he was in light chinos with a crisp crease and his shirt was pressed with precision – the collar wouldn't dare fray. The outfit needed a tie, and it was known Keen missed those strips of fabric. Under the table, Keen shifted. Charlie glanced down, saw the polished penny loafers. *Where did you even get those things these days?*

'You were told to come directly after you'd eaten.'

Charlie didn't move, didn't speak, simply regarded the old man. In his late sixties, Keen had a full head of hair the same steely grey as his eyes.

'Why didn't you?'

'I needed to brush my teeth.'

'And speak to Teddington?'

Charlie shrugged. 'She's a screw, but she's not stupid. She saw people were watching me after your message was delivered. She wanted to know what was going on.'

'What did you tell her?'

'That I didn't know what you wanted,' Charlie returned easily. 'I couldn't very well just kick her out of my cell.'

'There's plenty of men in here feel the same way about private time with her,' Keen observed calmly. 'That's why she doesn't go into cells alone. Until now.'

There was a query implied in the tone of that statement, but without an explicit question, Charlie wasn't going to respond.

'Why is that?'

Charlie shrugged again.

'I thought you were a smart boy, Charlie. I'm disappointed in you.'

Charlie figured he'd survive, but there were no guarantees.

'Word has it, you're working for Winehouse now.'

'Does it? I was offered time on a gardening detail. It was a reasonable alternative to the gym time I never get.'

Charlie watched Keen's developing smile and thought about crocodiles.

'If you wanted gym time, you only had to ask.'

'I went through the official channels.'

'Charlie,' Keen's look was almost hurt, 'haven't you learned yet, boy? I am the official channels.'

'And I don't take sides.' Charlie looked back, unashamed and undaunted. 'Now, if you had a reason to pull me up here, do you want to get to it, or shall I just go back to my book?'

'What did Winehouse want?'

'Didn't York tell you?'

This time, there was something more genuine in Keen's smile. 'Yes, but I can't believe Winehouse would ask you to look into who killed Tommy.'

'Why not?'

Now, there was a much darker tone to Keen's look. 'Because Tommy was one of mine,' Keen said. 'He was a good boy, and I liked him. Winehouse had him killed. I want proof. And I want you to get it.'

Chapter 7

Laying on his bunk, staring up at the ceiling, Charlie considered his situation. He didn't necessarily believe either Winehouse or Keen when they claimed to have no involvement with Tommy's death. In his experience criminals were a bunch of untrustworthy liars. His gut, his knowledge as a cop, told him neither Winehouse nor Keen were lying this time. But, instinct and truth weren't always the same thing, and believing they were could make a good cop a fool. However, if Tommy's death was down to either Keen or Winehouse, what benefit was there in getting him to investigate? It was a puzzle. Then again, it had been a long time since he'd had to use any investigative skills. It wasn't likely he'd need them in the future, but now was the time to brush them off. Of course, it was possible some hidden third party was pulling strings, looking to destabilise the place.

Buoyed by a quick glance at the pictures on the wall, Charlie rolled off the bunk and grabbed an old sweatshirt, pulling it on as he stepped onto the landing.

Breakfast was over, but there were plenty of inmates still down in the common area. When he'd gone down to get breakfast, Charlie had checked the work rota. His name wasn't on it today.

That was hardly surprising. Now that Winehouse and Keen had given him his orders, they wouldn't do anything more for him, unless he did something for them. If he came up with the answer one of them wanted, that one would, or might, consider him a friend, but to the other, he would be an enemy. The third option was do nothing, but that way he'd make two enemies.

Then there was Teddington, and the unknown 'rotten statesman'. The rotter would eventually hear about what he'd been asked to do, and that was unlikely to go down well. If the rotter was a screw, which was likely, both he and Teddington had the power to make Charlie's remaining prison life rather uncomfortable.

Though, it was questionable what they could do to him. They couldn't deny him visits, letters or works duty; he didn't get any. His prison property was the same basics he had been issued with – part of his self-imposed penance. And he'd already worked out a self-contained exercise programme that he used in his cell. All that was left was socialisation, library and study time, and access to cash. He would like to think he wasn't that bothered by any of these minimal luxuries, but they were humanising. He would miss them, if they were denied.

Socialisation. It was pretty much just Baker who talked to him in here. *What about Teddington?* He pushed that image away. Teddington was off-limits. There were rules.

So, there was little incentive from officialdom, and only one stick. *One bloody great stick.* Piss off the screws, and they could deny him parole. The more time he spent in here, the less chance he had of Oscar remembering him. His brow creased with the knowledge Oscar was unlikely to remember him now anyway. Three years out of five was too much, and Charlie knew he'd never really make it up to the boy, but he would try.

He looked around the prison. Three layers of cages in this wing alone. Over 150 men, who didn't want to be here. If the inmates decided to turn against him, they could get real nasty. Knocking food from his hands, was the least of it. The food in here was hardly *a la carte*, but he didn't want to starve. So far, he'd suffered no real physical abuse, but it was always possible. Even in the outside world, the nature of male urination always exposed a man's vulnerability. In here that could lead to – things he didn't even want to contemplate.

He sighed. Was physical harm really his only concern? It wasn't a huge worry. He could handle himself one-on-one easily enough. Only, if an attack came, chances were it wouldn't be one-on-one.

Since doing nothing was not an option, Charlie figured he'd better do something. Elbows on the landing rail, he surveyed his surroundings. Teddington wasn't in sight, but she'd been on afternoons, so if she was on shift today at all, she would be in later. *If* she was on shift. He couldn't remember if she had already worked two or three afternoons. He was fairly sure the shifts here were runs of three, then changed, but he hadn't paid enough attention to work out the system. His policy since arrival had been head down and no getting involved – let nothing touch him.

He no longer had that luxury.

Resigned to an unpleasant fate, Charlie pushed away from the rail and went in search of Baker.

* * *

Charlie chose a slow steady pace for the return journey to his cell; it wasn't like he had anything to get back to. He projected an air of casual isolation, feigned disinterest. As he lingered, he spotted Robbins. Robbins and Teddington usually worked together. She wasn't in view, but another woman was. Charlie recognised Rebecca Fry, a parole officer. Mousy to the point of obscurity, Fry had never made much of an impression on him, but now, something Baker had told him last year came to mind. *She likes a bad boy, that one. Be good to her, and you could get out early.* There had been no other rumours, at least not that he'd heard. She'd just arrived for a session with one of the inmates; the buff files she carried were probably parole applications and preparations for life beyond these high walls.

He guessed she had felt the weight of his gaze, because she turned to him as he passed. There was something cold and calculating in her eyes. No surprise there, no one treated him as human anymore. Except, maybe the one screw, but only maybe. It wasn't that he was treated badly; merely he was made to feel like scum. Then again – he mentally shrugged, as he moved on – he had killed a man. He *was* scum. There again, it could be he was punishing himself for what he'd done. Time to move on, and get over himself.

The cold suddenly warmed up and Fry stopped in front of him. 'I have an opening. Four o'clock. We can sort out a few things for you.'

Not sure what needed sorting for him, Charlie had no idea what to say as Fry's quiet steps took her away. Literally shrugging the moment off, he continued his journey.

Halfway up the stairs to the first landing, what he glimpsed stopped his heart. The skip was momentary, and when it started again, his ticker raced like it was sprinting for the finish line. He couldn't afford to give the game away, but his legs felt boneless, his feet like lead weights. He continued the familiar course back to his cell. Eyes front and centre, he turned left, then left again to the line of doors, but all he could see was that glimpse – Teddington manoeuvring with two men through the airlock arrangements of the entry doorway onto the open area beneath him. A third of the way along the landing, he reached his cell. *Not them.* Had he the luxury of slamming the door, he would, but he had to act normally, had to leave that door wide open.

He heard measured steps coming up the stairs in triplicate. A quick look over his shoulder showed the other inmates were out on the landing, watching the trio's movements. Anything new in this place generated observation and speculation. Charlie took several steadying breaths and returned to the open doorway, doing what he needed to do in order to appear like any other inmate.

Leaning with a forced casualness, Charlie watched first Teddington appear, and then, the two men behind her. His heart hammered as they turned at the top of the stairs. They were heading towards him. Of course, they were heading towards him; the men were so obviously police, it was painful to behold. They had to be here because of Tommy, and Tommy's cell was three down from Charlie's own.

He watched Teddington lead the way. Her eyes flicked to him as she approached, but showed nothing. Next in line was an older man, his authority stamped over his every feature, his every movement. He didn't acknowledge Charlie with so much as a glance, but Charlie knew this man would know he was there. A lack of reaction was not a lack of observation. Bringing up the rear, the younger officer caught sight of Charlie and did a double-take, turning his head as they passed. Charlie saw an instant surprise turn into a cold, dark hatred. Then, the man turned away, head held high.

Charlie got the message.

Scum.

This time, it bounced straight off him. He wasn't going to just accept that, not anymore. He was the same man he'd always been; it was his circumstances that were different.

They moved on, and Charlie waited. He looked across the way and saw Steven Morris staring back, the old lag was watching him way too close for comfort. For a moment, Charlie returned the gaze, then he stood erect, shrugged towards Morris, and moved back into his cell, where he went into his exercise routine.

Halfway through the first set, he became aware of the body in the door. Not wanting to get caught out Sanchez-style again, he lowered himself to the floor. Morris stood in the doorway, his hands in his jogger pockets. Moving as usual. Though, unlike many, Charlie understood the difference between fiddling and early stage Parkinsons.

'They your lot?' Morris tipped his head in the direction of Tommy's cell.

Carefully, Charlie got to his feet, overshadowing Morris by nearly a foot. 'What would my lot be?'

'Coppers,' he sneered.

'I'm not a cop,' Charlie stated, 'I'm a killer, remember? That's why I'm in here.'

'Once a cop, always a cop,' Morris parried. 'They friends of yours?'

'No.' It was surprisingly easy to say. 'They are cops, though. You're right about that. Given that Tommy died in here, there's bound to be an investigation. Odds are, it needs to be seen to be independent of the prison staff, so they've had to bring in outsiders.' Charlie shrugged. 'Procedure, probably.'

'See, you still think like a pig.'

'Thanks.'

'That why you've been asking about Tommy?'

'What can I say? I guess I'm irredeemably nosey.'

Morris considered him for a long moment. Charlie wasn't sure he liked the apparent sneer behind those eyes. 'Watch your back. You don't want Leo finding out.'

Then, Morris was gone, and Charlie frowned, as he returned to his exercise.

Leo?

Alarm bells were ringing, but he wasn't sure why.

* * *

Teddington tried not to sneer. She wasn't impressed by either Detective Chief Inspector Piper or Detective Sergeant Carlisle. She never claimed to be anything other than a guard, didn't expect them to treat her as an equal, but she did expect to be treated with a little common courtesy, not condescension and disdain. Most of all, she didn't appreciate their obvious lack of interest in the case. A man had died, for God's sake. Leading them out of the cell block, it grated that they had spent more time joking with the Governor than looking at Tommy's accommodation. They'd only given the most cursory glance to where he died – in a cleaner's cupboard.

The Governor's implication that the whole thing should be 'dealt with, quietly and efficiently' hadn't exactly encouraged her, either. *A whitewash at Whitewalk.*

She led them back to a side room off the wing. The now-redundant administration office had been assigned for police use. Here, Tommy's few belongings had been gathered and set out.

When they reached the office, Piper indicated Carlisle should precede him, and then stepped into the doorway when

Teddington moved to join them. 'We'll call you, if we want you.'

'You do that,' Teddington snapped. 'I'm just twiddling my thumbs after all.'

'Miss Teddington.'

Taking a deep breath, Teddington stopped mid turn, and faced the DCI. 'It's *Mrs* Teddington, but you should call me Officer Teddington, as you have all my male colleagues.'

The DCI acknowledged the point with a slight tip of his head. 'If it is more convenient for you,' he stepped aside and raised a hand into the office, 'perhaps you could join us now, *Officer* Teddington?'

Suddenly, that was the last thing she wanted to do. She squared her shoulders. *You pushed him. Now, deal with it.* She stepped inside, stopping in the middle of the office. She found the sound of the door closing behind her surprisingly ominous.

Looking forward, she met Carlisle's steely gaze and felt her skin crawl, as Piper walked around her, pulled out the one chair in the room, and carefully sat. He took a moment to clear the area off the desk immediately in front of him, before turning to look up at her.

'You were on duty when Thomas Walters died?'

'I cannot confirm that.' She kept her chin up and her eyes on Piper.

'Why not?'

'Time of death is currently unknown. All I can confirm is I was on duty when his body was found.'

'Where were you at that time?'

She took a calming breath. 'C-Wing.'

'Doing what?'

'My job.' She knew that wasn't the question. 'Checking all was quiet, keeping an eye on the inmates, ensuring there were no disturbances, generally being the required presence of authority.'

Piper returned her gaze with blank gravity.

'What about Bell?'

Teddington turned to Carlisle and frowned. 'What about him?'

'What was he doing?' the younger man asked.

'When?'

'When Walters was found.'

Her frowned deepened, and she shrugged. 'Exercising, probably. He does a lot of static exercises to pass the time. Or possibly reading. He does a lot of that too.'

'He was near Walters?'

'No.'

'You're sure?' Carlisle demanded.

'Yes.'

'Why?'

'Because he was in his cell when the alarm was raised. All we had to do was close the door.'

'Did he know Walters?'

Teddington felt the waves of abhorrence emanating from Carlisle. 'Everyone knew Walters.'

'Everyone?' Carlisle called her on the point.

'Well, okay, most people.'

'Bell?'

She considered it. 'I would have thought so, but I can't be sure. Bell keeps himself to himself. As far as I know, he doesn't smoke, have a drug habit, or need any of the services Tommy used to provide.'

'Teddington,' Piper asked, 'is it possible to get a decent cup of coffee in this place?'

'There might be a filter brew going in the staff canteen. Otherwise, the stuff from vending machine is drinkable.'

Piper turned to Carlisle, a flick of the head indicated the door. The younger man straightened, his flat lips compressed. He wasn't impressed at being dismissed. As he moved away, Teddington watched him.

'You know where it is?' When he shook his head, she followed him to the door and pointed. 'Down there, turn right, second door.'

'Teddington.'

The sound of Piper's voice brought her up short. It really was a distinctive voice, not especially loud, though she suspected it could be, but mostly, what she heard was iron-hard authority. She turned back to him.

'Close the door.'

'Which side would you like me on?'

His look told her she was testing his patience. 'This one.'

Carefully closing the door, she returned to her previous position; feet shoulder-width, hands behind her back, chin up, eyes on Piper. She found him quite a formidable presence. *Probably what makes him a good DCI.* He was watching her too closely; she suspected he saw more than she'd like.

'How many men in here?' he asked, as he leaned back.

'This wing has one hundred sixty-three.'

'How many is it designed to hold?'

'One hundred thirty.'

'Who shares with Bell?'

She'd expected questions about Tommy, not Bell. Her skin was starting to crawl. *Had contacting Bell been a mistake?*

'Er, no one at the moment. His last cellmate was released earlier this week. None of the others want to move in with him.'

'You give them the choice?'

'Not always,' she admitted. 'But, there are still other cells available to be assigned, and so far, they have been, and Bell's cell hasn't.'

'Why?'

She shrugged and tried not to frown. 'Assigning cells is down to the receiving officer. I haven't processed any of the new arrivals, so I cannot define on what basis any of them have been assigned where.'

Piper regarded her. His lack of expression made her stomach flip. *What is he thinking?*

'What is your relationship with Bell?'

Teddington felt her jaw drop; her brows rose before they descended to a slight frown. She had no problem meeting Piper's direct gaze. 'He's an inmate, I'm a guard.'

Piper rose to stand directly in front of her. Their eyes were almost level, and she knew he wouldn't miss anything. She swallowed.

'He's a man, you're a woman.'

'How observant, sir.'

'How sarcastic, madam.'

They glared at each other. Teddington rarely disliked anyone. To hate took effort, and she wasn't prepared to waste that. Her feelings were darkening, but for once, she wouldn't hide that, and she glared straight back into Piper's eyes.

'I don't even want to think about what you're suggesting, but let me be clear. I am a prison officer. I am responsible for the security, supervision, training and rehabilitation of the men in this facility. Bell is self-contained, non-violent, quiet. In the three years he's been here, he's taken and passed five computer courses, one in literature, another in nutrition, and is booked onto another starting next month in mechanics, which I personally hope he won't be able to do. He is, frankly, a model prisoner. He takes up very little time, makes few demands, and gets on with the fact that he's in here. Honestly, we all wish more were like him.'

'Why do you hope he won't be able to do the mechanics course?'

Did he really need to ask? 'He's served three years of seven. Because of good behaviour, the recommendation has been made he be considered for early parole. He'll be out in six months anyway.'

'Who made that recommendation?'

'Prison Officer Robbins.'

'The officer you're usually partnered with?'

'Yes.'

'Not you?'

She didn't like the implication. 'No.'

'Why not?'

She shrugged hoping it looked more nonchalant than it felt. 'Robbins spoke first, but most of us agreed.'

Piper watched her, scrutinised her. She had no idea what he was thinking. 'Do you know why Bell's in here?'

'He killed a man.'

'Do you know who that man was?'

She remembered processing Bell into the prison. The details would be on his file. She even remembered seeing headlines about him, but she hadn't been that interested at the time, and she wasn't bothered now. 'I don't need to.' Now, she frowned at Piper. 'Why all the questions about Bell? You're supposed to be investigating Tommy's death.'

'If Walters was killed, it was either by a con or a screw.'

'You've eliminated the Tooth Fairy, then.'

'You've taken an adversarial stance, Officer Teddington. Do you really think that will hide your guilt?'

'No!' She dragged in a breath, clenched her jaw, and closed her eyes. *Get control.* 'I'm not guilty. I've nothing to hide.'

'Nothing?'

She couldn't quite meet his eye, so she scowled at his mouth, her own lips tight. 'I am a trained, respectable individual, and I take exception to being presumed guilty until proven innocent. And since we've been talking about Bell, why don't you asked me how may bent "screws" we've got locked up for anything, let alone murder?' Finally, she was able to look him in the eye, and she was willing to bet hers were full of fire. 'You've heard of pots and kettles, right, Detective Chief Inspector?'

Whatever Piper would have said, Carlisle halted it by returning with two coffees. Piper hadn't changed stance, he hadn't even moved, but Teddington knew he had shut her out.

'Trusting is a difficult choice,' his voice was almost a whisper. Then, he stepped away. 'That's all.'

Teddington bristled at being dismissed with a brusque flick of his wrist.

* * *

Charlie wasn't sure what he was doing in the room. Another dull grey room. The posters, which were supposed to be "motivational," were as flat as everything else. Not that it mattered, he was more concerned about Teddington and Piper. Mostly Teddington. The images his imagination had created last night weren't as fleeting as they should be. *Focus on the case.*

The door closed behind him and metal turned. He twisted in his seat, eyes on Fry behind him. She was in her early thirties but dressed like she was in her sixties. Not to mention thick glass frames which weren't doing her any favours. They also didn't change the magnification of her eyes, so he wondered why she needed them. Fry's hand was on the lock. Seeing his interest, she smiled and stepped away from the door.

'Don't want anyone disturbing us.'

Probably not, she was a parole officer after all and details discussed in here were of no concern to anyone but them. He was surprised when her hand slid across his shoulder. She leant down to say close to his ear, 'This is our private time.'

He sat back in the hard plastic chair. He was in prison, he didn't have anything private any more, all there was was time. As she moved away, that hand brushed down his arm. He wasn't sure what to make of that. Felt like an invasion of his personal space.

Ha!

Personal space was another joke in here.

Fry sat her side of the desk with her buff file – well his buff file – in front on her. There was little of note about the woman. Except that Twin Set and pearls didn't really suit her or the situation. She tipped her head up to smile at him.

'Rather warm in here, don't you think?'

It was unnecessarily warm in the small room with no windows; he glanced at the radiator. It was on full. When he returned his attention to her, Fry was stripping off the cardigan, her breasts, as average as they were, pointed straight at him. The fading bruises on her left upper arm were a surprise. He'd seen such things before. Fingerprint bruising. Usually a sign of a battered wife. Sometimes of BDSM. He glanced at Fry's hand. She wasn't wearing a ring.

'So, Mr Bell, Charlie, you don't mind if I call you Charlie, do you?'

Her hands were crossed over the paperwork, elbows in. He imagined how it would look if Teddington did that. 'Fuller' was the word that came to mind. He concentrated more on Fry's eyes, realised she had asked him a question and shrugged. There were worse things she could call him.

There were a number of procedural questions, but he wasn't paying much attention. It really was warm in here, stuffy and uncomfortable and he could feel sweat beading on his upper lip, the crew neck of his sweatshirt felt suddenly restrictive, not allowing air to cool him. He'd need a shower when he left at this rate.

'Perhaps you should make a statement of what you would like to do when you're free.' She looked up at him. Her hand was on her pendant now. Running it back and forth along the chain. Drawing attention to her décolleté might work better if she was actually displaying cleavage. 'If you were free to do anyone you wanted, what would it be?'

He must have misheard. She had to have said anything he wanted. The problem was that the only thing he ever wanted to do was the one thing he'd thrown away when he'd killed a man. She was expecting a response, he shrugged.

'Have you given any thought to where you'll go when you leave here?'

He hadn't really. His house and furniture had been sold to pay for his defence lawyer. The only living relatives he had were his parents, and his father had made it very clear that he was *persona non-grata* there. All his old friends were coppers, and he could hardly turn to them after what he'd done. 'Not really.'

'I'm sure I could find you a bed.'

He flinched, feeling her foot on his calf. She shifted on her chair, looking through his papers. There really wasn't that much to look through. It was a narrow desk, so their knees were close together, he wasn't surprised when she shifted and he felt the heat of her foot against his leg again.

'A halfway house you mean?'

'Probably,' she acknowledged. 'I know it's not a great prospect, but I will do what I can. I'll do whatever I can to ensure your comfort.'

He nodded vaguely. The phrases these parole officers used. There was probably a directive somewhere about 'ensuring ex-prisoner comfort on return to civilian life,' or something. He figured it was safer not to respond this time.

He frowned, noticing her feet were outside his. His legs weren't closed, which meant hers would be wide open – a flash of fantasy zipped down his spine. The images he'd conjured of Teddington replayed across his mind. Played havoc with his breathing and blood flow.

'Charlie?' Fry leant forward again.

Focus. Jesus. Cold shower time.

'Is there anything I can do to improve your comfort here, Charlie?'

Someone probably could, but it wouldn't be Fry and it wouldn't be whatever she was offering. He thought of Teddington again as sweat rolled down his spine. Definitely time for a cold shower.

'Everything's fine as it is. We done here?'

Her lips pursed, her eyes taking on a surprisingly hard glare. 'Apparently.'

* * *

The inmates were back in their cells by nine, and Teddington was ready to call it a day. One of their last jobs was to ensure every cell door was locked. It wasn't difficult; the men were free to continue to socialise, if they wished, but the presence of the police, the questions many had been asked, had left the place in a more sombre mood. It was a state of affairs Teddington recognised as unusual. If she wasn't too exhausted to think from nights of limited sleep, she'd be more worried. Who was she kidding, she was worried. She was just too tired to do anything about it.

A couple of the hardier lags joked about having her locked in with them, but it was at best half-hearted.

'Can I have a word?' Holden was talking to Robbins; his bunkmate was already on his bed, immersed in his latest comic book.

'What is it?' Robbins asked.

The mechanic with a talent for liberating top-end cars looked meaningfully at Teddington. 'It's kinda personal.'

As Robbins turned to her, Teddington took a deep breath, rolled her eyes, and moved along. The next three cells were already closed. She checked they were locked. She paused at the fourth door. Partridge lay on the bottom bunk, his hand down his pyjama bottoms, and the tent pole effect obvious. As Teddington appeared, he smiled at her, working harder.

'All for you, sweetheart.'

Stony-faced, she closed the door, as he jerked and cried out.

The next cell door was open, she looked in on Bell. He was sitting at the tiny desk. Like Gandalf in Bilbo's hobbit hole, she thought. He was staring at an A4 sheet of paper, but his pen lay unused.

She stopped by the door and he lifted his head. A number of questions scrolled through his expression. Teddington was torn. She wanted to ask if he'd discovered anything, and she wanted to warn him about DCI Piper, but how?

'Why do you put up with that?' He nodded towards the wall. Towards Partridge.

She shrugged. 'It does me no harm, and boys will be boys. You've been in here three years, you gonna tell me you never?'

His crooked smile and lifted brow reminded her of what he'd said in the garden.

Her own stomach tightened at that idea. 'What are you writing?'

'Statement for the parole board.'

She frowned, 'Not usually necessary.'

'No.'

The silence stretched. She tipped her head. 'You haven't written anything.'

'No.'

'Why not?' For a second, she didn't think he was going to answer.

'Miss Fry,' Charlie said, 'suggested it might help if I made a statement about what I intend to do once I'm out.'

'And what do you intend to do?'

Charlie shrugged and leaned back. 'That's the problem. I don't know. I can't exactly go back to my old job, can I?'

'Not really, no.'

'So, what's the alternative for an ex-cop convicted of murder?'

'Coding? You did well in that.' She shrugged. 'Bring a sense of realism to the GTA-type games?' He didn't look any more convinced than she felt. 'At least, you'd be able to see your son,' she pointed out. 'You might not've been a good cop, but you could still be a good father.'

His laugh was short and bitter. 'I was a great cop, but Cathy's never gonna let me see Oscar now.'

'Why not? What happened between the two of you?' She told herself it was just professional curiosity.

'It was good while it lasted, but when she found out I was cop …' He shrugged. 'She said she didn't need that kind of pressure in her life.'

Teddington got the distinct impression there was more to it, but now wasn't the time. 'You're still the boy's father. You have a right to see him.'

'Do you seriously see any court being willing support my claim?'

Probably not, sadly.

'Winehouse and Keen had the same question as you.' He sighed. 'Which suggests neither was involved, but I can't trust either of them.'

She checked the landing a moment. 'Fair enough, but I'd trust Keen over Winehouse.'

Charlie frowned. 'Why?'

'Known him longer.' There was a lot more to it than that, and the way Charlie considered her suggested he was far from convinced by her nonchalance. *Not such a bad cop after all.*

'In here?'

'He was here before I was.'

His frown was deepening.

Damn it. She didn't want him asking those kinds of questions. She needed to get away from him, before she said something she shouldn't.

'Who's Leo?'

Teddington looked to the side, as she heard movement behind her. She glanced back to Charlie. The only answer she could give him was a tiny mute shrug, before she closed the metal door, her gaze clashing with his one last time, before she locked him up.

Chapter 8

Sleep was elusive. Charlie lay on his bunk, flipping through the child's drawings. They weren't from his child, couldn't be, but it had been good to think, even for a little while, that they might be. It was good to think of other things as well, and though he hated imitating that nonce Partridge, he closed his eyes and pictured Teddington.

His dreams were full of her. And blood. And Tommy's death.

Waking before dawn, he knew he wouldn't sleep again. He got up, paced, tried reading, tried exercising – nothing held him. He tried to work out who was lying about Tommy.

Maybe they all were.

Leo.

For three years, he'd watched the delicate balance of power between Keen and Winehouse, grateful he'd always managed to stay on the outside of it. What surprised him was the current lack of reprisals. Neither Keen nor Winehouse were making a move. The heightened tension was obvious, but they were both keeping their boys on a tight rein. Everyone was more afraid of Leo than Keen or Winehouse.

While he had no idea who Leo was, he had heard the name whispered with fear and respect a few times this last year. Having reached the wall, he sighed and pivoted. Pacing barefoot to the door, he worried about his predicament. He considered yesterdays second interview, when he'd been sitting across the table from Piper and Carlisle. The chilling procedural correctness. It was worse than it had been three years ago, at least then, he had been guilty.

The few steps between one wall and the other was too few. Charlie was getting dizzy going back and forth, so he slumped down on the lower bunk. How much did Teddington know? He guessed not much, given yesterday's conversation. Conversation; that was a joke. He knew there were places without surveillance cameras, where inmates would nip for a little 'private time.' Hell, some of them just went to their cells. But, that was impossible with Teddington. Everyone knew she didn't enter the cells alone – she couldn't risk doing so again. Still, he needed to talk to her. She'd been on for three days, so he wouldn't see her again for another three. He had plenty of time to figure out how to engineer a meeting.

Dropping to the cold floor, he shoved the problem to the back of his mind with press ups.

The door was unlocked at 8:30. He finished the set he was on, stood, washed himself, brushed his teeth, dressed, and went down to collect breakfast. He was vaguely aware of the two officers on the ground floor as he paced down the stairs, but he paid no attention.

'Hey, Officer Teddington!'

Charlie lifted his head at hearing the shout from one of his fellow inmates. This time he looked at the officers; Teddington, and some new guy.

'You must love it 'ere,' the heckler called. 'You're 'ere as much as the rest of us.'

'Thankfully not, Holden,' she returned with ease. 'Just covering while Richmond takes some time.'

'Not at Her Majesty's pleasure, I 'ope.'

'No.' She smiled. 'Lucky sod's just on holiday in Bermuda.'

'What bank did he rob?' This time, the call came from the other side of the hall, from another body further down the breakfast line than Charlie.

'Unlike you, Fellows,' Teddington laughed back to the inmate, 'he didn't. He just worked and saved.'

'Who's the newbie?' Holden asked.

Charlie had been wondering the same thing. The new officer trailed behind Teddington on her circuit. He looked young to Charlie, not much taller than Teddington, fit but not overly muscular. *Wet behind the ears.* He sighed. Everyone was a new guy sometime in their lives; he shouldn't be so quick to judge.

'This is Officer Dyer,' Teddington announced. 'And, yes, he's new, but behave. Show him what good little innocents you all really are.'

'Innocents?' Dyer asked.

'Oh, yes,' Teddington assured him, light-heartedly. 'They're all innocent men, wrongly accused. Didn't you know?'

She didn't laugh, but her smile suggested she could, as various cat calls backed up the claim.

Charlie had made it to the head of the line to be served shrivelled bacon and rubbery eggs. With Teddington here, he'd have to find a way to talk to her.

Eating alone in his cell, Charlie couldn't think of either a reason or place he could get her alone. He took his breakfast things back down and checked the garden rota. He wasn't on it. He checked the gym rota. He wasn't on it. He lingered, but no one was willing to talk to him. Baker was slouching in his doorway, they made eye contact, then Baker tipped his head. A mute and minor invitation. Taking his time, Charlie moved over.

'You get questioned yesterday?'

'Course.' Charlie kept his voice low, as he put a shoulder to the wall and looked down at Baker.

'They weren't interested, were they? It was cursory. They don't wanna know who did in Tommy.'

Charlie watched Baker; the man was simply stating his own impression. 'Maybe. At this stage, it'll all be procedural. For all either of us know, they got something from someone else, following other leads.'

'I don't see anyone missing, either, do you?'

Charlie considered who he had or hadn't seen. 'Partridge?'

Baker shook his head. 'In with that Fry woman.'

'He can't be up for parole yet, surely?'

This time, Baker shrugged. 'Dunno, don't care. I'm just sick of the little wanker's stories about who he fucked and how. He reckons he could fuck Fry and Teddington and still have enough left over for a cock sucker. Even claims to be halfway to proving it.'

'The bloke's a delusional twat,' Charlie muttered, but he pushed off the wall. This wasn't a conversation he wanted to maintain.

Heading for his own room, he glanced up a landing. Keen, hair darkened from washing, was as nattily dressed as ever, and flanked by Runt, as he returned to his room. No one would ever get the chance to accost Keen in the shower. Keen briefly met Charlie's eye. There was no signal, inflection, or acknowledgement. Then, the older man was gone.

'You not in the garden today?' Charlie asked Teddington, as she allowed him out into the exercise yard.

'Not my shift, remember? It's Richmond's. I'm just covering.'

Charlie nodded and walked on. This was too public. He took long, deep breaths. With the exercise yard on the other side of the building from the garden, this air was fresh. The sun was warm on his face, and he stopped, tipped his head up, closing his eyes. All the better to enjoy the moment of peace.

'Perkins is up to something.'

Charlie let his lungs and shoulders deflate. *So much for peace.* When he opened his eyes, Baker, whose mutter had shattered the moment, had moved on. Charlie stepped forward. It was no more than he'd been doing in his room, but at least, he wasn't having to reverse direction every few steps out here. Running his eyes around the men, he was on the second pass before he spotted Jack Perkins.

The insignificant nonentity was an annoying thug, a bully, in for the attempted murder of his young wife, now ex-wife. Charlie recalled what he'd heard. When they married, he'd been 19 and she'd been 16. After four years of abuse, she'd left him, and he'd gone after her with a carving knife. Rumour was, she'd finally snapped and struck back, damn near killing Perkins, and in Charlie's opinion, the near miss was a shame. She'd have got off on a plea of self-defence.

As he watched, Perkins walked taller today, strutted. He was up to something, all right. He had tormented on his wife. He'd been known to pick on some of the weaker inmates, but he wouldn't have attacked Tommy, knowing Keen protected Tommy. Charlie was sure Perkins wasn't so lucky. He tended towards the Winehouse camp, but wasn't really part of the circle. So why was Perkins talking to Mohr? Mohr was definitely one of Keen's.

'Didn't you get Mohr on a stabbing?' Baker surprised him by jogging up and asking.

If only. 'Nah, he wasn't one of mine,' Charlie advised.

'But, he's in here for a stabbing in't 'e?'

Charlie shook his head. 'Mohr likes to cut people, but there was never enough evidence to convict him. Witnesses suffered inexplicable amnesia before coming to court. He got caught out in a pub brawl. Grievous Bodily Harm. He's been in seven months; he'll be out in three.'

He let Baker move on, but stopped in the corner, watching Perkins, and wishing he could get that moment of peace back.

'If all you're going to do is stand around brooding, you may as well be in your cell.'

Charlie angled himself to face Teddington. She didn't look happy. In fact, she looked tired. Her hair was, as ever, pulled back into a tight bun at the nape of her neck, he could see no makeup, but tiny red pinpricks of old acne scars, her humanity betrayed by the laughter lines starting to spread around her eyes. There were piercings for earrings she never wore; her only jewellery was a cheap sports watch. Her uniform was boxy and hid any femininity, except for the obvious fact she had breasts. He tried not to think about her breasts, concentrating on her hazel eyes, instead. She was intelligent, and sometimes, when she regarded him, like now, her eyes completely penetrated him.

'Even murderers are allowed fresh air.' He kept his voice down.

'No, really?'

He reared slightly, such narkiness was not like her. Apparently, she knew it, too. She took a moment to close her eyes and released some tension.

'Sorry.'

His shrug was as small as her apology.

'There are no Leos,' she almost whispered. 'There's a Lyons in A-wing, but he's in confinement.'

'You checked for middle names?'

Her eyes narrowed. 'No, Lucas Charles Bell, I didn't think of that.'

He winced. He hadn't heard his full name since being processed in here. He'd never liked being called Lucas, even insisted his parents call him Charlie, much to their disgust. He should have trusted her to be thorough.

'I also checked aliases and birth signs. Unfortunately, that gave too many to be useful.'

He really should trust her. 'The staff?'

'I've no access to the personnel records, but no Leos I know of.'

'Murder weapon?'

Her bottom lip moved in unspoken negative. 'I was told it's police business now.'

Charlie nodded. Her hands were more tied than his.

'How long did you serve with Piper?'

Charlie tightened at the sharp question. 'Ten years. How did you know?'

'Carlisle's reaction. Piper's lack of. You were a DS, right?'

He nodded.

'His DS?'

He nodded again.

'Carlisle a DC, then?'

'I taught him the ropes.'

'No wonder he feels betrayed.' She stepped around him. 'Keep an eye on Perkins. He's up to something.'

The temptation to watch her walk away was strong, but instead, Charlie returned his attention to Perkins. The younger man stood alone, and Charlie went over. He saw him coming, and there was a moment of fight or flight reaction, then he puffed himself up, fight-ready. Charlie wasn't bothered. Perkins might get gym time, but there was no real contest. He looked down at the shorter man. There might once have been something handsome in those features, but it had been sneered away.

'I don't know what you're up to, Perkins,' he said, 'but everyone's noticed, so drop it.'

'Everyone?' he threw back. 'What, like Teddington? You into her, or what? She a good screw?'

Charlie clenched his jaw, wanting to punch that snide face. Instead, he leant down and spoke very carefully. 'Keep sucking Winehouse's dick. Maybe he'll protect you, but he won't always be watching. I will.' Charlie had the satisfaction of seeing Perkins' eyes widen in fright, and his face drain of blood, before Charlie walked away.

An hour later, he was in his cell, sitting at his table. He'd given up on the statement. Teddington's suggestion of coding ran shivers through his soul. He could do it, but he didn't fancy spending the rest of his life in an office. He'd spent too much time locked up in here to be locked up out there. The problem was, all the things he could think of that he would like to do, were out of the question, because his criminal record precluded them. He'd killed a man in cold blood, knowing he'd serve time for it, but he hadn't thought beyond that as to what the decision would mean once he was out. He'd face the outside world when he was part of it again. Something would turn up. It was all too late to whine about it now.

Instead, he picked up a book and tried to read it. Someone moved past the open cell door. By the time he'd glanced up, they were gone. He could still hear footfalls. Morris was on the opposite landing. For a moment, the two men's eyes met. Morris shook his head, before turning away.

Charlie frowned. *Odd.*

He put down his book, stood, only to be forced back by the impact of a body thumping into his. Sight and sound assailed him as the cell seemed to contract, the closing door echoed, and finally, his brain registered.

His shoulder blades protested being slammed against the wall. Teddington had crashed into him, her eyes wide, full of surprise, and coloured with fear. His hands on her upper arms, she righted herself, and quickly glanced over her shoulder to see who'd pushed her. He looked, too – Stanton and Mohr.

Mohr had a hold of Dyer by the hair. Dyer was on his knees, a fresh, red line of blood running down his nose where the bridge had split from his being thrown against the edge of the bunk. Mohr had a shiv to Dyer's throat – a toothbrush melted over two long halves of a razor blade. Stanton, a burglar and one of Winehouse's men, stood to one side. He held what had once been a blunt dinner knife, but was now a sharpened blade. The cell door was closed, and there was a good chance others guarded the outside to prevent interference. Charlie suspected Perkins was one of them.

Dyer blinked, his fists clenched, his body tensed for action.

'Don't!' Teddington commanded. 'Mohr doesn't need a reason to cut you.'

The police training in Charlie kicked in. He appreciated Teddington's understanding, her attempt to keep the situation as calm as possible, even though he could feel her trembling with fear.

'Go on, then,' Stanton said. 'Fuck her. We all know you want to.'

Charlie wasn't sure how to react. 'What?'

'Fuck her. Come on, man, we 'aven't got all day.' Now, Stanton turned to Mohr. 'Get him over the bunk.'

As Mohr moved Dyer, that shiv still frighteningly close to his carotid, Stanton turned back to Charlie. 'Think of it as a present from a friend.'

Charlie didn't have those kinds of friends and didn't want this kind of present. But he knew what he had to do. He glanced down at Teddington, who was staring up at him in a dangerous mix of fear and rage. His hands were tight around her upper arms; she wasn't going anywhere until he let her. Over her shoulder, he could see Stanton cutting the back of Dyer's belt; Teddington wasn't the only intended rape victim.

As she started to struggle, Charlie's grip tightened even further. He pulled her off her feet, pushed her around the table, backed her into the wall. He tried not to slam her too hard, but he had to make this look good. Her eyes flicked to Stanton, went wide to see Dyer's shouts muffled by the pathetic depth of mattress, as Mohr pushed his face down, held him for Stanton. Pressing his body against her, Charlie bent his head, apparently mauling her neck, and whispered in her ear.

'Donkey.'

With a surprising burst of energy, Charlie pushed away from the wall, swinging Teddington bodily as he did. She kicked out viciously. Her well-aimed heavy boots connected hard with Stanton's head – he fell to the floor without a sound. Charlie was vaguely aware of Teddington staggering against the wall, as he let her go and moved, his fist connecting hard with Mohr's nose. The shiv clattered to the floor. Mohr fell against the door, the smack of his head resounding heavily. He was down but not out. Charlie stepped over Stanton's limp form, took a bunch of Mohr's shirt in his hand to drag him up, so he could punch him again. Three years of pent up frustration over took him, and he lashed out.

'Charlie.'

He hit Mohr.

'Charlie!'

This time, Teddington's voice reached him. He turned to see her kneeling on the floor, a wad of sheet clamped to Dyer's throat. The man lay awkwardly, his whole body shaking, sheet rapidly turning red. Charlie dropped Mohr, letting him fall. Dyer needed medical assistance, and he needed it now.

Only the screws had keys, so the door couldn't be locked. He yanked the handle with every ounce of adrenaline-fuelled strength he had. Two bodies fell towards him. A fist in the face stopped one in its track, the other caught and turned, running away.

Charlie stumbled out onto the open landing, seeing a half dozen officers stampeding towards him. *When had the klaxon started ringing?*

Any other thought was impossible as a thousand volts buzzed through Charlie's body, and he fell quaking to the landing floor.

Chapter 9

Charlie blinked, he was on his back in his cell, waking up. *Just a dream.* Some dreadful nightmare. *Why am I on the lower bunk?* His knuckles ached, and he could feel the bruise across his right bicep where he'd hit the guard rail before slumping to the floor.

'Teddington.' He sat bolt upright as he said the name.

'She's fine.'

Charlie's head jerked to his left. His eyes widened to see DCI Piper sitting in his chair, reading his copy of *The Vivero Letter* by Desmond Bagley. It might be old, written in 1968, but it was still readable. The DCI closed it and looked at the cover.

'Not his best,' he observed.

'I prefer *High Citadel*.' Charlie considered moving to stand, but he wasn't sure his legs could take it. Instead, he simply lay back down. 'Actually, I'd prefer anything more modern, but beggars can't be choosers.' He took a deep breath. 'Dyer?'

'Not so good,' Piper advised. 'Lost a lot of blood.'

'Tough first day.'

'Yeah.'

'Stanton and Mohr?'

'Secure hospital facilities. I'll be interviewing Stanton later, but they aren't sure about Mohr. You pretty much broke every bone in his face.'

'He wanted to rape, possibly kill, both Dyer and Teddington.'

Piper let that hang in the air.

Charlie stared up at the slats of the upper bunk, wondered where the mattress was. The image of Dyer bleeding out flashed before his eyes. The original mattress was a bio-hazard now. He was probably laying on his mattress; it had to be much easier to bring the mattress down than to put him up. He took a deep breath, running a mental check list. Plenty of his body hurt but none of it bad. Bruised but not broken. 'Who was outside?'

'Jack Perkins and Richard Finlay. Both are helping with our enquiries.'

Charlie frowned. 'This makes no sense. Finlay and Mohr are Keen's boys, Perkins and Stanton work for Winehouse. Why are they working together?'

'Don't you know?'

Charlie turned and looked at Piper. 'No. Do you?'

Piper didn't respond, but he didn't move, either. Charlie knew there was more to come.

'What's your version of events?'

As he clinically related what had happened, Charlie tried not to remember how good it had felt to have a woman pressed against him, how good her apple scent made him feel.

'Why say donkey?' Piper asked when Charlie finished. 'Why not just tell her to kick?'

Charlie smiled. 'Because I needed a second's pause while she figured out what I was telling her to do and got her in position to do it.'

Piper made an odd sound before he stood.

'I take it I'm not getting parole any time soon.'

Charlie tipped his head to the side to look up at Piper standing over him. He couldn't read his old friend's expression. That wasn't good.

Piper's hands went into his pockets, he took a deep breath, huffed it back out. 'That's undecided. Mrs Teddington is stopping short of calling you a hero, but she has stated if it had been any other prisoner in here, she doubts she would have survived.'

'Mrs?' Charlie hadn't known that. He huffed. 'Of course, she's married.'

* * *

Charlie groaned as the door was opened. He'd put the mattress back on the top bunk, but now, he regretted it. His body ached more now than yesterday. Charlie couldn't exercise, both his knuckles and his bicep protesting too much to even consider it. Hungry, he went down for breakfast slowly. As soon as he stepped from his cell, it was obvious everyone was avoiding him. They wouldn't even meet his eye – apparently, an exclusion zone had been put around him. Still, on the bright side, it meant he had plenty of room, no risk of jostling today, his aching flesh thankfully acknowledged. He got his food tray, ate mechanically. As he returned his crockery, he jumped at the metallic clang of a food tray hitting the floor. He turned to see Holden staring, slack jawed, at something at the far end of the floor.

'Officer Teddington!'

Charlie shifted, stopped. Shock had him rooted to the spot.

Teddington.

He blinked, his jaw felt slack. Teddington looked exactly as she had yesterday. Sanchez loomed at her side.

'Holden.'

The greeting and the tone were absolutely neutral, she looked exactly as she always did. It was like yesterday had never happened. *Good for her.* Charlie wasn't going to admire it, or be proud – those were emotions for her husband. Not him. He wasn't going to admit his guts twisted with jealousy knowing she went home to a husband every night. Hadn't she mentioned a kid, too?

'We weren't expecting to see you today.' Holden had the attention of the wing, voicing its common thought.

'Why not?' she asked. 'I told you yesterday I'm covering for Richmond. Now, you'd better clean that mess up.'

As she moved on, the suspended moment broke, normality returned. Released from his unexpected paralysis, Charlie returned his tray, before heading for the notice boards.

'You're not on the lists,' Sanchez told him, as the two officers approached from the other side.

Charlie turned and looked at him, the animosity he'd shown the other day was still clear, as was the protective aura he was projecting around Teddington. She didn't look overly appreciative. 'Quiet day for me, then.' He shrugged.

'You should be able to get some reading done.'

Charlie was still frowning over Teddington's odd remark, as he returned to his cell.

* * *

Teddington paced the floor, acting normal as far as she could. Her insides were knotted. She was jumping at nothing; every shadow was a lurking attacker. Nervous system stretched tight, she wasn't sure how she was going to make it through the shift. Having Sanchez watching her like a hawk was both a blessing and a curse. He had her back, which seemed like reassurance, but was he waiting for her to mess up?

The Governor had suggested she take the day off, but there was no one else available to cover Richmond's shift, which would have meant restrictions for the inmates. Huffing, she continued her pace, watching the men, wary of anything unusual. Or usual. It was exhausting. When Sanchez stopped to pass the time with a couple of inmates, she stopped, too, careful to be neutral with them, but her mind was far from on the job. It was nearly eleven when she finally spotted Charlie leave his cell, library book in hand. *God that took him a while.*

'Didn't you mention wanting to speak to Fellows this morning?' she asked Sanchez, as they moved away from the chat.

'He's not going anywhere.'

She smiled up at him; prison humour was wry at best. 'He's not comfortable around women, either, particularly me, for some reason.' Despite knowing that reason, only Fellows shared the secret, and she intended to keep it that way. 'You go have your chat.'

'You'll be okay?'

This time, her smile was more genuine, at least she hoped it was. 'I'll be fine. I'm a big girl, and I've been doing this enough years now, so please, I don't need babysitting. We both have jobs to do.'

The separation was a relief, but she had to stop herself from running, as she headed towards the library. She hated feeling more vulnerable today than she had yesterday.

At first, she thought the library was empty, but the librarian was speaking softly to another inmate, helping with some textbook he was looking through.

Teddington moved to the fiction section, not surprised when she saw Charlie browsing there. He turned to her, as she approached. She stopped closer than she normally would, but it wasn't close enough, not like yesterday. She could feel the heat coming from him, felt it generating heat inside her. Meeting his eyes, she could see the guardedness in him.

'You okay?' she asked.

'Why wouldn't I be?'

She felt her hackles rise. 'Oh, I don't know.' Aware they could be overheard, she kept her voice low. 'Several thousand volts being shot through you for a start.' She was sniping at the one man in the whole place who didn't deserve it. 'But, why should I care?' *This isn't good*, the thought cut through her, she pivoted away, but his hand clamped on her arm, spinning her back, keeping her with him.

'You shouldn't,' he ground out. 'And I shouldn't do this, either.'

She saw it coming, he leaned down a placed a quick hard kiss on her lips again, and again, she didn't even think about stopping him. Then, they were just glaring at one another. She closed her eyes. Felt the sigh of his breath on her face, and his hands fell away from her arm. But, he didn't go anywhere. When she opened her eyes, they both seemed calmer.

'Teddington?'

A huge lump blocked her throat. She struggled to plough through this battlefield of emotion, pushing aside the desperation to hug him, the simultaneous need to run away. She struggled to find any coherent thought.

'Why come in today?' he asked.

'Richmond's off.' She shrugged. 'No one else to cover.'

'Wasn't a case that you had to prove to yourself you still could, then?'

Her heart hammered, her jaw slackened. Dear God, he could read her like a book.

He glanced over the top of her head; his eyes clouded. When he looked back at her, she wasn't sure if he had her pinned or mesmerised.

'Those drawings?' he asked. 'Your kid?'

Pinned. And on the ropes. She had to swallow, before she could answer. She shook her head. 'I'm sorry, I didn't mean to hurt you.'

'I miss him.' He shifted his eyes away. 'I'm just another worthless Dad, who didn't get to see his son's first day in school.'

'What about the man you killed? Did he?'

Hating herself for saying that, she marched sharply away.

* * *

Teddington felt every nerve had been stretched to the limit. Avoiding Charlie for the rest of the shift had been easy; he'd pretty much kept to his cell, and she'd kept out of it.

Her skin crawled at the way the men looked at her, whispered behind her back. If they did. She rubbed the nape of her neck. *Paranoia?* After yesterday, she couldn't be sure. Her hand wasn't as steady as she'd like by the time she signed out and got to the locker room to collect her bag.

She was struggling to get the locker to close properly when Sanchez appeared by her side. Like her, he had changed out of uniform. Unlike her, he looked ready for a night out. She wasn't sure she had the energy for a night in.

'Saw you talking to Bell earlier.'

Teddington tried not to react. Just because he had seen them talking, didn't mean he'd seen them kissing. It probably meant he'd seen them pass the time of day at lunch. 'I spoke to a number of the men today. Several of them expressed sympathy for what happened. A few even wanted gory details.'

'I've been hearing gory details.'

Sanchez spoke easily, but when Teddington faced him, she didn't feel overly easy. Sanchez was a few inches taller than her, broad, honed. And somehow, he made her feel less comfortable than Charlie had, which was ridiculous. She and Sanchez had been friends for years. She sighed. Clearly, she wasn't going to get away until he'd made his point. 'What gory details?'

'The ones that have you snogging Bell.'

She let her jaw drop, not at all surprised by the low register of Sanchez's tone. He wasn't happy. Nor was she. She wanted to brush it aside, but she had to be careful. 'It's not a new accusation, for me or other female members of staff. Come to think of it, I've heard it about some of the male officers, too.'

'But, is it true this time?'

She gritted her teeth and took a big breath, calming herself before she snapped at him. As she swallowed, she opened her eyes, speaking as carefully as she could. 'I can assure you, at no time have I "snogged" Charlie Bell.' She wouldn't call either of those two kisses 'snogs.' 'In fact, I'm kind of hurt you, of all people, would think that. I thought you respected my professionalism, our friendship.' Even if she wasn't showing much of either today.

'I do.' Yet, he still managed to sound accusatory. 'It's just—' He looked away, colour rising in his cheeks.

'Just what, Enzo? I don't snog inmates.'

'You don't snog staff, either,' he grumbled, 'however much any of us asks you out. And you've been divorced for four years. Why won't you at least come out on one date with me?'

Now she looked away. 'You know why.'

'No. Oh, I know all the useless excuses you can come up with, but you've never given me one good reason for not actually dating me.'

'You're too good a friend. You're like the brother I'm missing. I don't want to screw that up.'

He groaned.

'All right,' she sighed, pushing her hair back with one hand. 'Okay, let's say we do go out, we have a nice time, like we have hundreds of times over the years, as friends. Then at the end of the evening, what if we don't go all the way? Would you accept that? What if it didn't go well, what if we had an awful time? Would we still be friends enough to work together?'

'I can take it slow.'

The sincerity in his eyes, the want, was all so very tempting. *What if it went well?* she wondered. *What if we have a great time, end up in bed and having fun? Would that be so terrible?* 'Kiss me.'

He reared. 'What?'

As shocked as he was by the request, so was she. 'I said kiss me. Properly. Let's see if there is any point in starting this.'

Put on the spot, there wasn't a lot else he could do. Sanchez checked there was no one around them. His right hand came up to her face, his palm warming her skin, as he tipped her head towards him. His left hand snaked around her waist. She closed her eyes, as he leaned in, joining their lips, and pulling her against him. Teddington let her hands wander up to his shoulders. She kissed him back. When she felt his tongue probe into her mouth, she opened up. He was a good kisser, great technique, but something was missing. He was the one who finally withdrew, eased his hold, and, for a moment, he looked terribly sad.

'You just didn't feel that, did you?'

She swallowed and shook her head. 'Sorry.'

His hands fell away from her.

'It's not you,' she said, stopping him when he moved away. 'And, no, that's not a sop. It really isn't you. It's me. It's what happened … it's what could've happened yesterday. You're a good friend, but you and me dating, that's a bad idea. Me dating anyone's a pretty awful idea. I'm just not worth it.'

It was an empty truth which echoed through her hollow insides.

* * *

Teddington lay back in her bed and wondered what the hell was wrong with her. Enzo Sanchez was a good man. Maybe that was the problem. She wasn't worthy of a good man. Was that what kept pulling her back to Charlie? He wasn't a good man. She closed her eyes and hated herself for that thought. Yes, he had killed, but he wasn't evil. She knew that. Instinctively, she knew he wasn't, at heart, a bad man. She didn't know what had made him kill. She still hadn't looked up the file to know the details of what he'd done, but she was sure whatever it was – he'd been driven to it.

She sighed, and hated herself. Maybe she was just romanticising him because he'd kept her safe. Something she still hadn't thanked him for. No, if she was going to be honest – and she should be with herself, even if she couldn't be with anyone else – she was making him something he wasn't in her mind, because when he'd pressed those all too fleeting kisses on her, something inside she'd thought was dead woke up, and started howling with need.

Chapter 10

Feeling sick to her stomach, Teddington pulled her car to the edge of the curb and parked a couple of houses down from the one she was interested in. It had taken all morning, and some activities she shouldn't know how to do, but she couldn't risk one call or a PNC search. There couldn't be a paper trail back to her – nor even an electronic one.

Looking around, the street wasn't as affluent as she'd expected, given the name Briar Avenue, but it wasn't a hole, either. The semi-detached houses were built in the 1980s, to fulfil some yuppie need for property ownership, but they were small, barely a metre between each coupling, and the front and back gardens were little more than pocket handkerchief size.

When Teddington felt her lip curl at the distinct lack of curb appeal, she forced it back down, and told herself not to be such a snob. She'd been lucky with her home, family, and upbringing; not everyone could say the same. Halfway down the length of the road, there was a gap between the houses where the developers had had an unusual moment of altruism, and installed a playground. Paint peeled from the climbing frame; only one of the three swings was still in use, even the chains from the other two were missing. There was a barren area that might once have had a roundabout, but that was long gone. The very air seemed to slump in sadness.

Teddington chewed her bottom lip. The longer this took, the greater the danger of discovery. She checked the address she'd scrawled. 17 Briar Avenue. Looking across the street, she saw the right house. It wasn't great. The lawn, where it still clung to life, was mostly moss and weed, the windows needed cleaning, and the white uPVC of the door needed a good wipe down, but it wasn't the worst-kept property in the street. The gutters were still in place, and there were no missing or obviously patched tiles on the roof. Something about the house looked lifeless, though, like it was shut up.

All she wanted was to see Oscar safe and well cared for. She owed Charlie a little reassurance, at least. Actually, as she sat with her hands on the steering wheel, she told herself she didn't owe the damn man anything. He was a convict, who'd lost touch with his son because he'd killed a man. She didn't owe him *anything*. She reached for the ignition, but didn't press it. As a mother, she knew the pain of being separated from your child; whatever she might think of Charlie as an inmate, he was a human being. He deserved to know his son was healthy.

Stymied by her own vacillations, Teddington sat for another half an hour, watching number seventeen. There was no movement in or around the house. A woman walked by, a pushchair directed by one hand, a small boy grasping the other. The boy was still very young, with a head of full blond curls. Teddington couldn't help the small smile that tipped her lips as he turned to his mother. *What a little cherub.* He looked so cute in the bright blue jumper of his school uniform. Teddington checked her watch – 3:09. Maybe that was why there was no one in number seventeen – Cathy might still be picking up Oscar from school.

The mother and the two children had walked past number seventeen, and were heading for the playground.

Teddington frowned. They couldn't be, could they? No.

But …

The boy was about the right age, blond like Charlie. Charlie hadn't had any contact with Cathy since going inside, and that was three years ago. She had no idea what Cathy looked like, no idea what kind of woman Charlie would find attractive – she discounted herself; that was situational only. So, it was altogether possible this small family was the one Teddington wanted to see. She smiled and hoped so as the smiling little boy rushed to the swing.

The mother had turned the pushchair now, and Teddington could see another little bundle, apparently asleep in the chair. From the appalling frills on the bonnet and fuchsia pink of the baby blanket, she assumed it was a girl. Her guts knotted, and her heart twisted. She watched them and hoped. Then, she looked to number seventeen.

As much as she wanted to just drive away and tell Charlie his son was well, she had to be sure. Lip between her teeth, she stepped from the car, taking care to lock it before heading to the playground.

The woman looked up, offered Teddington a frown. It took Teddington a moment to realise that as a woman without a child entering a playground, she was to be considered a risk. Teddington knew this was a standard over-reaction to stranger danger, the ridiculous perception any childless adult caught looking at a child must be a paedophile, media headlines and propaganda over taking the truth. Still, even perceptual un-reality had to be dealt with.

Sticking her hands deep into her jacket pockets, Teddington walked into the fenced area and sat on the bench to the right of the gate, as far from the family as possible. Swallowing hard, she thought of all the things that should be, and weren't. In the end, she couldn't bring herself to look at the boy anymore, staring instead at the odd spongy-form surface of the playground.

'Hey.' The voice made Teddington jump, and she looked up at the woman who was now frowning at her. 'You alright?'

'Fine.' Teddington nodded.

'Why you crying, then?'

Fighting around the lump in her throat, Teddington put her hands to her face, surprised to find out she was indeed crying.

'You sure you're okay?' the other woman asked, bring the pram over with her, sitting next to Teddington, though on the far end of the bench.

Teddington nodded again, sighing out the hurt. 'Yeah. I'm fine. Sorry. Didn't want to upset anyone.'

'S'alright.' The woman looked over to her son, who was now busy exploring the pipe work on the climbing frames.

'He's a cute kid,' Teddington observed. 'This his first year in school?'

'Yeah.' The mother smiled, as she looked over at him.

'He enjoying it?'

'Oh yeah, Cruz loves it.'

'Cruz?' Teddington queried.

'Well, if it's good enough for the Beckhams.'

'Yeah, no, great name,' Teddington apologised. 'Sorry, it just surprised me. I didn't mean to imply there's anything wrong with the name.' So, this wasn't Cathy, and that wasn't Oscar. 'Cruz is five, right?'

The other woman nodded, as she checked the blanket over the little girl was tucked in well enough.

'Does he, do you, know Oscar, then? Oscar Hamilton? They'd be about the same age.'

'Oscar?' the woman frowned up at her. 'You mean Cathy's kid?'

Teddington nodded, noting just how clouded the woman's face had become.

'You from the Social?'

Teddington frowned as she shook her head. 'No. Why would I be?'

'You're not a friend of Cathy's?'

Teddington was overly aware of the thin ice she was on. There were a number of ways she could go with this conversation, and they all had their hazards. She had to make a call on who this woman was, what her relationship with Cathy would be, and a guess which route was the most likely to get her the information she needed. All that ran through her mind in a nanosecond. 'No,' she said, 'but I know Oscar's father.'

Something darkened on the woman's face.

'His biological father.'

That news was surprisingly easy on the other woman.

'I just want to know that Oscar's okay. Don't want to interfere, or get involved or anything. I just want to be able to tell his dad the boy's doing okay.'

She watched, the other woman was frowning, kept glancing nervously toward the houses.

'Is he doing okay?' The swell of bile in her gut told Teddington the answer wasn't going to be "yes."

The woman swallowed and turned haunted eyes to Teddington. 'I haven't seen Oscar in a year. He didn't start school in September.'

Teddington frowned. 'Did they move on?'

This time, the woman shook her head slowly and licked her lips. 'We just haven't seen him. A few months ago, Cathy was obviously pregnant, and now, she's not, but none of us have seen the baby, either.'

Frozen dread washed through Teddington. She twisted to the house. Fear stretched every nerve. She couldn't sit by and do nothing. The draw of that house was too much. She absently thanked the woman, as she stood and walked to the front door of number seventeen.

Teddington saw the doorbell, but got the distinct impression it wouldn't work. Instead, she rapped hard on the door and waited. For a second, she thought she heard something, but if there was a sound, it didn't repeat. Dismissing it as her own imagination, she knocked again, harder and longer.

No response.

Again, harder, longer.

This close, she could smell something sour emanating from inside the house. She stepped back, looked around. All the windows were secure. Turning, she saw the woman from the playground had her son in hand, and was pushing the pram back along the street. For a second, their eyes met, but the woman turned away quickly, hurrying into a house up the road.

Returning her attention to number seventeen, Teddington moved down the side. There was no barrier to the back garden, so she went that way. The windows and door were all locked. She knocked again. She went to the windows and looked in. *God, what a mess! Little wonder that woman asked if I was from the Social.*

Moving back to the front of house, Teddington took her mobile from her bag, hesitating. If she did this, she couldn't hope for anonymity anymore. Some things were more important. She rang 999. Though her heart and stomach were churning turmoil, she was sure this was the right thing to do. When the answer came, she asked for the police and gave them all the details she could, including her own. Hanging up, she was left pacing the length of the street, terrified to hang around the house, as she waited the thirteen minutes for a patrol car to appear.

Too worried about what was happening inside number seventeen, she didn't consciously register the two police officers, only they were there, and appeared to move in slow motion. Didn't they understand a child's life was in danger?

'Miss?'

'Hi, you have to break in, there are kids in there. They're in trouble.'

'Your kids?'

'No!' Teddington was too worried to care about the insult. She took a deep breath and tried again. 'This is the residence of Cathy Hamilton. She has a son Oscar, five, but no one's seen him in a year. There may also be a young baby in there. Go up to the front door, and you'll smell how bad the place stinks. Go to the back door and you'll see what a mess the place is. It's a health hazard. Those kids are in danger.'

She watched the man look past her and at the house. He didn't appear any more impressed than she had been. 'What makes you certain there's a kid in there?'

'I heard something,' she said. The more she had thought about it, the more certain she was. She also figured this was not the time for sheepishness. 'I'm pretty sure it was a child's cry.'

She knew procedure; she knew what she'd told them was sufficient grounds for them to break into the house. The two exchanged a glance and walked up to the front door. They knocked, got no response. The taller one, the one she'd spoken to, tried the handle. Nothing. They disappeared around the back. Soon enough, they returned. The shorter stockier one raised his foot and kicked at the door.

The whole frame gave way and collapsed into the hallway of the house.

Three different exclamations of disgust harmonised. The smell assaulted the senses. A number of flying things escaped the rancid prison. Teddington watched as the two officers each covered their noses and mouths with one hand. All three stared into the interior. It was dark, dank. There were piles of papers and magazines in the hall. Black mould crept up the wall like a deranged finger painting, a dirty protest.

The two officers exchanged a look; one pulled a torch from his belt and switched it on, checking the balance of the door before he stepped up and into the house. The second officer followed him. Teddington watched, as they passed the stair well and looked into the other rooms.

'What do you think you're doing?' the shorter one asked when she followed them over the door.

'Bedrooms.' She pointed upward. 'If there are kids here, they're probably upstairs.'

'Hey, you can't go up there!'

But, he couldn't stop her, and Teddington couldn't stop herself despite her disgust.

She picked her way between the trash and the clothes on the stairs. She didn't dare touch the banister; the thought made her skin crawl. There were things growing on the rubbish at her feet, creatures scuttling at the intrusion of humanity. She could smell sour sweat, stale beer, stagnant cigarette smoke. Illegal cigarette smoke.

She covered her nose and mouth with both hands, desperately trying not to gag as she reached the tiny landing. Unflushed toilets. Filthy nappies. Rotting food. At least she hoped it was rotting food. Anything could have died in this.

'You shouldn't be in here.'

But, the police officer at her shoulder managed to sound like he was glad she had gone up first. For a second, they gaped in shock into the open door of a messy front bedroom. *Puts Tracey Emin to shame.* The bed was buried under a heap of clothes, rubbish and drug taking paraphernalia. In the silence of their shock, they heard something from the closed door to their right.

'Could be a rat,' the man said.

Teddington doubted it. The hope she heard in the man's tone might echo her own wishes, but she was too realistic to see hope here. Hardly able to breathe, Teddington felt like she was just an observer, watching a horror movie play out, knowing what was about to happen, and screaming at the screen not to go in there. Every fibre of her being wanted to pull back, yet it was her hand that grasped the handle. She pushed the door open. For a suspended moment, she couldn't move, as the horrific scene etched itself into her memory.

The smell was overwhelming. The officer beside her retched, throwing up on the landing. Thin curtains hid the scene from the sun's sight, but she could see the piles of detritus around the room. Full nappies lay open on the floor, crawling with flies, their drone the only sound. The blue packaging of a nappy pack was the only colourful thing in the room, its colourful image of a bright smiling baby at such odds with what Teddington was seeing, and struggling to comprehend.

In the big, once white cot, was a baby, flies and maggots crawled over its many-days dead body, and right beside it, Teddington was staring into the white wide eyes of an emaciated five-year-old, his stomach bloated painfully.

'Call an ambulance.' She pushed the words out, as she stepped into the room. She searched for a blanket, but there wasn't one. Instead, she took off her jacket, held it to her chest with her chin, as she reached inside that child's prison and picked up the desperately thin boy. He was freezing cold, the filthy t-shirt clung to his tiny frame, and she could feel nothing but skin and bone as she picked him up. Acid tears burned her eyes, her throat ached, her nose ran, as her heart twisted to hold such a fragile creature. She wrapped him in her jacket, giving him what warmth she could as she cradled him as easily as a newborn.

She headed out, having to hold the sticky rail to be sure she didn't fall with such a precious cargo. She could already hear the ambulance sirens. As she took him down, the boy just looked up at her, big eyes, scared and hopeless. She sobbed as the second police officer helped her carefully over the broken door. Again in the fresh air, Teddington fell to her knees, still cradling the boy. She was shaking, all the memories, the tattered emotions crashing in on her. How could any mother do this?

Then, the paramedics were there, taking the boy, asking her questions which she would never remember. Pain was ripping her apart. 'Don't let him die.' She knew she was repeating the desperate phrase, as the paramedics got the boy into the back of the ambulance, and the police officer held her back.

'You're not family,' he told her gently. 'You can't go with him.'

She turned to the man. He was right. She wasn't family.

But, she knew someone who was.

Chapter 11

Charlie had gym time.

He'd looked at that list first thing and had had to grab the nearest guy and get him to confirm he was in fact reading what he thought he was reading. What surprised him was the man he'd grabbed was Winehouse's lackey, Paul, and when he'd confirmed what Charlie hadn't expected, he delivered a message from Winehouse.

'Sometimes the rot starts at the leaf and works its way down.'

The obscure-message-of-the-day didn't help Charlie much.

Charlie walked out of the showers, fresh and clean, dressed, and feeling human for the first time in a long time. He used the towel to rub his hair as he walked back to his cell. After folding his towel, he sat on the bare slats of the lower bunk to think.

There were two treadmills in the gym. He'd taken one and started running. He hadn't run in ages, running on the spot in his cell wasn't the same, but he cranked up the machine and really stretched his legs. God, it had felt good. He was glad he'd kept up the exercising, the stretching; he wasn't running to his best, but at least he was running, even if he was getting nowhere. Then, Keen had come in.

'Slow down, boy. No demons out to get you here,' the old man had said, as he took up the treadmill beside Charlie.

Charlie had slowed. He had listened to what Keen had to say, not least of which seemed to be a thank you for helping Teddington. Which made no sense, and just added to the questions he had about the pair of them. What made instant sense was what Keen told him.

'Condensation starts at the top of the shower. If you want to stop it dripping down, clean the ceiling.'

He'd have to be an idiot not to get the message, but just how high -

'Bell.'

Charlie was yanked out of his thoughts, surprised to see Sanchez in his doorway.

'Get up. You're coming with me.'

This won't work out well, Charlie rose. When he was told to put out his hands, he did nothing but scowl as cuffs were slapped on him.

'What's this about?' he demanded, as Sanchez pulled him forward, along the landing and down the stairs. Other prisoners were staring, jeering, as he was led away. At the exit, he went through the first door. Another officer was waiting on the far side of the double barrier. Senior Prison Officer Turner. As soon as Sanchez locked one door, Turner undid the other.

This was wrong. Charlie glowered as he was led out; they never did anything this quickly. If there was paperwork to be done, Charlie didn't see the signatures. He was led out to a waiting transport and bundled into the back. His stomach gripped.

'What's going on?'

Sanchez neither answered, nor met his eye, as he secured him in place, before knocking on the back of the cab. The vehicle was on the move before Sanchez sat down.

This was so wrong. Worries and fear caught Charlie in a maelstrom.

He pulled at the cuffs; they weren't going anywhere. 'What the *hell* is going on?' he demanded of the two silent officers.

'You'll find out soon enough,' Turner told him.

This wasn't going to be good. Charlie's heart pounded as hard as if he was still running on that damn treadmill. 'Can't you tell me anything?'

The two men exchanged a glance. The only thing Charlie could read was their discomfort. *Oh, God, this is bad.*

'There's been an emergency,' Turner told him. 'We're taking you to the hospital.'

That didn't tell Charlie anything. What kind of emergency? Oh, dear God. The only person he knew in hospital was Mohr. Had the man died? He leaned forward, elbows on knees, covering his face. Dear God, had he killed again? *Once in cold blood was bad enough. Have I unintentionally beaten a man to death?*

No, wait. If Mohr was dead, why would they be taking me to the hospital? The police station, yes, but not the hospital. And if this was about Mohr, where were the cops?

This had to be something else. *Think man, think.* His family, then? No, they had pretty much cut him off. Of immediate family, there was only his parents. They didn't talk, but that didn't mean he didn't care. *Oh, please, let nothing have happened to Mum or Dad.*

These thoughts and a million more, each worse than the last, crowded his mind on that endless trip. When at last they stopped, Sanchez unlocked the grill door Charlie was sat behind. They rearranged the cuffs so he was linked to both Sanchez and Turner. It was an awkward way to get from the van, but it had to be done. There were uniformed police waiting for them at the back entrance to the hospital, and they led the way through the corridors.

The scent of too much disinfectant assailed Charlie. He tried to think of why he was being brought here, but all his years as a cop didn't help make sense of it. He knew they were reaching the end of their journey when he saw the way barred by double doors that stated 'No unauthorised entry.' There was a woman standing to the side of the hall.

Trained to be observant, he automatically catalogued her appearance. She wore low heels, a soft jersey knit dress, the deep burgundy throwing red highlights off long wavy hair that hung softly unfettered around her face. Her head was bowed; he couldn't see her to recognise her. Her shape was good, all woman; the curve of her ankle and calf showed she kept fit. The way she hugged herself suggested she was in pain.

A doctor in scrubs appeared at the door.

'Mrs Teddington?'

'Yes?'

When the woman looked up, stood away from the wall, Charlie felt like the world was shifting. That was Teddington? What was she doing here? What was the doctor telling her so quietly? Given the way her hand went over her mouth, it couldn't be good.

Finally, the doctor looked up saw the police and prison officers and their charge advancing on them. Charlie was utterly at a loss to understand what was going on. When Teddington looked to him, her eyes were wide and watery. She'd been crying for some time. *Devastated*. It was the only description that fit.

The doctor tapped her on the upper arm. 'No more than two.'

Teddington turned to the doctor. 'You can't stop him–'

'Family only, and no more than two.' With that command, the surgeon turned away.

When Teddington turned to the approaching men, her eyes went straight to Charlie. She looked haunted. He didn't understand.

'We can't let him go in alone,' Sanchez pointed out.

'Then, don't.' She put out her own right hand. Her look to Sanchez was challenging. When the man hesitated, Charlie saw the muscles in Teddington's jaw working. 'There isn't time to piss about.'

Sanchez looked to Turner, who nodded. Only after Sanchez's cuff was moved to Teddington, did Turner release the cuff on his own right wrist.

'What's going on?' Charlie demanded, even as he followed Teddington through the double doors. Inside, they entered the theatre area. The scrubbed surgeon, pointed them to another door. Teddington moved swiftly, nearly dragging Charlie, who was suddenly reluctant, not daring to think about what might be in that room.

Then, they were there.

White tiles, steel fixtures, and in the midst of all the cold sterility, the body of a child under a blue sheet. A tube ran under his tiny nose, but led nowhere. Butterfly needles were taped overlarge on the small frame; intravenous drips fed him saline and the last of a bag of blood. A heart-rate monitor beeped a weak heartbeat.

'No.' *It can't be.* He felt a gentle hand taking his. 'No!'

He couldn't hold himself back, and in two strides, he was at the bed. His hands reached out, his head shook. *How could this be his beautiful boy?* Someone was strangling the air from his lungs, a vice encircled his skull, like it would split.

'Why aren't the doctors in here?' he knew the answer. 'Why aren't they helping him?'

He wasn't the only one struggling with emotions; he could hear it in the words being torn from Teddington.

'There's nothing more they can do. They said there was a blockage in his intestines. They removed it. There was necrotic tissue …'

'Oh, Oscar.' Tears poured from him, as he took the tiny form in his arms. There was no weight to the boy, as he lifted him against his heaving chest. 'Daddy's here.' But, the boy was so small, taller but thinner than when he'd last seen him, three and half years ago. Charlie was inarticulate, emitting a high keening, as the world tore out his heart and trampled on it.

The sound of the heart-rate monitor changed, emitting a single unbroken tone.

He was barely aware Teddington stood before him, her hand on his, her fingers softly stroking back the boy's hair. Charlie took no notice as the doctor quietly turned off the monitor.

The loss of that sound cut Charlie from the world. He was shaking, and he fell to his knees, Teddington doing what she could to control the fall, but he didn't care about the pain, as his weight fell full on his patellae against the linoleum floor. Teddington there beside him, sobbing with him, half cradling him, half cradling his son.

Someone was trying to take the boy away from him. Again. He wouldn't let them. He couldn't. Her words were soft in his ear. She was pulling him back; she was here. The child was taken, leaving him bereft in every way. Her arms wound around him, holding fiercely. The coldness receded, as human warmth reached him. But, it was a moment only, and one he rejected. He was too numb.

There were footfalls. New hands, stronger hands reached him, pulled him. He was drowning, and he didn't care. Her words were in his ear again. He wanted to retreat from it all. She was trying to help, but what help could there be now? He pushed her away. Her yelp reached through the numbness followed by pain, as a fist connected heavily with his jaw. Finally, he turned. She was looking lost and small, her eyes wide, and, as the cuff was removed from her wrist, he could see tears mixed with blood around her eye.

Chapter 12

*I*t's over.

The words echoed around her brain. Teddington sat quietly, while an emotional war tore her insides. The plunging depths of finding Oscar had abated to numbness for a blissful moment, but now, she was completely connected and feeling, fully functional. Now, she had to face the consequences of her actions, and she had an all too clear idea of what that meant.

Teddington sat in the outer office with the Guv's secretary, Vera, the only indication of her turmoil the occasional gurgle from a stomach so full of acid she couldn't eat. Neither woman spoke. What could they say? Teddington had broken every rule, stepped way over the bounds of her responsibility. The moment when Charlie had punched her replayed. He'd looked desolate one second, furious the next. He'd punched her. The boys had subdued him. He'd knelt where they'd held him, desolate. She knew the feeling.

'Send Officer Teddington in.'

Teddington was vaguely aware of the voice, though its significance didn't sink in until Vera called her by her first name. Jolted back to reality, Teddington stood. Her knees felt spongy, but she steeled her spine and returned to the Guv's office.

Peter Jones was a solid man. Tall and square, like he'd been crafted out of building blocks. His full head of hair was still dark, not a single grey. She suspected it might not be entirely natural. Every time she saw it, she thought of Play-Doh moulds. Usually that made her smile. Today, it didn't touch her.

Jones wasn't alone. The personnel advisor was there, too. She felt odd being here, but not in uniform; that hadn't happened before. Her stomach clenched, threatening revolt. Luckily, she hadn't eaten since finding Oscar yesterday, so there was nothing to throw up. Being a prison officer hadn't been an ambition of hers, but now she was one, she found she enjoyed the job, and she didn't want to lose it. Worse was, knowing that if she did lose her job, there was no one to blame but herself.

Feeling hot and cold, and numbly terrified, she stepped up before Jones' desk and stood, waiting for him to speak. Though she didn't look directly at the man next to Jones, she could tell he wasn't best pleased. His lips were an angry, compressed line. Her concentration was on Jones. His face was as sour as overripe lemons, his look as acidic. She swallowed. This would not be good.

'We have discussed this at length.'

The bells are tolling.

'Your actions represent a complete failure of protocol.'

Even his voice was solid, the ominous tone of a hanging judge. She imagined a square of black cloth on his head, as he sentenced her career to death.

'We have taken into consideration your years of good service and your personal circumstances.'

No matter how much she swallowed, the metallic taste at the back of her throat wouldn't shift. The bile in his tone was making her nauseous.

'You are to be given a formal warning.'

Warning? Wasn't it gross misconduct, leading to instant dismissal?

'At this point, a suspension would be in order,' the personnel advisor added. 'However, staffing levels are very tight, so you can consider yourself lucky to retain your job, but understand this, Officer Teddington, going forward, you put one foot wrong, and you will be out of the Prison Service. For good.'

Skin. Teeth. Of.

'Yes, sir. Thank you, sir.'

* * *

Something clawed at Charlie's guts, tearing him apart, ripping him open from the inside.

Guilt.

It consumed him. Left him so completely empty, he was helpless, utterly incapable of doing anything. He heard the key in the cell door, but he didn't care if it was locked or unlocked. Open or closed, made no difference. He didn't pass through it. It had taken the last ounce of his strength to get to his top bunk, and he'd only bothered with that because the bloodied mattress of the bottom bunk had yet to be replaced. He lay there, awake or asleep, not noticing if it was day or night, ignoring calls to meals.

'You have a visitor.'

Charlie heard the voice, even recognised it as Sanchez, but took no notice. He never had visitors; they must be talking to someone else. He just continued to lie on his side, staring at the wall. Staring at a child's drawing. But, not one done by his child. His fingers rested on the waxy surface of crayon.

'Get up.'

He didn't even have a picture from his own kid. Now, he never would. He pressed in and scrunched up the picture.

'I said, get up!'

Heavy hands fell on his lower legs, swung him round with such force, Charlie had to move, catching himself on the edge of the bed to avoid falling. He sat, staring sullenly at the floor. Sanchez stood in his peripheral vision, but Charlie didn't have the energy to face him. 'I don't get visitors.'

'You do now.'

The voice was dark and full of a disgust he hadn't heard from Sanchez before. It was no more than he deserved. He was hollow. The one reason he looked forward to getting out of this place had been stolen from him.

'I don't want –'

'I don't give a crap what you want, Bell,' Sanchez snarled. 'Get off your arse.'

There was little point in arguing, so Charlie slid off the bunk, and followed Sanchez to the visiting room, even though it wasn't visiting hours. Only one table was occupied, so it was clear who his visitors were, though he didn't recognise the man, nor the woman in black. Not, at least, until she looked up, and he saw Teddington. She looked every bit as wretched as he felt, her face unusually pale, and not just because of the contrast with her nightly garb. There were dark rings under her eye and a scab in her right eyebrow.

'I do that?' he asked as he sat, his fisted hands resting on the table top.

'Not important.'

It was to him. He wasn't much of a man, but he'd never hit a woman before. He wondered if there was even an ounce of decency left in him. He hung his head, studying the table between his hands.

'Charlie, this is Michael Levi. He specialises in family law. He's prepared some papers for us.'

Us? Now he did look up. *Why would she speak about 'us'?* 'Why?'

She averted her eyes momentarily. He could see she was steeling herself to get this right, to deal with whatever his reaction might be. 'I need your power of attorney to have Oscar's body released, and make arrangements, for burial or cremation.'

'No one burns my son.' His anger blazed.

'Okay.' Her voice was unusually quiet. 'Burial it is, then.'

With that, his anger dispersed as quickly as it had arrived.

'You need to sign this.' Levi pushed some papers and a pen across to him.

It was automatic to flick through, but he didn't take any of it in. He let the papers fall, staring blankly.

'If you don't sign,' Levi was all business, 'the boys will be buried by the State in a pauper's grave.'

Oscar deserved better than that. Charlie picked up the pen and signed.

'Thank you,' Levi said, taking the papers and stuffing them in his bag, as he turned to Teddington. 'I'll let you know if there are any developments with the other child.'

'What other child?'

'Thank you, Mr Levi,' Teddington said nothing more, as the lawyer left.

When they were alone, she couldn't quite meet Charlie's eye.

'Is there anything in particular you want me to arrange? Burial, but what about flowers? Any preference for the coffin? A gravestone, marker? Is there a particular religious pathway you want followed? Your file says C of E, but …' Her voice had trailed off.

He shook his head. 'Whatever.'

'Charlie?' Her hand went over his on the table top.

'No touching.'

The dark voice came from behind him. He'd forgotten Sanchez was still there.

Unable to look her in the eye, he concentrated on her hand. She drew it back. He watched as she clasped her hands together, so tight the knuckles turned white. So close. Inches that might as well be miles.

'What's that, Charlie?'

He didn't respond.

'Charlie, what have you got in your hand?'

He couldn't tell her. He opened his fingers. The paper crackled, as he released the pressure. She shifted slightly. There was a pause. Perhaps she needed permission. He didn't know, didn't care.

Teddington reached out and took the paper. As she opened it, her groan was pure pain. She lay it flat, smoothed her hand over the picture. It would never flatten now.

'Jesus, Charlie. I am so sorry.'

The lump in his throat stopped him responding. He should tell her it wasn't her fault. Only, it was. He was blissful in his ignorance, until she'd brought those pictures and dragged him into hell. Because of her, he knew he'd stuffed up. Royally.

'Charlie?'

Unable to bear the sight of that picture, he closed his eyes, compressed his lips. Averted his head, from her, from Sanchez.

'Charlie, I've been told you aren't eating.'

Her voice was stronger now.

'You haven't shaved, or washed, since they brought you back. Christ, you're still in the same clothes.'

He remained silent, trying to block the painful memories. 'Charlie?'

What did she expect? What response should he make?

'Charlie, you have to take care of yourself.'

'Why?'

'Because,' her voice cracked, and she had to start again, but she leaned closer, almost whispering. 'Because I can't bear to see that same look of hopelessness in your eyes that I saw in Oscar's. Please. Please, don't give up.'

'You have no idea.' When he turned to her, he was snarling. 'All the time I've been in this place, I believed out there, somewhere, was something good I'd done. That I'd left a son, who could have a better life than I did, be a better man. Now, there's nothing.'

He glared at her, but one blink, and his vision cleared. As she stared back, her eyes wide and her lip slightly parted, he realised he wasn't the only one lacking hope. He forced his face to relax. She didn't deserve this. Something clicked.

'What other child?' he asked.

She closed her eyes and looked away, he heard her swallow, saw her hands clench. She was so close. He reached out, covering both her hands with one of his.

'No touching.' This time, the warning was full of menace.

He sat back, numbness replaced the moment of futile anger. 'What aren't you telling me?'

Drawing in a steadying breath before she looked up at him, Teddington licked her lips. 'Oscar wasn't the only child I found.'

He didn't know what she'd seen or been through, but he could see the horror of it in her eyes, hear it in her tone. He didn't understand, but some part of the man he had been was trying to kick his way back. 'Tell me.'

She had to swallow, to lick her lips, gather herself before she could meet his eye. 'There was another child, another boy. This one only a couple of mo—' her voice cracked. She had to clear her throat to finish. '-months old. He was already dead when I got there.'

He stared at her. Could she really be saying what he thought she was saying? He waited for more. It didn't come. 'Tell me.'

She shook her head. 'That's it, that's what I found. Two children. A dead baby and a dying child.'

It wasn't all she'd found.

'The baby …' Again, she had to pause to force herself to say what was being said.

This wasn't a side of Teddington he had ever seen before. Usually, she was so calm, never fazed by anything the inmates could throw at her. She was struggling with the situation as much as he was, taking it personally. He couldn't fathom why.

'It would appear the birth was never actually registered. As far as we can tell, the baby didn't even have a name. We don't even know who the father is.'

He frowned. 'What's Cathy say?'

Her eyes locked with his, and he didn't want to define the darkness he saw. He hoped to God that loathing was not for him.

'Ted—?'

'She's not been found.'

Charlie blinked, struggling to understand. 'Pardon?'

Carefully controlling her breathing, Teddington searched the ceiling for a script that wasn't there. 'The house was shut up, and the police haven't found Cathy yet. Neighbours say her boyfriend, who they assume to be the baby's father, was last seen about a month ago, storming out of the house, but they don't even know his name. Apparently, it was normal behaviour for him, when he wasn't pushing drugs. They didn't want to know him. Cathy wasn't exactly popular, so all the neighbours cared about was that she wasn't causing trouble anymore. They hadn't actually noticed she was gone.'

Charlie didn't know what to say. 'I can't believe ...'

'Then, don't.' Finally, Teddington sounded as sure and steady as she usually did. 'We don't know what happened. We don't know where Cathy is. Frankly, I don't care. I can't see how she could come up with any reasonable explanation for what she did. I'm only sorry I didn't do something sooner. I've known for a while you had a son, I should have checked –' Again, she swallowed and looked away. 'Maybe I could've –'

'Don't.'

Charlie froze at Sanchez's warning. Only then, did he realise he'd reached for her again. He turned his head, closed his eyes. Sanchez was just doing his job, but it was keeping Charlie from the human connection he needed. That was the true punishment of prison. Instead, he turned back to Teddington. He didn't understand why she was taking this quite so personally, but he appreciated that she was. 'This isn't your fault, either. You had no reason to check. Why did you?'

She covertly peered around the room. 'After giving you this,' she flattened out the twisted sheet as best she could, 'I felt bad. Like I'd cheated you. Then, you,' her eyes slid up to Sanchez again, 'you helped me when ...' She couldn't say it, and he didn't need her to. 'I just – I wanted ...' She had to try again. 'I thought you deserved the truth, so I went to check on Oscar, thought I'd be able to come back and tell you he was getting on fine, happy, healthy. You know, normal.'

Only, he wasn't.

'I have to ask,' she said at last, 'if I'm allowed to bury the two boys. Are you okay with them being buried together, or would you rather they be buried separately?'

Charlie didn't want to even think about that. He buried his head in his hands, bunched them in his hair. Curling his fingers round, he pulled, like he wanted to yank his scalp off. It hurt, but it couldn't compete with the demons tearing up his guts. Part of him said, 'Crawl away, ignore the world,' another part said, 'Man up, and get on with it.' 'I can't think straight.' *How pathetic could he get?*

'It's okay.' She was sounding like her again now. 'I know it's not easy. I'll do what I can. But, you have to get through this, too.'

Get through what? Losing his kid? She didn't understand. She was a mother. *What, what would she know about it?* 'How?'

'However you can.'

He let his eyes meet hers, watching as she flicked her gaze to Sanchez, then back to him.

'For me.'

The words were so low, he didn't know if she said them or if he imagined it. Even if he was imagining it, he didn't care.

She left, and Sanchez led him back to the cell.

'I didn't know I'd hit her,' he muttered, as he stopped in the cell.

Force spun him, his back hit the wall, a solid iron bar pressed into his oesophagus. Sanchez's forearm pinned him down, all but cut off his breath.

'I did, you bastard. I saw you do it. And you ever raise a hand to her again, and I will beat seven shades of shit out of ya.'

Looking at the hate in the officer's eyes, the malice of his tone, Charlie only questioned one thing. 'Why haven't you?'

Suddenly, the hate disappeared, the venom neutralised, and Sanchez's arm moved away from Charlie's neck. 'Why risk my career beating you, when you're busy beating yourself up?'

The door slammed shut, locked. He was alone with his thoughts. He didn't know how to get through this, but he would. For her.

Chapter 13

Teddington had had to get up and leave. She couldn't stand to watch a man she'd always considered strong, looking so broken and beaten. Not when it was her fault. Sort of. She left, but she couldn't go home. She couldn't face sitting alone in her room. She couldn't face talking to her mother, either. Some places didn't bear visiting.

She passed Chris Roberts as she walked out.

'You look like shit.'

Teddington couldn't help but smile. 'Feel like it, too. Thanks.'

'You still coming tonight?' Roberts surprised her.

All she could do was frown at him.

'Drinks for Turner's birthday, remember?'

With everything else that was going on, she'd completely forgotten.

'Oh, come on. It might cheer you up. After all you've been through, you probably need a break.'

'Well, I could do with a drink.'

It couldn't hurt. For three days, she'd been able to think of little other than that hell she'd found poor Oscar and his brother in. It was with her every moment of every day, awake or asleep. She needed to at least try to think of something else, and a birthday celebration seemed the perfect opportunity. She'd told Charlie he had to look after himself, and she needed to take her own advice. 'I warn you now, I might be a bit of a downer on the mood. Feel free to kick me into touch if I am, but I'll be there.'

Unable to face going home, Teddington headed into town. Window shopping was less gratifying than usual. There were a couple of hours to go before she met up with the guys, so she wandered. The big department store in the middle of town was always good for that. Casting only the most cursory of glances over the offerings, all the colours, the bright and the shiny, she circled the sales floors. Then, one thing caught her eye – a little white bear with a blue bow. It was in her hand before she even thought about it. Its fur was so soft.

Her throat ached, and she blinked back tears, remembering another little bear, one with a pink ribbon. She had to have it. Oscar had to have it. She stroked the bear again, looking at the shelf. There was another stuffed animal, a small rabbit. That came, too. Even a boy with no name deserved something cute.

She took the two tiny toys to the counter.

An hour later, she was talking to the pathologist. As she talked, he looked over his half-moon glasses at her. His narrowed eyes, the set lips, the slight frown that could have been deep wrinkles, she wasn't sure. The only thing Teddington knew was no matter how she put the request, his face didn't soften. In the end, she resorted to nothing more than begging.

'Please.'

'It's most irregular.'

'There's nothing regular about this case,' Teddington pointed out. 'Please. It won't hurt anyone.'

'It won't help the boys.'

'I know,' Teddington admitted. It was too late for the boys, but that wasn't the point. 'But, it'll help me.'

The old man sighed, shook his head. Teddington's heart sank further than she thought it could possibly go. His lips pursed, as he reached out a liver-spotted hand and took the rabbit and then the bear. 'The bear for Oscar, the rabbit for the baby, right?'

'Thank you.' She struggled with the words in relief.

'Hmm.' He looked at her, head inclined. 'Now, get out of here.'

* * *

'You okay?'

Teddington turned to look at Sanchez, as he slid onto the bench seat beside her in the Farmers Arms. 'I'm fine.'

He moved in close, closer than she was comfortable with. 'You look like you've been crying.'

She drew in a breath. 'Have,' she admitted.

'Because of *his* kid?' Sanchez just about avoided sneering.

'Because two children died unnecessarily, and you know why that gets to me.' She wasn't going to admit what she'd done, tell him, or anyone, about the toys, but that had helped her.

'But, why are you arranging the funeral? That's above and beyond.'

'Same reason, you know that. Besides, there's no one else to do it. Look, Enzo, can we forget all this for tonight, and just enjoy the evening?'

He picked up his beer and handed her her wine. 'Okay.' They clinked glasses and relaxed.

Over the next half hour, the crowd grew to include Chris Roberts, Nigel Turner, and Will Norman, then Teddington was surprised to see Len Robbins. Teddington knew he liked to go for a drink after work, but she was sure he'd declined this celebration. He got a round in for the group and joined them, the additional pints and wine taking up most of the space on the table they'd gathered around. It was warm and comfortable. They embarrassed Turner with an inappropriate gift and a kiss-o-gram.

Free flowing conversation jumped from politics to TV, to girlfriends to the state of the roads now the M20 was being dug up – again; jokes about the European Traffic Cone Mountain made Roberts laugh so hard he snorted his beer. Teddington felt a lot of the pressures and troubles of the last few days ease away, the strain between her shoulder blades releasing.

They were all still laughing, when her gaze moved up and she saw the pub's TV screen. The sport had been interrupted for the news, and she saw the action, as a blonde woman was escorted into a police building over the banner headline, 'Catherine Hamilton arrested for infanticide while holidaying in France.' So, that was Cathy. She could sort of see what Charlie might have seen in the woman. *But how could someone who looked so normal have done what she had done? Who goes abroad and leaves their kids to die?*

That washed the smile away.

'Not tonight.'

She turned when Enzo whispered in her ear. She didn't remember him putting his arm around her shoulders, or when she'd leaned into him. But, he was close and warm, and a good friend. He was right, too. She was involved, but she shouldn't be that involved. She smiled at him. 'Okay.'

His kiss surprised her, but since he was the one who turned and dealt with the cat calls from the others, she just sipped her wine, and let the tension go. Her smile didn't even falter when she spotted the odd look on Robbins' face.

Inevitably, as a group that had come together because they worked together, they ended up talking about work.

'Thank God Richmond's back next week. We can get back to more normal shift patterns. Overtime's good, but I'm knackered.'

Teddington wasn't sure who had said that, but as a murmur of agreement ran round the room, she looked up. 'How'd he afford it?'

The group looked at her like she was bonkers.

'No, really,' she said. 'A couple of months ago, his wife couldn't afford to replace holed shoes, so how did he suddenly afford the kind of holiday I can only dream of?'

'Maybe one of his horses came in,' Robbins offered. 'Not really our business.'

'He's got family all over, maybe one of them paid.'

'Anybody else think the Wing's gotten more subdued lately?' Norman asked.

'Hardly surprising,' Robbins suggested, 'given what's been happening.'

'Yeah,' Norman agreed, still frowning. 'Only, it started before Tommy. It was getting quieter then, too.'

'Quieter, yeah,' Teddington agreed, thinking about it now, 'but not calmer. It was like the place was holding its breath. Tense, waiting for something to happen.'

'Well, something did happen,' Roberts agreed. 'Tommy topped himself.'

'No, he didn't.' Teddington hadn't meant to say that out loud, but the men all turned to her, some pints suspended by their surprise.

'It was suicide,' Robbins stated.

Teddington shook her head. 'Can't be. If he'd killed himself, where's the thing he cut his guts open with? If he'd been going for hari-kari, the weapon would have been with him – it wasn't. Someone took it; that means murder.'

'That's for the police to worry about,' Sanchez spoke too brightly.

Teddington felt the tightening of his grip. He was warning her off. *Why?*

'Anyone heard how Dyer's doing?'

Teddington felt Sanchez try to head the conversation elsewhere; she raised her hand and slapped him lightly on the chest, stopping him in his tracks.

'Dyer's doing okay,' she offered. 'I dropped in to see him this afternoon. He's still sore, and the cut's going to take a while to heal. It'll leave a scar, but he'll be fine. Physically. Not sure he'll ever be the same though.'

'None of us are, after something like that,' Turner pointed out. He'd been caught out by a group of prisoners a few years ago, and had the scars to prove it.

'Do you reckon he'll come back?' Roberts asked.

'Backroom, maybe.' Teddington shook her head. In all honesty, she couldn't see Dyer ever setting foot inside Blackmarch again, but he might just surprise her.

As the conversation moved on, she felt Enzo snuggle her into the crook of his shoulder. She wasn't sure how to take it. She tensed.

'Do us both a favour.' His voice was a low warning whisper in her ear. 'Just go with it, okay?'

Unsure how she should react, Teddington pulled her head back to look at him, only to have Sanchez claim another kiss. She didn't know what he was playing at, but after their last encounter, she knew it wasn't the obvious. Which was why she kissed him back, her hand rising to his neck. The tips of her fingers feeling the soft short hairs at the edge of his hairline.

The cat calls got worse, pulling them apart. Roberts was even clapping, Turner and Norman laughing.

'Well, that proves all the rumours about you and Bell are bollocks.' Norman laughed, tipping his drink towards them before he emptied the glass. 'Anyone else for another?'

* * *

'Okay, then, what's going on?' Teddington asked Sanchez, as they stopped by her front garden gate. It was gone two in the morning. After the pub, someone had had the great idea of going to a night club. They'd shared a taxi back, since they lived in the same street.

'What?' Sanchez leaned towards her. Despite the number of drinks, she knew he wasn't that drunk; every other one had been water.

'You know what I mean.'

He shrugged. 'I just got this over-powering urge to protect my oldest friend. Keep you safe. D'ya mind?'

She minded the prevarication, but not particularly the action. She kind of appreciated the protection, the closeness she'd been missing. Right now, she needed it. She shook her head. 'As long as you know it can't go anywhere.'

He nodded, rather sadly. His hands moved to her face, brushing her loose hair back. 'You sure?' He kissed her again. When he pulled back, he looked even more sorrowful. 'You're sure.' With a half-smile, he left her, crossing the road walking the two houses up.

She watched his retreating back, before heading up the path to her house. He was a good man. It was a shame she didn't feel more for him. But, she wasn't going to drop the fact he wasn't telling her something – now just wasn't the time to pursue it.

Chapter 14

'Surprised you're in,' Turner remarked, when he saw Teddington come in for handover.

'That's rich.' She laughed. 'You're the one who was three sheets to the wind last night. How did you make it in this morning?'

'Urgh.' He rolled his eyes. 'Threw up when I got home. Peggy made me drink a pint of water, then fed me Resolve this morning, before kicking my worthless hide out of bed.'

Teddington smiled. 'She's a great woman, your wife.'

'I'm a lucky man,' he acknowledged. 'I know. Better get her something on the way home.'

'I'd suggest flowers *and* chocolates.'

'I'm thinking a new bathroom mat, after what I did.' Turner laughed.

With the arrival of the rest of the afternoon shift, conversation turned to the business of handover, not that there was much to hand over. As had been observed the previous evening, things had become very quiet.

As she and Robbins stepped into the Wing, Teddington looked around. All the doors were open and back. She avoided lingering on any one door too long. There were a few people milling around, but not as many as she might have expected. She did spot the newbie, though.

The unofficial assessment of Matthew Pearson looked about right: cocky little bleeder, who had a lot to learn and didn't yet know it. He was talking to Morris and a small knot of other men. That was a good sign. Morris cooperated with Keen, and should help teach the boy a thing or two.

Hearing their arrival, Morris looked up, so did Pearson. He looked surprised to see a female in uniform. Robbins turned away, heading towards the board as he had a notice to add to it. Teddington met Pearson's leer, knowing she couldn't be the first to back down.

'Wow, a female screw. This'll be fun.' Pearson puffed up with pointless bravado. 'What do you think, guys?'

That was when he noticed what Teddington had seen all along. The general quiet of the wing had turned to stony silence. Although not one of the men had moved, they were distancing themselves from Pearson.

Pearson glanced around, saw what had happened, and was a lot less courageous when he turned back.

Teddington paced over to face him. 'I am Officer Teddington. You, Pearson, will refer to me as *Officer* Teddington. You will show me, and all my colleagues, respect. You've just arrived and have a lot to learn. I suggest for your first lesson, you understand this; six days ago, two inmates, both bigger and scarier than you, tried abusing me. They will remain in hospital for the foreseeable future.'

Satisfied his whitening face showed he had got the message, Teddington turned and walked slowly up the stairs, heading for level two, pacing her way towards Keen's cell.

* * *

'Your girlfriend's back.'

Charlie stared at the ceiling. 'Teddington's not my girlfriend,' he pointed out. He hadn't spoken to anyone but Teddington since he'd held Oscar while he died. And Sanchez, he admitted to himself.

'Then, how come you know who I'm talking about?' Runt sniggered. 'Look, man, I couldn't give a toss myself, but Keen thought you might want to know … the new guy, Pearson, was insulting her. Keen thinks he needs a lesson in respect.'

There were any number of people capable of that. Runt, Paul, him, Sanchez, Teddington herself. But, there was one point he wouldn't give in to. 'I don't do Keen's dirty work.'

Runt shrugged and pushed away from Charlie's door frame. 'That's your problem all over, mate. But, hell, it's your life. For all I care, you can stay up there and rot in your bed. Just like your kid.'

The words stabbed him deep in the heart. Rot in his bed. Just like his kid. Charlie closed his eyes. Bile rose in his throat, but there was nothing in his stomach to fetch up. He hadn't eaten any more than he'd spoken, less, in fact. He didn't know much about what Teddington had found, he hadn't watched the news broadcasts, but Morris had come over and told him what they were saying.

The two children, one several days dead and the other dying, had been found in a – as Morris had put it – complete shit-hole. The names of the officers and the civilian who'd called them in were kept out of the press, but there were enough people around to know who it was, and that Teddington's involvement not being public was something of a miracle. He wondered if Piper had anything to do with that, but he'd never know, so he didn't worry about it. The police had had to trace Cathy to the continent and bring her back. In handcuffs.

Once, when he'd been a constable in uniform, he'd attended a house where a body had been rotting for a week. The sight and the stench had stayed with him, and he recalled it now, the knowledge making Morris' descriptions all too real.

'One day.'

Charlie's eyes snapped open. How long had he been torturing himself with those images? Eternity was probably what he deserved. Turning his head, he found he was staring straight at Teddington.

'What?'

'You have one day. If you're still behaving like this tomorrow, it'll be classified as hunger strike, and we'll call the psychotherapists.

End up in a straitjacket, and not only can you kiss goodbye to any parole option, you'll not be allowed to attend your son's funeral. Which is Wednesday, by the way.'

With that, she stalked out.

'What about the other one?' he asked, pushing himself onto his elbows. 'What about the baby?'

She paused in the door and turned back to him, sorrow warring with the blank mask she was trying to maintain. 'Working on it.'

* * *

Working on it.

Charlie stayed on his elbows and watched the empty doorway. *One day? Psychotherapists?* He'd had to see a few of them after what he'd done. *No hope of parole? What did that matter?* He had nothing to get out for.

Working on it.

When he'd walked towards her at the hospital, Teddington had been crying her eyes out. She'd been the one who had found the boys. She'd arranged for him to be with his son at the end, when Sanchez and Turner had been prepared to hold him back. She'd been the one trying to help him when Oscar passed. And he'd hit her. She'd been doing everything she could to take care of funeral arrangements. And all the time, she'd obviously been in pain. If what Morris had told him was even half true, then she had walked through hell for his boy. She was still trying to help the other child, to whom she had neither connection nor obligation. But, he had an obligation to her now. He owed her.

And as for missing Oscar's funeral?

No way.

Carefully, Charlie lowered himself to the floor. He had to hold on to the bunk, as an unexpected light-headedness threatened his balance.

Standing like that, his gaze fell on the back of his hand. His skin looked pale, almost see-through, appearing to hang from nothing, the veins threaded blue and thin. The hands of an old man. Self-loathing shuddered through him, as he hung his head and stepped over to the tiny metal sink. Putting the plug in, he started the water running and prepared to shave for the first time in four days. Glancing up, he recoiled from the man in the mirror.

Dirt darkened hair pointed all over the place, matted and sticking up, as if he didn't even own a comb. Dark shadows underlined sunken eyes, his cheekbones too prominent, the darker blond of his beard only serving to highlight the pallor of his skin, doing nothing to hide the hollowness of his cheeks. Disreputable. Disgraceful. Dishonest. That was how he looked. *What happened to your self-respect?* He sneered at the man in the mirror. He'd promised himself he'd get through this, for her. He was letting them both down, and deserved a kick in the arse for it.

Turning off the tap, he leaned down, soaking his whole face in the warm water, only just able to get his head into the basin. Releasing his breath in a steady stream, he felt the bubbles run across his rough cheeks. He could just stay here, never draw breath again, drown in a basin.

No, you can't. Grow up.

He hadn't done enough for his son. Hell, he hadn't done *anything* for his son, but there was one last thing he could do, and he wouldn't fail Oscar this time.

Besides, he thought, as he began the process of scratching thick hair from his chin, he knew even if he tried topping himself, he wouldn't be successful. The fight-for-life instinct was too strong – at the last second he would pull back. If he did manage to maintain enough control not to pull back, he'd black out anyway, fall out of the basin and survive. Which would put him on suicide watch, and ensure he missed Oscar's funeral.

As he shaved, he noticed his stench. Well, dealing with that should fill up another ten minutes.

It wasn't until he came back from the shower block that he noticed the books on his table. Thinking about it, they had been there before he'd left; he just hadn't bothered registering them.

Putting his used clothes to one side – he'd do the laundry later – he sat down and looked at the three books. They had all been read, but remained in good condition. Lee Child, *Killing Floor*. Steven Leather, *Hard Landing*. Jasper Fforde, *The Big Over Easy*. The first two he'd already read, both of which were slightly unsuitable, given they each involved the main character spending time in jail, but he picked up the last. The blurb on the back made it sound like a comedy. He put it down. He wasn't in the mood for amusement.

While wondering why they'd appeared, he had a fairly good idea of who would have left them there. Just in case, he flicked through the books and out of *Hard Landing*, a small note fell.

Please don't give up.

Same handwriting as before. Teddington. He doubted she'd meant this to make him feel like a louse, but it did. Oscar wasn't the only one he had let down, nor was Teddington, but she was the last one left he cared about not letting down. Pulling on a plain marl sweatshirt, Charlie moved out to the landing. No one was hanging around. That was unusual. He looked down. There was activity on the ground floor, preparations for serving the evening meal, but the usual crowd that would gather wasn't there yet.

Charlie frowned. The place wasn't usually this quiet. All the doors were open, and through some of them, he could see inmates sitting quietly. Morris was at his table, playing cards. Only Runt was visible on the second floor, standing guard outside Keen's door. Teddington was on the ground floor, talking to Benny York, who was showing her something in a book. Charlie suspected he was having trouble reading – one of the reasons York was in here was the rage that boiled over when people called him retarded because he couldn't read properly.

Catching movement from his peripheral vision, Charlie saw Robbins walking down the landing, possibly having come from Hart's cell. The two men watched each other, as Robbins steady pace brought him closer. It was no surprise when Robbins stopped close enough to speak to him.

'Dragged yourself out of your pit, then.'

Charlie considered sarcasm, but it felt too much like effort. 'Yes, Officer Robbins.' He wasn't usually so formal, but something in the air suggested he should be. 'Did I miss something?' he asked, looking around, his eyes inevitably drawn down again. 'Everything seems … quiet.'

'It's just peace and order. Nothing to complain about.'

Charlie frowned. 'Officer Robbins? Shouldn't you and Teddington be on a run of night shifts about now?'

'We are. This is a double shift for cover.'

Robbins looked down, following Charlie's line of sight to see it squarely on Teddington. Charlie sensed his tension, then, with a sigh, the man seemed to relax.

'At the best of times,' Robbins told him, 'I'd suggest you give that one up, but she's with Sanchez now.'

Charlie frowned, as Robbins moved on, he looked down at Teddington. Her and Sanchez? Made sense. But, if she was with Sanchez, why had she kissed him?

Okay, he'd kissed her. Both times. But she hadn't objected, hadn't reported him, there'd been no come back. Hang on, wasn't she married? Charlie couldn't see her as the cheating kind, but married, with Sanchez, kissing him? None of it made sense. Another puzzle to solve.

As Robbins moved away, Charlie moved to Hart's cell. Hart was sitting on the lower bunk rubbing his stomach.

'You alright?'

'Fine.' The way the word was squeezed out proved the man a liar.

Charlie frowned. 'Did Robbins punch you?'

Now, Hart looked white for a different reason. 'No.'

Charlie knew a lie when he heard one.

'Piss off, and keep your gob shut.'

He also knew there was nothing he could do. Charlie continued on until he reached Winehouse's cell. Winehouse himself was also at the basin, shaving before the last meal of the day.

'Sorry for your loss,' the older man stated.

Charlie leaned against the doorframe. He wasn't sure what to do with such expressions of sympathy, but figured he probably wouldn't have to get used to it in here. 'Thanks.' He let Winehouse splash water on his face and start dabbing at the damp, before he spoke. 'What did I miss?'

Winehouse stilled, considering. 'What do you mean?'

Charlie held the regard, steady and direct. 'Things are different, quieter. What's going on?'

Shrugging and returning to his facial care, Winehouse was keeping a nonchalant demeanour.

'Well, you and Teddington did manage to beat the living daylights out of Stanton and Mohr, and with that coming right after Tommy's death … I guess everyone's just a little more subdued than normal.'

Charlie watched as the older man took up an aftershave balm, smoothing it over the recently cleared skin. All the time Charlie was overly aware of the fire on his own neck and face. That was what he got for not shaving in four days.

'Here.' Winehouse threw him the small tube, which he deftly caught. 'Looks like you need it more than I do.'

Pressing a little of the ointment onto his fingers, Charlie began to rub it into the sorest parts of his neck. 'Thanks.'

'Keep it.' Winehouse waved away the return. 'There's not much left, and I already have the replacement.' As Charlie continued to soothe his burning skin, Winehouse tidied up the tiny bathroom space and wiped his hands. 'So, now you're back in the land of the living, I trust you'll be back to finding out how Tommy died.'

It wasn't the highest thing on his to-do list, but he guessed it was there, somewhere. 'I wasn't getting anywhere. Don't forget most of the men in here still think of me as a copper, one of "them."'

'To be fair,' Winehouse smiled at him, 'you did have involvement in the cases that put a fair few of them in here.'

'Only a couple are left,' Charlie pointed out. Most of the men he'd put away had either completed their term by now, or had been transferred to a training prison or closer to home. A couple had actually been deported.

'That's enough.' The dark tone came from outside the cell. Charlie was suddenly aware Winehouse's favourite bodyguard, Paul, was behind him. Without thinking about it, he'd put himself in a position of vulnerability, but moving now would be a public acknowledgement of that fact.

With a slight shrug, Charlie let the point pass. 'Thing is, I do ask, and most of the time, the answer's two words with three f's.'

'You didn't get that as a cop?'

'As a cop, I could fall back on threats of time in a cell. That's rather redundant here.'

'Back then, you wore the handcuffs of legality.' Winehouse shrugged as though it was the easiest, most obvious, thing in the world. 'A few days ago, you beat Mohr to a pulp. You don't think you've got anything to threaten them with now?'

It hadn't occurred to Charlie that such notoriety would be useful, but then it hadn't occurred to Charlie that that was what he would be notorious for. He didn't like the idea of acting like – of being – a thug. But, it was a reputation that might have its uses.

'So … what about *you* answering some questions?'

'I didn't see anything.'

Charlie looked at him levelly. 'Do I need to beat it out of you?'

Surprisingly, Winehouse's smile widened at that. 'You haven't left your cell for days. That means you haven't eaten in days. You'll be weakened by the loss of your son and the lack of sustenance. Right now, Paul could beat you to a pulp. Hell, right now, one lucky punch, and I could beat you to a pulp.'

'Have to be a damn lucky punch. I'm still twice your size.' He watched Winehouse pulling on his shirt, buttoning the carefully pressed item. 'You might not have seen anything, but in four days, you've probably heard what I haven't.'

A minute later, Charlie was careful to leave Winehouse and go to collect his meal alone. He didn't need anyone thinking he'd chosen a side.

He would have to get his arse in gear, if he was going to get to the truth of what had happened to Tommy. But, if he did, what would he do with the information? Piper was working on it – what likelihood was there he'd find something Piper couldn't? The shadow of the man he used to be mentally bitch-slapped him for that one.

Thanking the server for his overcooked vegetables, Charlie headed for his cell. The dinners here were never the best, and he hadn't expected to want anything, but as soon as the cooking smell hit his nostrils, the hunger hit his stomach. As bad as the food was, it was, quite literally, a feast to him, the starving man. Glancing up to the top floor, Charlie figured he'd need to go see Keen after he'd finished his food.

'Do you like thin ice?'

Looking up, a forkful of limp carrot halfway to his open mouth, Charlie saw Teddington entering his cell. He put down the fork and closed his jaw. 'Why am I on thin ice, Officer Teddington?'

'You finally get up, get clean, and the first thing you do is go to Winehouse?'

'He was closer,' Charlie pointed out, ignoring the technicality, and re-gathering veg on his fork. 'I'll see Keen after. So, you and Sanchez?'

She frowned, 'Where did you hear that?'

'Robbins. What's your husband say?'

Her look was harder now, her lips compressed. On a man, Charlie would expect that look to precede an attack. He wasn't sure how to take it, as Teddington stepped up to the other side of the table.

'The coroner has agreed to release Baby Hamilton to me. The boys will be buried in the same plot, but different coffins. I trust you're okay with that?'

Suddenly, the lump in his throat wasn't just the burnt offerings. The pressure of those two lives closed in on him. His fault. 'Why didn't you tell me how bad it was?'

'Are you okay with the arrangement, or do you want separate graves?'

There was a tight-pinched tone to her question. Her jaw was clenched, lips pressed together. She wasn't okay with all this. Any of it.

'You didn't answer my question.'

She swallowed, shooting him a hard, warning look. 'Nor will I. I don't have much time. The arrangements?'

He nodded.

'Right, well. I'm not on during the day again till Friday, so I'll see you at the funeral.'

Chapter 15

Charlie's suit was brought out of storage. He hadn't worn it since the trial. He had to pull the belt a notch smaller, but the shirt and jacket were tight across the shoulders and around the biceps. Apparently, he really had been working out a lot.

Sanchez and Richmond had been assigned to escort him to the funeral.

'Good holiday?' he asked despondently, as Richmond put the cuffs on him.

'Great, thanks.'

The mood was way too dour to allow anything more. They went through processing, all the necessary procedures and forms, then, to the back of the van. Charlie saw the hideous irony of attending his son's funeral from a prison van. If he hadn't been in prison, he would have exercised his right to see Oscar, and he would have kept the boy alive.

His fault.

He'd chosen to do what he had done, to cross the line, to become a killer. Oscar had paid the price.

The drive to the cemetery was lost in pointless self-flagellation. He couldn't go back, couldn't change things. All he could do was try to do better from here on in. Then, Richmond was opening the cage, cuffing their wrists. As he stepped from the van, he was surprised to find Teddington standing talking to Sanchez. It was a punch in the gut to see how natural they looked together, how damn good Teddington looked, all in black, smart and demure, incredibly attractive. Her hair was up, but much softer than the way she wore it in work. There was a handbag at her side, but the shoulder strap ran beneath her jacket. When she turned her head to look at him, her neutrally glossed lips parted slightly. She stepped over to him, stopping his progress past the door of the van, and when she spoke, her voice was low and tight.

'Apparently, the local TV and press have no respect, they're filming. So, don't react to them. Don't speak to them.'

He nodded his understanding; no words were getting past the lump in his throat anyway. She lifted up her right hand. Richmond looked from it to Sanchez, who nodded silently, and the cuff was moved to Teddington's wrist. As he watched, Charlie noted she wore a thumb ring, but no wedding ring. There was another on the third finger of her right hand, a ring with an amber-coloured stone. Could be amber, could be topaz, he wasn't knowledgeable enough to know which. Looking at her again, there were matched stud earrings, and a similar pendant resting in the small V neckline of her black silk blouse.

She looked up at him. 'Okay?'

How the hell was he supposed to be okay? They were about to bury his child, but he couldn't expect her to understand how that felt. No parent could, until they had to, and he wouldn't wish this on his worst enemy. Of course, he wasn't okay. He nodded in answer to her question.

'Good.' She stepped back, and they were side by side. As they moved around the van, she whispered, 'Miss Hamilton is also here.'

Another punch to the gut. But, he could see the flashes of photographers – photographer, he amended; there was only one. He spotted the cameraman as he moved beside Teddington towards the waiting graveside service, the two tiny coffins flanked by pall bearers he didn't know. As they approached from one side, he saw the other prison van beyond the grave, and from this, appeared first one burly uniformed female officer, then Cathy, then a second officer. None of them looked happy; angry would be closer to the point.

He hadn't seen Cathy in years; she'd lost too much weight, and gained the sunken eyes and sickly pallor of a junkie. That explained a lot. She was so different from the vibrant young woman he'd had an affair with. Was this his fault too? Was there anything he could have done differently to help her, help them? *No,* that annoying voice in his head reminded him. *Once an addict always an – Oh, shut up.*

Their steps carried them forward, and Charlie barely registered the movement, as Cathy looked up at him, hate in her eyes, but as she glanced to Teddington, the hate overflowed. Her nostrils flared, her lips drew back in a snarl, and she pulled at her restraints looking to attack.

'You bitch!'

Teddington stopped, so Charlie had to.

'This is your fault!'

Charlie couldn't allow that, but as he took breath to respond, Teddington moved, her left hand on his chest, standing before him, her eyes blazing a warning. Her words were low, forced through lips that barely moved, she didn't want the over vigilant camera crew hearing.

'Do not jeopardise your parole.'

He clamped his jaw, as Cathy cursed vilely at them in words and ways that could teach a soldier a thing or two. He unfurled his fists and looked down to Teddington. With a small nod, he indicated his readiness, and her tiny acknowledgement was grateful, as she moved back to his side, and they paced calmly down the gentle incline to the graveside.

He was aware that Sanchez and Richmond flanked them, but they kept a discreet distance back. He wasn't about to run, not when he was still cuffed to a serving prison officer. That was what he had to bear in mind. She was here as a matter of duty; she wasn't here because she cared about him. It wasn't Teddington and Bell; it was Teddington and Sanchez. That was how it should be. To be fair, it should be Teddington and Mr Teddington, but he wasn't in a position to judge. He watched Cathy across the way.

Cathy was why they were here; her and her habit, her inability to be a decent mother. She had killed any affection he'd once had for her, and now, she had killed the last thing he cared about – his son. She had killed another man's son, too. With any luck, that poor bastard didn't know, wasn't having to suffer the pain Charlie felt at burying his child.

Cathy continued mouthing off, and the officers at her side did nothing to stop her. Peripheral vision showed the camera crew were focusing on Cathy. Her explosion would make the best story. It was the priest who reproached her; an old man, his hair white, his face lined by years, but his spirit was strong, and so was his sense of right.

'If you don't calm down and show some respect, I will have you removed.' Apparently, his voice was strong, too.

'Fuck you. They're my fucking kids, you can't fucking ban me from my own kids fucking funeral!'

There was so much wrong with that statement, Charlie didn't know where to begin.

'Cathy!' His bitten word seemed to get to her. Although she continued to glare and snarl, she stopped chafing at being handcuffed, and she shut up.

As the vicar began the service, Charlie let it wash over him. As the two tiny white coffins were lowered gently into the ground, he was aware tears streamed down his face, but he couldn't stop them; he didn't want to. Oscar deserved more than his tears, and he had no pride left to salvage. As his eyes shifted, he became aware Teddington was doing everything she could to control her own tears. They still sparkled in her lashes.

There was an odd sound then a thud. An open palm appeared in his peripheral vision. Numbly, he looked around. Officer Richmond was laying on the grass, his eyes open, and blood leaking only slightly from the bullet hole in the middle of his forehead. That odd sound repeated.

Everything happened at once. Teddington calling first for Richmond, then Sanchez. As time seemed to slow, Charlie turned to see the other officer was down, red colouring his white shirt, flowing from his back on to the grass. Distantly, women were screaming. There was a pull on his left wrist – now, Teddington was down.

'No!'

He knelt beside her. Her jacket was newly torn, blood flowed from her right shoulder. She turned to face him, white with shock. The ground beside her exploded under the impact of another bullet. A bullet from a silenced gun. That was what the odd noise was. They were under fire.

Charlie didn't even have to think about it. The handcuff wasn't coming off, and he had to get out of here. Scooping her unceremoniously up, he threw Teddington over his shoulder and headed for the only cover he could see – the prison van. The window screen spider webbed, then shattered, and the dead driver slumped forwards.

Charlie turned towards the other van. The vicar was crouching, the far off mutter of prayer spilling from his lips. The camera crew had disappeared, but the camera remained on its tripod filming. The female guards and their charge were already bundled inside their van, but as Charlie took two steps towards them, the vehicle sped off, and the grass at his feet exploded again.

Charlie ran.

He dodged behind grave stones, zigzagging his way towards the thick trunks of a line of oaks at the edge of the cemetery. Breathing hard, he turned into the protection of one heavy tree. He was trying to think.

'Charlie?'

Thank God. Twisting, Charlie bent and put Teddington on her feet. She leaned against the trunk, still needing him to hold her upright. Her skin was pale and glazed with sweat against the blood flowing up her neck and face from being upside down over his shoulder.

'My car,' she managed. 'Black Golf, there.'

He turned to see the small car waiting on the roadside outside the cemetery boundary wall. The brick wall was only three feet high, so he picked her up again, the carry awkward with them being cuffed. Richmond had the cuff keys. His long legs carried them quickly to, and over, the wall.

'Car keys?' he asked, Teddington still over his shoulder. But, as he stepped up, he heard the car automatically unlock.

He put her on her feet and yanked open the door. With haste and no concerns about propriety, he half threw Teddington in. As she scrambled across to the passenger seat, he climbed in, saw the pushbutton start. It had been over three years since he'd driven, but with adrenaline pumping through his system, he didn't even think about it.

The car shot out of the space and flew down the road, as though the legions of hell were on their tail. For all Charlie knew, they were.

Chapter 16

Pain, pulsing, writhing, alive. It stalked through Teddington's world. She wanted to back away from it, but she knew she couldn't. She had to hang on, no matter how difficult. She could feel weight on her, the harsh breathing of another being; something was pulling at her shoulder, something else at the unhurt one.

Forcing her head forward, she opened her eyes, but her sight was blurry. Logic told her Charlie was going through her shoulder bag.

'Don't have the cuff keys.'

'Not looking for them,' he told her. She felt so slow. He sat back and figured out how to use phone, before she worked out what he was doing.

'That can be traced,' she pointed out.

'I'm counting on it.'

As she watched, he dialled and mentioned the name Piper. Her car fob and house keys hung from his little finger. He gave a succinct report on what had happened, and the fact he hadn't had any part in it. He said he was calling from Teddington's phone. Teddington had no idea what he was playing at, as he slipped the phone under her driver's seat. He spoke to her, but she couldn't figure out what he was saying. His hands were cold on her face, the light tapping was his attempt to rouse her.

She was slipping away. *This is it.* She'd just seen her oldest friend slain, a colleague murdered. She was handcuffed to a convicted killer, and she was slipping towards death. A stupid smile pulled at her lips. *Hell of a way to go.*

She closed her eyes.

* * *

'Don't you bloody dare die on me,' Charlie growled.

Between the close confines of the car, the new tightness of his clothes and the damn handcuffs, pulling her from the passenger seat so they could get out was the damnedest thing – but he managed it. He was sweating, as he kicked the door closed and managed to lock it. As he'd promised Piper, he left the keys under the front wheel arch. He shifted again, and put her over his shoulders. A fireman's lift was the only way to carry her, given how they were cuffed.

He'd parked on a passing spot in a quiet country lane, but the police should be here soon enough to collect the car after that call. He headed across the fields, knowing exactly where he was going. He passed through the twenty yard deep run of woods, and stopped facing the house. He'd dearly like to put Teddington down; she was a solid weight pressing on his spine – he prayed she wasn't a dead weight. But, with the cuffs, putting her down was pointless; he'd just have to take her up again, and that would take too much effort. Instead he bore the weight and watched the house. There was no one in; exactly as he'd hoped. The old Land Rover was parked out the back. As usual, the vehicle was covered with mud, both licence plates obscured. Sometimes, knowing the local lowlifes was an asset.

Charlie ran across the open ground, the gravel on the driveway crunching beneath his feet. He reached the vehicle and tried the driver's door. It wasn't locked. He pulled the door open, and with more care then he'd shown anyone in a long time, he eased Teddington from his shoulders and into the seat then across of the other side of the vehicle, before he could get in properly himself.

He paused one second to wipe her hair from her forehead. 'You hold on,' he told her, but she was inert.

His heart hammering for a million reasons, he checked the ignition, no keys, but they fell into his lap when he pulled down the sun shade. He crunched the gears in his haste to get out of the farmyard and on the road. He watched the road, overly aware

Teddington was being yanked about like a marionette every time he changed gears.

'Hold on, babe. I'll get you to help.'

* * *

Teddington was cold.

Something was pulling at the skin of her shoulder. It didn't hurt, but it wasn't comfortable. It was the cold that was getting to her. Her right breast felt odd. Reluctantly, she turned her head and opened her eyes. Things didn't form right; they were just shapes, blobs of dark and light. She blinked. A man was leaning over her.

'Charlie?' She didn't like how weak her voice sounded.

'Sorry, my dear. He's next door.'

She didn't recognise the voice. Fear gripped her, and she blinked again. Each time, her sight was getting clearer. She tried to raise her head. The man gently held her down.

'Don't move, or you'll end up with a really nasty scar.'

Looking down, she saw her blouse had been unbuttoned, the cup of her bra pulled down, her whole right breast exposed – unnecessarily, she thought, since the wound was several inches higher.

'You a doctor?'

'Was a surgeon.'

Maybe she'd lost a lot of blood. She certainly felt lightheaded. 'Was?'

'Yeah.' He put down an implement she didn't want to think about, and took up a needle. Again, she looked down. It was a fairly neat entry hole he was sewing up.

'How bad?'

'Messy, but nothing vital hit. Chipped your scapula, but I removed the fragment and the bullet. Take good care of the wound, and you should get full use of your arm back, but you'll need to take it easy for a few weeks.' He snipped the last stitch, put the needle aside, and returned with dressings. 'Do you want it?'

She frowned. 'What?'

'The bullet?' He pressed surgical tape in place.

'No!' She was disgusted. 'Wait. Yes. Yes, I want it.'

The doctor smiled down at her. 'Sure now?'

'Yeah.' She nodded gently. 'I might even get my name engraved on it.'

'Good idea.'

She wasn't overly impressed he was staring down at her exposed nipple, which looked very erect in the chilly room. She reached across and pulled up her bra. The black lace didn't leave her much better off.

'Can't blame a guy for looking.' He smiled, as he reached for another thing off the tray behind her head.

'Is that why "was"?'

He took his time deciding his next words. 'No. That's because I like kids.'

She could see he had a syringe now. 'Isn't that good in a doct– oh.'

'Don't worry, I don't, I can't do anything about it.'

She didn't understand, and she told him so, as the needle pricked her skin. He pulled down his trousers, showing her genitals. She blinked again. He didn't have a penis. Or testicles. The sedative kicked in, and the world turned black.

Chapter 17

The field was beautiful, lush and green, and the sky was blue – a perfect summer's day. Only, it wasn't. The sky darkened around the edges, thunder clouds rolling in. The air was turning wintery, blowing cold over her right shoulder. Her friends were a long way away, waving at her. She waved back. Was it? Could it be?

She started walking towards the figure. Then there was another. Richmond. She hadn't seen them in so long. She started walking faster; there were other people there, her grandparents, her uncle Sid, Great Aunt Louise. One by one, they were jumping into a hole. She saw them disappearing, as she drew nearer. All going now … Richmond. Sanchez. She saw her father. He was carrying something.

She moved closer. A baby girl.

Sasha.

Her father was moving towards the hole, taking Sasha with him.

Now, she was running.

'Sash—'

Teddington sat up and gasped for air. Someone was stabbing a red hot poker through her shoulder. Crying out, she fell back onto the bed, her left hand jerking up to grasp her shoulder, but it only came so far. She was jarred to a stop, cold metal biting into her wrist.

Fully alert, she took in her surroundings. The room was dark, the window boarded, admitting only the merest hint of light. She was on a metal frame bed, with a thin mattress and thin pillow – a thinner blanket over her. *Good God, is this what the bunks in prison are like?* The door crashed open. More light came in than her eyes could cope with, so she turned her head and closed her eyes.

* * *

Charlie put his hands deep into his trouser pockets, as he paced in the tiny front room of this tiny flat in an abandoned apartment block. The apartment was miniscule, consisting of the world's smallest kitchen, a bedroom, and a shower room. All of which opened directly off a living room where a cat would struggle to stretch, let alone be swung.

He scraped his hair back. Twice as many steps as in the cell. He felt like shit – all this was his fault. There were limited options, and the woman in the adjoining room was stuck with him, through no choice of her own. Then, he heard her cry out, and ran to the door, pushing it open but not entering.

'Teddington?'

'Charlie?'

He could see her outline on the bed. He wanted to go in, didn't dare. 'You okay?'

'Not really.' The conversational nature of the words was darkened by her sarcastic tone. 'Not only does everything hurt, it seems someone's *handcuffed me to the bloody bed!*'

He couldn't blame her for being angry. The pain however, was one problem he could do something about, but not yet. He was already leaning on the door jamb; now, he rested his forehead on the wood, grateful for the cold, for the unexpectedly still sharp edge in this otherwise dulled interior, as it dug into his skin.

'You said you were a mother,' he broached the subject that had been gnawing at him. 'Who will be looking after your son? Or daughter?'

She didn't answer immediately, probably didn't trust him with the information.

'Daughter.'

A dead tone. She didn't want to talk about it. He could respect that. But, he wasn't going to. He knew now, more than ever, the importance of protecting your children. Shame he had learned that lesson too late. But, Teddington did know those things. She cared about people.

'Who's taking care of her?'

Again, he had to wait for the answer. When he heard it, he couldn't believe it. 'What did you say?'

'I said God!' This time, her voice resonated sharply. 'God is looking after her.'

The last twisted off in a pained tone. Charlie knew there was more to it, but he didn't understand. 'Teddington?'

'Sasha died, alright?' she snapped out of the darkness. Charlie's gut turned over. Then, more softly, Teddington went on. 'Cot death. She was four months old. That's why my husband threw me out, divorced me. Why I came back here.'

He heard the bitter snort of a laugh.

'That's how I ended up a prison officer.'

And that was why she had felt Oscar's death so keenly. Closing his eyes, he bowed his head. *God, what had he done?*

'I'm sorr—'

'Don't you dare.'

He hunched. She didn't want his sympathy. Why would she? Right now, she was his unwilling prisoner. All he could do was stand in silence, and fruitlessly wish things were different.

'*Was* there a dickless doctor, or was that just part of the nightmare?'

The smile was involuntary. Teddington sounded like Teddington again. She bounced back well. 'That's the Doc.'

'Friend of yours?'

'Difficult to say.'

'What can you say?'

He closed his eyes and tried not to think of it. 'We found kiddy porn on his computer, but he'd already castrated himself, so he gave it up, and testified against five other paedophiles, those further up the distribution chain. He got himself struck off the medical register and never practiced again. He's buried himself, doing God knows what, but he leaves the kids alone, and he's not troubling anyone.'

'He took care of me?'

'He was a good surgeon. Low loss rates. You should be fine.' He wasn't entirely sure who he was trying to convince.

'Why did you do it?'

'You needed a doctor.'

There was a stunned silence. 'Not *that*, you prize twat. Why did you arrange your escape from your own son's funeral? Why did you arrange to kill my friends?'

The air rushed out of his lungs. *Am I really hearing this? Does she really think? Ask? Of course she asked. Why wouldn't she think that?*

'I had nothing to do with it.'

'And why should I believe that?'

The sob in her voice clawed at him. He struggled to find the right answer. 'Because, it's the truth,' he told her. 'I went to that cemetery for Oscar. Christ, Teddington, you never even told me what cemetery it was. How could I arrange anything, when I didn't even know where I was going until I got there?'

She was quiet.

'Say something.' He needed to hear her voice.

'Why did you run?'

'They were shooting at us.'

'Were they?'

'What?' He heard a noise, and looking in, he saw her swing her legs over the edge of the bed, pain clear on her face, as she held her right arm awkwardly to her side. He moved to pick up the syringe, before going to stand beside her.

'What the hell is that?'

'Painkiller. The Doc gave it to me. Do you need it?'

She considered. 'Maybe later.'

He nodded and held it in his hand. *Louse. Shut up.* 'I swear, the only thing I was thinking about at the funeral, was my son. I was as stunned as you when the shooting started.'

Unable to look at her, he stared at the blank wall instead. Peripheral vision told him her head was bowed.

'I can't believe they're gone,' Teddington spoke into the silence. 'Richmond was so pumped after his holiday. His missus was happy, he was happy, his world was all right. And Sanchez—' Whatever she was going to say, it caught in her throat.

'Sorry.' *God, that sounded so lame.* 'I know you were close.' And every word sounded lamer.

'Close?' A bitter laugh stabbed him. 'We've known each other since we were eleven,' she said quietly. 'Our parents moved into the same street within a few days of each other. We started secondary school together, and because the rest of the class had already made their friends, we ended up sitting together for most of our classes. It was hardly surprising we became friends. He even introduced me to Ward.'

'Ward?'

'Edward Teddington. My ex-husband. We were in uni then, different courses, but same uni. When Teddy and I moved away, Enzo helped us. He was best man at our wedding. When Teddy kicked me out, and I came back to live with Mum, we met up again. Enzo still lives – lived – in the house he bought off his parents when they moved to Italy. He was the one told me there was a job at the prison. He helped me prepare for the interview.'

Charlie didn't know why she was telling him all this, but he was grateful she was. He felt he should say something, despite the jealousy tightening his throat. 'Little wonder the two of you were an item.'

'We weren't.'

He reared, then, peered down at her head. Her eyes were directed forward now.

'He just made out we were in the pub when we were celebrating Turner's birthday. Enzo said it was safer for me.'

Charlie sat down, beside her, uncertain how many more hits he could take. 'Safer? Why?'

She shook her head. 'No idea.' She frowned at him. 'If you didn't arrange it, why are we still alive?'

'What do you mean?'

'Well, Richmond got a bullet through the brain, Sanchez in the chest. They were kill shots. But, I was hit in the shoulder. No lasting damage. And you weren't hurt at all.'

Charlie's expression blackened. 'You may never regain full use of your arm, and chances are it was a miss because you moved.'

She shook her head. 'No. Think about it. Someone good enough to take out the others shouldn't have had any problem killing me. Must have been a proper sniper. But, I'm not dead. In fact, the biggest worry I have is picking up something nasty from this mattress. You do realise how disgusting this place stinks, right?'

He couldn't help smiling. Typical woman. Been shot, dealt with the Doc, but complains the accommodation is filthy. Before he formulated a response, a noise outside caught his attention and he stood, moving to the other room.

* * *

Teddington tensed. If anything happened, there was nothing she could do about it; after all, he'd left her handcuffed to the bloody bed! And he'd taken the painkiller with him; something she needed right now. She tested the bonds, but her wrist was going to break before either the cuff or the bed did. She looked back through the open doorway. Charlie's shoulders were tensed. Then, she heard a door opening. Charlie visibly relaxed. He reached in and pulled the bedroom door towards him, though he stayed in the doorway.

Left in darkness, Teddington held still and strained to hear. It wasn't actually that difficult; a little muffled, but audible.

They exchanged a few minor pleasantries, but quickly got to business.

'What the hell's going on?'

'… an't be sure.'

Though she could only make out the odd word of what the other man was saying, there was something oddly familiar about the voice; she just couldn't place it. Her heart hammering in her ears wasn't helping.

'… out of the way …'

'Why? What have I got to do with any of it?' Charlie was still by the door, so she could hear him much more clearly.

'… or investigation … used Officer Teddington as intended … solitary … is she?'

Charlie nodded. 'I took her to the Doc. He patched her up. But, this is hardly an ideal environment to recuperate in.'

'Then, you should have dumped me at a hospital!' Teddington shouted through. This was all such a mess, and keeping her with him made it worse. She could see the twist of his head through the crack in the door.

He didn't move closer, but he spoke over his shoulder. 'And how would I have got the cuffs off?'

'Stamped on my hand to break it, then slip the cuff off the resulting mess.'

'You'd never have use of that hand again.'

'It was my right hand, I'm left-handed, I'd've coped.'

'Now, you don't have to.' His voice was dark and warning. For once, Teddington decided to heed the cautioning tone and shut up. There was a pause. The other voice asked something before Charlie spoke again.

'Withdraw a load of cash,' he voiced what sounded like a half-baked plan, 'and go,' there was an odd pause, 'somewhere.'

Definitely half-arsed.

'You can't,' Teddington told Charlie, then, to head off an argument, added, 'you signed over power of attorney to me. You no longer have access to your bank account, only I do. Which is all going to make it look like I'm in collusion with you on this.' That hadn't occurred to her before. 'Bollocks.'

'The accounts are all locked now, anyway.'

This voice she heard all too plainly, but it was a third man, someone she didn't recognise. Not that she recognised the mumbler. Yet.

'Who's out there?' she asked. 'No, don't answer that. I'm better off not knowing.'

'They're people I trust,' Charlie told her. 'Friends I can rely on.'

'Really? What can you rely on them for? To take care of your son, so he doesn't starve to death?'

Good grief! How could she say such a thing? Still, there was no way to take the words back now, and a part of her didn't want to.

Their conversation lulled. There was an uncomfortable cough, then it picked up again. She couldn't make much out, but she pricked up her ears when she heard Charlie asking, 'Just what is his condition?'

'Serious. He's in ICU, but he's stable.'

'Who's stable?' And what did stable mean, anyway? Coma patients were stable; they could still be vegetative.

Charlie opened the door a fraction more and looked at her, careful to ensure she couldn't see past him into the room. 'Sanchez. The bullet missed his heart, and because the ambulance got to him so quickly, they saved his life.'

Teddington wasn't sure if she should laugh or cry – she did both. 'Thank God. How come the ambulance was there so quick?'

'Live stream from the news.'

Ah, she hadn't thought of that when she'd accepted the 10:15 slot the vicar had offered her, and for the first time, she was glad for the film crew. Charlie turned his attention back to the men in the other room, pulling the door closed behind him. Being left alone didn't seem important – for the moment, she needed to take a second to be thankful her friend was still alive. But, there was so much more running around her mind. She *had* to think.

By keeping her with him, Charlie had jeopardised her entire future. If he'd left her at a hospital, she could have claimed innocence, but now, she was so linked with him when she did get back to a normal life, the police would question her, want to know every detail of everything that happened. That was why she didn't want to know who those men out there were, who the Doc was. The less she knew, the less she had to hide.

'Teddington's theory, not mine.'

At the mention of her name, Teddington looked up.

'Without the bullet, we can't prove that.'

She didn't know who said that.

'Here.' There was movement, she guessed Charlie was retrieving and handing over her bullet.

'This is a .22,' the third man reported. 'Quite different from the .45s used on Richmond and Sanchez.'

Teddington's heart was hammering in her chest at the implications.

'Two snipers or just two guns?' she called through.

There was a small pause. 'Given the sequence of shots, could be either.'

'I was there, and I'm not sure of the sequence, so how do you know?'

Another pause. 'Television footage. The region saw it live; the country has seen the reruns. You made national news.'

'Shit.' This wasn't good. 'In that case, we have a real problem.'

'We didn't before?' Charlie asked.

'Don't be self-indulgent. This is partly your fault, too.' She was thinking; she liked to pace when she was thinking, but right now, that wasn't possible. 'Regardless of how many people were shooting, the fact is, they had distinct orders. Kill the guards, don't kill Bell or Teddington, just a minor wound. My being shot must have been in there somewhere, or there would be no need of the second weapon. But, again, the orders must have been quite specific. Right shoulder, bad, but ultimately minimal damage. Whoever gave that order, knows me. Probably quite well.'

Charlie looked in on her. 'What makes you sure of that?'

'Charlie, you've known me for three years. You've seen me sign various forms for you, but you've never registered I'm left-handed!

I was shot on the right. Even if I lose some range of motion, I'll not be crippled, because I do most things left-handed anyway.'

'Implications?' This was the second man, the one whose voice she couldn't quite place.

Implications were something she didn't want to think about. 'Someone wants us out of the prison, but not dead.' Which made her wonder, why? 'They probably want to implicate the pair of us in Tommy Walters' murder.'

There was a pause. 'How?'

'I don't know. But, throw enough mud and some of it will stick. Maybe I had access to the murder weapon. Then, there's Charlie's track record for murder.'

'What weapon?'

Again, something about the voice nagged at Teddington. 'I don't know. Not for sure. No one's figured out what the weapon was yet. That DCI Piper's as incompetent as he seemed, maybe he's even in on the cover up.'

'He's not.' Charlie sounded so certain.

'Ha! You didn't see how cosy he was with the Guv,' she growled. 'That aside, there are a couple of things it could have been, and whatever it was, it was in Blackmarch. I work there. I could have had access to it. At this point, it's just useful circumstantial evidence, but that doesn't mean more can't be fabricated, and that's got to be easier if neither of us is there and in the way.'

'What do you think it was?' the third man asked.

'Could be anything. A knife, a shiv, even a wooden stake. There …'

'There, what?'

'There are wooden stakes used in the garden – usually for holding strings across the veg patch. They disappear sometimes. They're only balsa wood, but they could be sharpened and used against a man.'

'Have any disappeared lately?'

She thought about it. 'One got broken about a week before Tommy died. I only got the smaller half back.'

'Have you reported that to the police?' the third man asked.

'No. I didn't think about it 'til now.'

'And if you had?'

Unsure how to say it, she swallowed, and decided honesty was probably the best policy, though she wasn't entirely sure why, when on the run with a convict and his 'reliable' friends. 'I doubt I'd have said anything.'

'Why?' the third man asked. 'You're on the same side as the police. You work with them.'

'Actually, I work with the Parole Service more. Rarely have actual contact with the police. Besides, at best, it's circumstantial. I'd only be putting my head above the parapet to get shot at.'

'There's something rotten in the state,' Charlie quoted.

'What?'

'Corruption,' Charlie told the unseen man. 'The only reason to target either of us, is we're too close to seeing who, what, and where. Me, because of the questions I've been asking about Tommy, Teddington, either because she's got unwitting access to the evidence, or because she's incorruptible.'

That made her smile. She'd never considered herself incorruptible. Charlie's faith in her was rather warming. 'Works rota.'

'What?'

'The works rota,' she said again. 'I was looking at it last time I was in. Tommy never worked in the garden or the workshop; he didn't like getting his hands dirty. Literally, he had a phobia about it. But, the day before he was found dead, he was on the rota for working in the garden.'

'When you were on shift?'

'No, that was my day off. I was officially on afternoons the day he was found, but got a call the previous evening, so Robbins and I were working a double the day he was found, to cover. So, I was in when he was found, but not when he would have been working, and maybe not when he died. I still have no idea of time of death, so can't say where I was then.'

'Who authorised the rota sheet?'

She tried to recall the officer on duty. 'No idea. I didn't get that far.'

Charlie opened the door wider, 'What d'ya mean, "you didn't get that far"?'

'I mean, I didn't get that far. I heard about him being on the detail after his body was found, but the only chance I had to look was earlier this week, at handover. I had the book open, but I was just doing the check when Enzo walked in, closed the book, and started all this nonsense about me and him being an item. Well … reinforced it. He'd started it in the pub before. Then, Turner, Robbins and Roberts came in. Couldn't look after that.'

'Enzo?'

'Enzo Sanchez,' Charlie supplied to the unseen man. 'The officer in ICU.'

Teddington ignored them, knowing they were talking but thinking this through. 'We have to go back,' she said eventually.

'Are you kidding?' Charlie argued.

'Never more serious. I don't want to run away from my life, but if I don't take you back, my career is over, and you'll be on the run for the rest of *your* life. It is, at best, a time-sensitive option.'

Apparently, Charlie wasn't in the mood to be persuaded so easily. He opened the door to see her as he spoke. 'You figure that someone in there is trying to set us up, but you want to go back into the lion's den?'

'Yes.' She stared at him in the dim light. 'Look, I don't know what's going on any more than you do, but if someone's prepared to go to all that effort to get rid of us, then, stirring them up–'

'Is a really bad idea.'

His expression largely covered by the fact the light was behind him, but she got the impression he was glaring. She tried another tack. 'Depends how we do it. If we just slink back, then it can all be hushed up, and anything that can be used against us will be … but your "reliable" friend out there says we made the national news, which means the public will be interested. Chances are, at some point, the police are going to call a press conference. If you and I turn up, and turn ourselves in under the glare of the media spotlight, if anything later happens to either of us, it's going to be obvious. It'll hit the headlines again, an investigation will be required, and the fear of that is what will keep the pair of us safe. If we keep running, this won't end well for either of us.'

For a while, silence reigned.

'She has a point,' the third man said.

Charlie drew in a breath, bracing like he was about to go into battle. He closed the door, and their words were completely muted. Feeling sick, the pain in her shoulder throbbing into her neck and head, Teddington let their words wash away from her. She really needed that painkiller. Hating the weakness, she carefully lowered herself to the bed, laying on her left side, her arm uncomfortable with the cold metal around her wrist.

The door opened with surprising haste.

'Teddington, are you—' Charlie cut himself off, 'Are you alright?'

'No.' She didn't like either the concern in his tone or the plaintiveness of her own. 'I need that painkiller now.'

Chapter 18

Teddington slept better than she had in a while. She woke with fewer aches and pains than before, and her mind quickly clouded with thoughts of what was to come, of the things that could go wrong. The pale glow from the moon shone in from the open doorway – just enough light to catch the outline of shapes. All of this was the excuse she gave for not realising sooner there was a weight over her waist, and a warmth behind her back. She was spooned against a virile male body.

After Charlie had given her the painkiller, she'd been aware of his talking, remembered him coming in after, helping her sit up to drink, telling her something about a press conference, but it was all a bit of blur. At some point, he must have come in and snuggled up behind her, though she didn't remember his doing so. For now, she enjoyed the additional warmth, the improved scent, but baser needs intruded.

She turned her head as far as she could towards him. 'Charlie?'

He murmured and snuggled closer.

'Charlie.' This time her voice was stronger, louder.

He groaned and opened his eyes, blinking, as he came awake, he picked his head up to look at her, a slow beguiling grin spreading. 'Morning, sweetheart.'

'Yeah …' She smiled. 'You can quit that right now.'

'Are you always this grumpy in the morning?'

'Only when I've been shot, kidnapped and handcuffed to a bed in a slum. Besides, I'm not even sure it *is* morning.'

He scrubbed his face with his hand, before checking the digital watch he wore. 'It's not. Just gone ten o'clock.'

'Take it the painkiller knocked me out?'

Charlie nodded. 'Doc said that might be a side effect.'

'It's also left me really dry-throated. Is there anything to drink?'

Charlie nodded, as he pushed himself up and shifted down and off the bed. 'We've food, too. Hungry?'

'Yeah.' Every muscle pulled, as she eased her feet over the edge of the bed. She was grateful she'd worn boots; they had stayed on and kept her feet warm. Teddington drew in some deep breaths, unsure if the spinning in her head and the rebellion in her stomach were just effects of movement or hunger, or the remnants of the drugs.

As she fought the nausea, the light in the other room increased; apparently, Charlie also had a lantern of some sort. When he returned, he carried the lantern over his wrist, along with a two-litre bottle of water and a carrier bag of food. With her right arm too sore to move and her left cuffed, Teddington suddenly saw the problem.

'Any chance you could uncuff me?'

He paused. 'I can't let you go.'

She couldn't help it, she rolled her eyes. 'Where am I gonna go? I don't even know where I am. Besides, I've been shot. It's uncomfortable just sitting here, so the jolting of running would probably hurt like hell. I've got a fuzzy head and early stage dehydration. *And* I'm wearing heeled boots, so no way could I run faster than you right now, anyway. Which means any attempt to get away from you would, frankly, be an exercise in futility. Uncuff me.'

He put the food and lantern on the end of the bed and reached into his pocket for the key, kneeling before her to release her wrist. His hands felt surprisingly warm against hers.

'God, you're cold.'

Apparently, he felt it, too.

He sat on the bed beside her and something snapped. The end of the bed shifted slightly, and the two of them froze, waiting for something more to happen.

'That didn't sound good,' Teddington observed.

'I'll check it out after,' Charlie promised, but she noticed he moved gingerly back to lean against the wall.

How little effort it took him to shift forward again and drag her back beside him, was a worry. Knowing he was stronger than her was one thing, realising how much stronger was another. She wasn't exactly the skinniest woman she knew, and she wasn't used to being treated like a lightweight, but she wasn't going to complain, either. His arm remained casually round her shoulders, and she appreciated the shared body heat.

He opened the bottle around her, letting her guide the plastic to her lips, so she could drink her fill first. It was welcome relief. Next were pre-packed sandwiches. They weren't the tastiest thing Teddington had ever eaten, but they were no less welcome for that.

'Your friends provide this?'

'Yep. Not exactly a feast, but better than nothing.'

'How did you contact them? When?'

'You sure you want to know?'

She thought about it, sighed. 'Best not.'

'Did anything I was telling you earlier sink in?'

She frowned. 'Something about a press conference tomorrow we could turn up to?'

'Eleven-thirty tomorrow morning, to be precise. DCI Piper will lead a press conference, telling the world what they know, and appealing for me to give myself up, or at least, give you up, since you must be in need of medical assistance.'

The frown knitted her brow again. 'How do they know that?'

He just raised his brows at her.

'Oh yeah. TV's great, huh?'

As they finished eating, he told her the plan. It was clear and surprisingly simple. Without complications, there was less to go wrong.

'Can I ask you something?' Teddington asked, picking at the last crust of her sandwich.

'Sure.'

'How the hell did you ever get involved with a woman like Cathy Hamilton?'

Charlie took a deep breath, then huffed it out. She suspected he wasn't going to answer her, reconciled herself to that.

'She and I were both trying to take care of the same teenager, to get him clean. She worked in a rehab centre, and I took him there. She was held up as an example of someone who had kicked the habit and turned her life around. She was there to help and inspire others. Given the nature of the place, I didn't think it was a great move to let on what I did for a living; it might have put people off. So, I lied by omission.

'After about three months, I told Cathy I was a DS, and she freaked out, screamed all sorts at me, chucked me out of the studio apartment she kept. I found out a little while after that the reason she liked working at the centre was that sometimes junkies who really wanted to quit would hand in their stash. She was supposed to log it all, and then, it would be turned over to the police for destruction. Only she would skim some off before logging it, and indulge her habit. Something she omitted to tell me. She managed to stay clean through the pregnancy, though.'

'Really?'

Charlie nodded. 'She had to be tested as part of the visitation rights case I brought against her. It showed she hadn't taken anything from the time she found out she was pregnant.'

'How would they be able to tell that?"

'Hair tests,' he explained. 'The drugs grow into the hair, so you can get a fairly accurate indication of when someone was and wasn't using.'

'Oh, interesting. And at least, it shows she wasn't entirely irresponsible.'

'No, but she obviously got back into bad habits at some point. After Oscar was born.'

Charlie balled up the wrapper of the sandwich he'd eaten and threw it across the room. It couldn't have been a satisfying shot. The plastic un-crinkled and fell within a couple of feet.

Teddington watched its insolent rocking, and said nothing. He was going through enough.

'When I did what I did,' he spoke softly, 'I knew I'd go to jail; I accepted that. What never occurred to me was without the threat of me taking full custody of Oscar, Cathy would start taking again.' Charlie pushed his hair back this time. It needed a cut.

'Oscar's death was not your fault,' Teddington told him softly.

The grunt Charlie replied with suggested he didn't entirely agree with that statement.

The conversation dwindled. Teddington shifted up, stood, stretching as much as she dared with her shoulder. 'I need the bathroom.'

'You don't need this one.'

Still, he led her to the bathroom, and she baulked but didn't comment when she saw the state of it. The stench was stomach-turning, but her innards had been empty too long to let go of food now. There were limits, she supposed, to what could be expected from an abandoned squat.

Only when she came out did she see that he'd been gentleman enough to move away from the door, to give her space, as well as time. He wasn't stupid, however, and still stood between her and the front door, the way out to whatever freedom there might be. But, when she looked up at Charlie, all the emotions came crashing in again. She couldn't abandon him. She didn't want to admit it, but she needed him. She moved into the room, and he crossed to her, following when she wordlessly returned to the dark bedroom. Once in there, he used the weak light of the battery lantern to check the bed.

'Just a broken slat. Should be okay for the night.'

She didn't move when he faced her. She wasn't sure how she felt about sharing a single bed with him. That, she admitted to herself, was a lie. She knew exactly how she felt about it, which was the real problem.

Then, he was right there in front of her. He moved, put his arms around her, drawing her gently against him, cradling her, carefully avoiding any pressure on her right shoulder. It would only take minimal effort to move away from him, but she didn't want to. No more did she resist when he tilted her head up to his. Kissing him was all too easy, his firm lips knew what to do, seemed to know what she needed. His taste was a drug, activating and thrilling every sense she had.

She laid her head on his chest. His heart thumped in her ear, beating as crazily as her own. 'It's not real.'

She made herself say it. Felt and heard his in-drawn breath. His arms held her, no more willing to let her go than she was to remove herself.

'What?'

'This,' she told him quietly. 'All this emotion. What you're feeling for me.' At least what she hoped he was feeling for her, since she knew what she was feeling for him. 'It's not real.'

'Feels real to me.'

She closed her eyes, and wished this was different. 'It would, but it's not. In the last three years, I'm one of only five women you would have seen in the prison, and the most consistent for being around. But, we don't really know one another, we don't know any of those little things you'd learn about someone you know socially for three years.' She took a breath. 'You don't even know my first name.'

'Ariadne,' he said.

She frowned, shifting to look up at him. 'How do you know that?'

'News reports.' He shrugged. 'My friends brought a paper when they brought the food.'

'Oh.' Made sense. 'But, see, it's a recent nugget, and only because of this ridiculous situation.'

He reared at the phrase, his hands falling away from her. 'So, explain why you feel it, too.'

She stepped away, but he grabbed her left arm, making her face him.

'Well?'

She didn't have an answer for the harsh demand.

'Ariadne?'

Oh, Lord, did he have to say her name with such seductive softness? 'I prefer Ari.' She took a breath, inclining her head away. 'You should keep calling me Teddington.' Her voice sounded dull, even to her own ears. Her breath shook. 'This is so impossible, you must see that.' If he did, he made no indication.

'Explain why you feel it, too.'

She couldn't, wouldn't admit the truth. So, she fell on the one thing she had left. 'Stockholm Syndrome.'

Chapter 19

Stockholm Syndrome.

The empathy of a hostage for a captor.

To grow attached to a person one is forced into close confines with.

The words cut at Charlie, as he lay in the darkness, staring unseeing at the ceiling. Numbly, in the wake of her hollow diagnosis, they had still lain down together, spooned again. Her weight, her warmth, was beside him, though her back was turned to him. His arm was around her waist, her hand lay on his forearm. She'd placed it there soon after they'd laid down. It had been a conscious act. Though the touch was light, he felt it demonstrated she needed him as much as he needed her. Or, maybe, that was just wishful thinking.

Maybe, she was right. Maybe, this wasn't real, but it damn well felt real to him.

The scent of apples still, just, clung to her hair, and he moved, burying his face in the soft tendrils. This sweet torture was all he was ever going to get; he was going to make the most of it.

'Charlie?'

In his dreams, she called to him.

'Charlie!'

That snap *wasn't* dreamt. He blinked and opened his eyes. The sun stood solidly to attention, as it cut through the gap between the boards and the glass. At some point, he must have fallen asleep. They were pretty much in the same position as when they'd laid down.

'Morning,' he murmured and squeezed her to him, morning glory aching his groin at the feel of her body against him.

'Charlie …' This time, her voice was soft, and he got the impression that she was luxuriating as much as he was until, 'You're lying on my hair.'

He lifted his head, and she shifted, turning to him.

'It's still not real,' she told him.

'Is.'

'Not.' But, she was smiling, and he liked that.

'Don't care.' He kissed her, anyway. He deepened the contact; she let him, kissing him back. He shifted, seeking to cover her body with his. She tensed, pulled away, took a sharp intake of breath.

'My shoulder.'

He must have pressed on it, hurt her. He eased off, but stayed close. 'I want you.'

'I can tell,' she said. 'But, it ain't happening. It can't.'

'I assure you, it could.' He was smiling, and so was she.

'Charlie, it's not that I don't want to, but before the day is out, you and I are going to be cross-examined by the police about everything that's happened, and I would like to be able to answer honestly that you and I have not had sexual congress.'

'Sexual congress?' He frowned at the cold phrase. 'I'd have called it making love.'

Her hand rose and stroked his face, making him feel the roughness of his beard growth. 'Doesn't matter what you call it. It's not happening.' She leaned up, kissed him once briefly, and smiled at him. 'Now, get off me.'

He obliged, but as he did so, he caught up the cuffs again and her left wrist.

'Hey!'

He handcuffed her to the bed.

'What's this for?'

He felt like a heel for the betrayal he saw in her eyes. 'Propriety's sake.' He walked away, he had to. Closing the door, shutting her away from him, he paced the room, dragging his fingers through his hair. Had he become her jailer? He was a fool. She was right.

It wasn't real. It couldn't be. Stockholm Syndrome was the best he could hope for.

He wanted to scream, to rail against the world, but he was where he because of the choices he had made, so railing was no more than a childish tantrum. The thing he wanted was right in front of him and he couldn't have her. Couldn't drag her down with him. Wouldn't ruin her life. Not that he could; Teddington was intelligent, mature, stable. She wouldn't let him drag her down. She was everything he'd ever wanted in a woman. She deserved better than anything he had to offer.

'Damn it!' He kicked out at the shabby chair, which skittered away and juddered against the wall.

'What did the chair do to upset you?'

Charlie turned, surprised to see Danny in the doorway. He wore soft denim and a navy zip-front hoodie. With his average height, mid-brown, medium-length hair, nothing distinctive about his face, he'd never get picked in a line up, and Charlie knew of at least six he'd stood in.

'All sorted?' Charlie demanded, as he swept up his tie, and slapped it around his neck. He grabbed his jacket, but it was no longer comfortable to put on.

'Course.' Danny was frowning at him, holding out a length of black cloth.

Charlie snatched it and stormed into the bedroom. Teddington was sitting on the edge of the bed, but turned at his explosive entrance, her eyes wide. He felt more than he wanted to, so clenched his jaw and strode the two steps to her. He bound her eyes without a word, yanking the knot tighter than he'd intended. A sharp intake of breath told him he'd caught her hair. Again, he unlocked the cuff from the bed. He contemplated the cold metal and debated his three choices: cuff her hands together, cuff her to him, or leave her free.

'Stand up.' Was that cold command really his?

She tipped her head to his voice, but he trusted Danny's binding was thick enough to keep her from seeing anything.

Carefully, she stood. She was too close. He moved her wrist behind her back, again, having to ignore the way her sharp breath pulled at him. He didn't want to hurt her. She wasn't a hostage, but he clamped the cuff around her other wrist all the same.

'Is this really necessary?'

He took a steadying breath. 'Yes. You can't see the man who's helping me, and if you aren't cuffed, you can't explain why you didn't just pull the blindfold off.'

'Oh. Okay.'

'You were the one who said you didn't want to lie to the police.'

'You know what, Charlie?' she snapped. 'I remember that. You don't have to remind me what an arsehole you are.'

* * *

When Charlie decided it was time to move, he took her upper arm to steer her. Thankfully, it was her left arm; the right was still smarting from being cuffed behind her back. He'd guided her through the flat, carefully telling her to watch out for door jambs or any other obstacle. His voice was harsh and distant. She shouldn't have called him an arsehole, but she was glad she had. They had to be distant now. The concrete staircase was wide, but she took it carefully, afraid she might fall. His hand around her arm was hardly the stabiliser she needed. The hostile vibrations coming from him did nothing to reassure her jellied knees.

Suddenly, they were in an open area. The air was fresher – no urine odour, sound didn't echo off the walls. She walked beside the steel silence of the man with her. The ground fell away, she was falling, she cried out at the sudden stop of being yanked back.

'Sorry,' Charlie said. 'There was a curb there.'

'You—' she bit down on the angry response.

'Arsehole,' he said. 'Yeah, I know.'

He talked her through getting into the back of what she presumed was some kind of people carrier, and she'd been all too aware of his constant presence, as he'd told her to lean forward, uncuffed one wrist, and settled her more comfortably, before he'd pulled a seatbelt across her. There was movement. A door closed, and Charlie was beside her. She heard the cuff ratchet closed, and presumed they were cuffed together again.

Then engine started, and they moved off.

She couldn't see the driver; she didn't want to. She sat in silence and waited, as they were driven to their destination. Getting out of the vehicle was harder than getting in. Only after the vehicle had left did Charlie remove the blindfold. He seemed oddly reluctant to remove the cuff.

'Neither of us are about to make a break for it,' she said. 'Are we?'

Charlie looked towards the open end of the alley, as if he was considering it. 'No.' Turning back, he uncuffed them, but wouldn't look at her.

Now, she was all too aware of him, as they stood close together, tucked out of sight in a blind alley beside an empty shop, just yards from the police station. Charlie had positioned them behind the big waste bins.

'Got to say,' she said softly, just to break the silence, 'you're introducing me to a whole new world of aromas.'

This time, his smile was more genuine. They had to take their humour where they could find it.

'Always like to broaden a girl's horizons.' The cheeky grin slipped from his lips. 'This isn't what I wanted.'

Me neither. 'What do you want?'

'You.'

She swallowed. 'Right now, that's not an option. Why is the conference being held on the station steps?'

'To make this easier for us.'

'But, what have the press been told?'

'No idea. That part wasn't my problem.'

No, but that made her wonder whose problem it was. How had he managed this? He had to have a contact inside the station. Of course he had a contact inside the station – he'd worked there before his arrest. But, as with so much of this, she was better off not knowing.

They had hours to wait, having had to get here long before any of the press did. She was cold and hungry, but the pain was bearable. At least he stayed close, sharing his warmth, keeping an eye on the entrance to this horrid place, making sure they weren't caught out. She breathed through her mouth, trying not to use her nose. She rested her head on his shoulder and closed her eyes, enjoying the warmth and smell of him, the nearness.

'What happened to my jacket?' she asked.

'You cold?'

'A bit, but I also want to know what happened to my jacket.'

He shook out the jacket he carried and hung it around her shoulders. 'I think I left it at Doc's.'

'Aren't you going to want this?'

He shook his head. 'To be honest, it's not overly comfortable any more. I've done too much upper body work.'

Don't think about his body! She untipped her head, in case he saw the flush on her face. She kept her eye line level with his chin.

'You need a shave.' She saw him smile.

'Yep.'

She moved to look up at him. 'Did you really kill that man?'

He stilled, froze. Then, carefully, he took a deep breath and lowered his head to look down at her. 'Yep.'

'Why?'

He paused, watching her. 'Isn't it in my file?'

She shrugged. 'I haven't actually looked. All I saw when processing you in was a statement of the crime for which you've been incarcerated, no details.'

'Makes sense.' He took a breath. 'Phillip Mansel-Jones,' he kept his voice low, he didn't want to alert anyone to their presence, 'was a scumbag of the worse degree. He had contacts everywhere, on every side.'

'Law included?'

'Possibly, but I didn't see any evidence. We believe even the legit businesses were laundering more money than they realised. Off the record, we knew what he was up to – drugs, guns, prostitution, smuggling, laundering. Kidnapping and rape. And the victims were getting younger. But, somehow, there was never sufficient evidence. We did everything by the book, and the bastard just kept slipping through our fingers. One day, we—'

He paused. Even four years later it made him so angry that talking about it was difficult. 'I finally managed to get a warrant to search his home. Hell, we tore that place apart and nothing. It was so clean – too clean.'

He clamped his mouth, and she watched the muscles in his jaw working. Everything about him was tense. 'He stood there and laughed in my face. Said any further action would be taken as harassment, and he'd have my badge. So, I backed off. Way off. Until—' He exhaled deeply. 'Ari, what happened, what I did, I did because I believed it was for the best. Phillip Mansel-Jones is dead. He can't hurt anyone else. Even with Rhys, his younger brother, taking over the empire, things are better out there.'

'But, if the situation was just going to continue with the brother, was it worth facing a jail sentence for?'

He nodded. 'His brother is scum, but not as bad as Phillip. Phillip would—' He averted his eyes. 'He had to be stopped. I stopped him.'

The tension he felt at the memory was obvious. His eyes, brows and lips were pressed tight. She rose on her toes, placed her lips on his. The tension eased. She felt his hand splay across her lower back. It would have been so easy to give into this attraction, but she broke the kiss. It wasn't real. She couldn't allow it to be real.

She flattened her feet, rested her head by his neck, felt him rest his chin on her head.

'Don't change your shampoo.'

She smiled. 'Why?'

'I like apples.'

'Didn't know that.' She smiled.

'Now you do.' He was laughing in spite of himself. 'See, we're learning all about each other. That's real.'

She laughed but didn't move away. 'Yeah well, things might get all too real if you knew who my Uncle Billy is.'

The moment of his tense stillness told her that he took that as a threat. Which was probably just as well. It didn't matter much right that moment. She closed her eyes and enjoyed the feel of his arms around her.

'Charlie?'

'Uh-huh?'

'Can I have your tie?'

He pulled back, frowning down at her. 'Why?'

'Because I'm getting cramp in my shoulder from holding my arm still.'

He swore, as he stepped back and switched his tie from around his neck to hers, carefully tying it, and then, slipping his hand under his jacket to ease her right wrist through the loop. 'I'm sorry.'

'What for?'

'I should have realised, should have thought.'

'It's okay,' she told him. 'What time is it?'

He checked his watch. 'Half-ten. The press have already started setting up.'

'Not long now.'

* * *

Not long now.

He took a deep breath, held her close, and rested his chin on her hair. This wouldn't last, so he closed his eyes, etched every image, committed each sensation to memory. Presently, he heard the clamouring, and then, the quiet. Taking her hand, he led her down the sunless alley. At the edge, he could see the back of the crowd. They were listening to the conference intro.

'Here,' Teddington whispered, twisting to let his jacket fall from her shoulder, revealing the makeshift sling, the tears in her blouse and the white of the dressing beneath, 'you'd best have this back.'

'Why?' He took the item anyway.

'People don't believe what they don't see, and in this case, they need to see that while I've been shot, I've also been taken care of, and that has to be down to you. Besides, I get the feeling I really won't need it out there, anyway.'

Teddington squeezed his hand. It was time to move, her grip eased, and they paced side by side toward the crowd. Then, he heard DCI Piper's voice.

' … as kidnap.'

'That is not what happened.'

Too late now.

Teddington's voice was cool and clear. Charlie could already hear the cell door closing in on him. For a second, there was stunned silence, then the press turned to them, and the journalists were clamouring, angling microphones towards them, a dozen questions all arriving at once. The crowd gathered around them, closed in. Charlie wasn't comfortable like this. This wasn't crowd control; the journalists moved too close, Teddington yelped when one of them knocked her arm.

'Move back!' Charlie's voice rang out, before his brain kicked in. Apparently, the instinct to protect over-rode his instinct to survive.

The crowd moved back, parting for them as Teddington moved up towards the station steps where Piper stood with an unreadable look on his face. Charlie followed. What choice did he have? The journalists were still asking questions. Teddington moved to face Piper, and Charlie moved further up the steps, overly aware of DS Carlisle glaring, and the uniformed officers moving in tightly around him.

Charlie watched, nothing more than a spectator, as Teddington stole the show. She held Piper's regard, then turned coolly to the crowd.

'A statement will be released later today.' But, as she turned to go into the station, a question rang out, asking how she felt about Sanchez's condition.

'Officer Sanchez was a good man, a competent, caring officer, and a dear friend,' Teddington answered. 'I already miss him, and I'm sure I will for years to come.'

'He's not dead.'

Charlie knew Teddington knew that, but her reaction was so good, no one else would ever have believed this wasn't the first she'd heard of it.

'What?' She leaned towards the man who'd spoken, swayed to the point Piper reached out to steady her. His grab brought her attention around to Piper, who looked much taller than her for the simple fact of being on the higher step. 'Sanchez is alive?'

Piper nodded.

'Thank God.'

It was a very good act, Teddington looking both devastated and relieved at the same time, and Piper equally well played the concerned officer, cutting off questions, and leading her into the station. The uniforms were a lot less gentle with him, hustling Charlie inside. Under the scowling gaze of DSI Broughton, he was forced toward the custody suite to stand behind another locked door.

* * *

Charlie stepped into the holding cell, and heard the door shut and lock behind him. He noted it was a different sound to the one in Whitewalk. He noted how it was a different sound to that he remembered from being on the other side of the door. Once upon a time, the only reason he'd set foot in this cell was to bring a suspect in or out. Now, he was the suspect. *Convict.* To be locked up in the very station where once he had worked had a bitter sting. But, it wasn't the first time.

The look Broughton had given him was cold and hard. Just like the last time they'd been face to face – shortly after confessing to murder. He had respected the Superintendent just as he had respected Piper, though with Piper there had also been a sense of camaraderie, friendship. Some of that at least had survived his fall from grace.

He took a deep breath. Disinfectant with a sour undertone. Someone had thrown up in here relatively recently, but it had been cleaned up. One of last night's drunks, probably.

The cell was smaller than his. He huffed a small laugh at that. Given the overcrowding and his absence, chances were, the cell had been reallocated. Tommy's bed had been reassigned quickly enough. When he went back, which would probably be a prisoner transfer later that day, he could have been moved anywhere. His personal belongings moved to a box, and if the screws were really pissed with him, which they were bound to be, it would take a while for him to get his stuff back.

Without room to pace, he stepped up to the narrow ledge and the blue plastic covered cushion. A quick check reassured him the smell was the only lingering vomit in the room, he laying down. Even with a cushion, the platform was hard and unyielding.

He knew how this would go. By now, Teddington would be being interviewed, probably quite gently, with the requisite tea and biscuit. Piper would get her the good stuff from the staff canteen, not the mess from the vending machine. She'd be well treated – after all, she was on their side. A fellow officer, if in a different vein. And she appeared most innocent; that it was as much a fact as a cover up just made things easier. She'd probably then be taken to hospital to get her shoulder checked out, though he doubted they'd be able to fault the work. They wouldn't be able to identify who'd done it, either – the Doc was in the clear, as long as they both kept quiet.

Given that Charlie was known for being impatient, they would leave him here to stew for as long as they reasonably could, and when they did interview him, it would be a solid job, completely by the book, go on for hours, and be less than pleasant. No decent tea for him.

Teddington could have no idea how wrong she'd been that returning was the best thing for him. She didn't understand the parole she'd told him not to jeopardise was now a pipe dream. He hadn't had anything to do with the shooting but that wouldn't stop the authorities, or the papers, blaming him. He'd be serving his full sentence now. If he was charged in connection with conspiracy to shoot Richmond and/or Sanchez, he'd do more besides. He huffed. Was that likely? A high-profile shooting, one man dead, another critical. They wouldn't let this lie. If they couldn't find anyone else, they'd find him. Piper might believe he was innocent, but Piper wasn't the only one he had to worry about.

He didn't want to think about what would happen when he got back to HMP Blackmarch. Against the odds, equilibrium had returned with both Winehouse and Keen; that didn't mean it would continue when he went back. And he was still no closer to figuring out who had killed Tommy. Then, there was whatever Teddington was hiding, about what was happening behind the scenes, and her relationship with Keen. *Why was she so ready to trust Keen above Winehouse?* Charlie wouldn't have favoured either. This was the part of being a cop he had always found most annoying. Myriad questions, few answers.

Laying straight, his feet and head touching the walls, Charlie crossed his hands over his belly. It growled; he ignored it. Closing his eyes, he thought about last night, about the comfort of just being that close to another human being. He had never told a woman he loved her; he'd avoided serious relationships. When he went home, it was to his own bed, and alone. If he took a lover, he tended to go to hers or grab a hotel; he hadn't wanted a woman with him in his own space. Cathy was the closest he'd ever come it a proper girlfriend, but he stayed at hers. She had never once gone to his house.

His parents had always had, hopefully still had, a solid marriage. They were the perfect example of what a couple should be. Of all his colleagues, only Piper had maintained a steady and exclusive relationship, the others were cheating or worrying their wives into paranoia and divorces. He didn't want to do that to any woman, or himself. Better for all concerned to keep them at arms length.

Only that wouldn't be enough with Teddington, with her he wanted … more. She was smart, strong, and kissed like an angel. Maybe she was right; maybe it wasn't real, just an intense situation, but it felt real to him.

'Get up.'

Charlie opened his eyes, directing his attention towards the door. Carlisle was standing outside, squinting through the viewing hatch. Charlie carefully moved to stand, his feet slightly wider than shoulder width, his hands open and wide, a few inches clear of his body to show he was no threat. Only then did Carlisle unlock the door.

The interview room had seen a lick of paint since last Charlie was in it, though, in fairness, he'd been on the other side of the table then, his own interviews as "the suspect" having been conducted in a different room. What surprised him most was Carlisle had left, and the only remaining occupant was Russell Towers, the lawyer he hadn't seen since the day after his trial, when he'd instructed the man not to bother with an appeal.

'I didn't call you,' Charlie observed as he sat down.

'No one did,' Towers advised in that upper crust accent that had grated on Charlie's nerves by the time the trial was over. 'I saw what happened and I knew you'd need a lawyer. My apologies for taking so long to get here. I had another meeting I couldn't get out of.'

'What time is it?' His watch had been taken away in the custody suite.

Towers checked his Rolex. 'Five-o-six.'

Six hours. How the hell had six hours washed over him so easily? 'I can't afford your time.' Paying the last bill had nearly bankrupted him.

'It's pro-bono.'

'Why?'

Towers took a moment to draw in a breath. He was obviously considering what he was going to say. 'I don't like losing.'

'Then, you should avoid all contact with me,' Charlie advised. 'This … *I* … am a lost cause.'

'I don't believe that, Mr Bell. I never have, and neither should you.'

But, he had to. He couldn't deal with the hope of anything more. 'Do you know what happened with Teddington?'

'I believe she was interviewed and then taken to hospital. Her injuries had to be checked and recorded.'

'Have you spoken to her?'

'No, but I will.'

Charlie didn't want that, but he wasn't sure why. His urge was to protect her, to keep her from anyone or anything which could upset her. That was ridiculous; he was the one most likely to hurt her. Look at what he'd already done.

'So, let's get to it,' Towers demanded Charlie's attention. 'Tell me everything that happened from the moment you arrived at the cemetery.'

* * *

'So,' Carlisle said, as he glared across the table, 'you expect us to believe not only did you have nothing to do with the shooting, you actually "took care" of Mrs Teddington while you were missing, including removing the bullet from her shoulder?'

'That is what my client said,' Towers pointed out. 'It is, in fact, what he has said at least three times, with further repeats for clarification on a number of points.'

'Not all of the clarifications have been clear,' Carlisle sneered.

Towers was steady in his regard of the younger man, then he turned to the older officer. 'Detective Chief Inspector Piper, I have to point out that it's becoming increasingly obvious Detective Sergeant Carlisle here has an issue with my client. This level of persecution is bordering on harassment.'

Charlie knew exactly what the problem was, too – the personal betrayal Teddington had so accurately diagnosed. He sat quietly and watched the interplay between the two men. He was beginning to wonder if he knew either. Carlisle was angrier than before, and even though he'd moved up a rank, he hadn't matured into the calm, assessing officer Charlie would have expected under Piper's guidance.

He turned to Towers, the man was sharp as a tack. How had he missed that before? *Too numb, probably.* He'd killed Mansel-Jones and given up, resigned himself to a particular fate, and had never considered the alternative, the possibility he might not serve jail time.

'Unless you have some sort of evidence suggesting my client is lying,' Towers continued, 'then, this interview should be terminated forthwith, and DS Carlisle here should be removed from any further dealings with my client.'

Piper checked his watch. 'Interview terminated at 1923.'

Carlisle clicked off the tape machine, and Charlie could see his clenched jaw, the narrowed, daggered look Carlisle threw him. It was Piper's steadier, unrevealing expression that had Charlie worried. Then, Piper turned to his younger colleague.

'Thank you, DS Carlisle.'

Carlisle recognised the dismissal when he heard it, Charlie doubted he understood it. Snatching a tape from the machine, leaving one for the lawyer, Carlisle left the room. Only after the door was shut again did Piper fix his gaze on Towers.

'Under normal circumstances, this is where I'd tell you your client is free to go, but that can't happen, in this case. Mr Bell will be held in custody here, and transferred back to Blackmarch in the morning. Is there any other business you wish to go through now?'

'No, I think that's all.'

'Good,' Piper said. 'Then, you can leave me to speak with Bell alone.'

Towers turned to Charlie.

'It's okay,' Charlie agreed. 'I can't go anywhere, so I might as well talk to him.'

Towers ensured all the formalities were observed before he left. Alone with Piper, Charlie faced his old boss.

'She's fine,' Piper told him. 'Being kept in hospital overnight for observation.'

'Did you interview her?'

'Yes.'

'Carlisle?'

Unusually, Piper allowed himself a half smile. 'She told him where to get off.'

An involuntary smile moved Charlie's lips up. 'I can imagine that.'

'Her story matches yours.'

'Did you expect anything else?' Clearly, Piper hadn't. 'What now?'

'You get a night in a cell here. I'm going home to my wife.'

Chapter 20

Charlie stood back in his prison cell. Same cell, all his stuff still here. Nothing missing, nothing even moved. He'd showered, changed. Jeans, tee and grey marl sweatshirt. His usual outfit. Comfortable. Nothing had changed. Had he even left? Had anything he thought had happened, actually happened?

It's not real.

He could hear Teddington saying it. Maybe she was right. He sat down at the small desk. Three books sat on the top. Lee Child, Steven Leather, Jasper Fforde.

He picked up *The Killing Floor*.

He was ten pages in, when he noticed it.

The place was quiet. Actually, it was more than quiet. It was library silent. Usually, sound echoed around the wing, bounced on the glazed bricks. He picked his head up, facing the door. No, he wasn't imagining it. There was an absence of sound.

Turning down the corner of the page, he closed the book and stood, crossing outside to the landing. Standing on the balcony, he observed his surroundings. Was he the only one left in the prison?

He could see Morris in his room, and headed around the landing, wondering when he had grown so heavy-footed. Every echo was now a harsh, recoiling scream. Though he couldn't see anyone, he had the unnerving feeling he was being watched.

Morris didn't look up from his own trembling book, as Charlie appeared in the door.

'Can I come in?' The door was wide open, but some respects had to be maintained.

'You best had,' Morris kept his voice low. 'Sit there.' The old man indicated the foot of the bed.

Charlie sat. When he went to speak, Morris raised his hand. He held his silence and watched as Morris turned the page, the bottom of the book rested on the table, controlling the worst of the shakes. Morris must be used to it. It looked like one of the last pages in the book, as Morris' eyes scrolled across the width. Charlie was rather surprised to see the cover – *Gone With The Wind*. Mentally, he shrugged, each to their own.

Finally, the old man closed the book.

'Good book?'

'Surprisingly,' Morris confirmed. 'Why did you come back?'

Straight to the point. Charlie liked that. 'It was the right thing to do.'

'Teddington persuade you of that?'

His nod confirmed it.

'Did you two …'

Although the question trailed off, Charlie understood it. He finally understood why Teddington was so insistent, so right. 'She'd been shot. I couldn't take advantage like that.'

'Most would.'

'I'm not most.'

'True,' Morris acknowledged, inspecting the younger man. 'What did you come over for?'

'I was in my cell, and it felt like …' he sighed, 'it felt like none of it had happened, no funeral, no shooting, no running and hiding. Like it was all just an overly vivid dream.'

Morris offered a bitter laugh. 'Well, if it was a dream, we all saw it played out on national TV.'

Charlie nodded. 'But, I was reading, much like you were, then, I noticed how quiet it is. Normally, you've got men wondering around, talking, you can hear TVs or games, conversations, sometimes arguing, sometimes even fighting. But, not today. Everything is *too* quiet.' Aware he was keeping his voice unnaturally low, Charlie looked to the door. There was no movement. He turned back to the older man, 'Quiet as the grave.'

'Which is what—' Morris' attention shifted to doorway. 'Officer Robbins.'

'Morris.' Robbins nodded, then turned a frozen gaze on Charlie. 'Back to your cell, Bell. Don't want you disturbing other prisoners.'

Charlie considered pointing out he wasn't disturbing Morris, but the hairs standing on the back of his neck convinced him that wasn't a good idea. So far, there had been no reprisals for his absence, but that didn't mean there wouldn't be. He turned to Morris, apologised, and stood.

'You've always had sharp vision, Charlie,' Morris noted, as he left.

He was wondering about the odd comment, as he felt Robbins push him in the back, moving him on.

'If I had my way, you'd be in solitary now for what you did.'

'Getting Teddington out of the firing line and removing that bullet?' Charlie threw over his shoulder, as he rounded the final corner of the landing and headed towards his cell. 'For saving her life?'

The nudge in the back became a shove, a hard one at that. He found himself stumbling into his cell, catching himself on the bunk as the door was swung shut and locked.

* * *

Lunch time came and went, without the door being opened.

Dinner time came and went, without the door being opened.

Charlie wasn't overly surprised when breakfast the following morning passed in the same fashion. He kept reading.

What did surprise him was, just as Reacher was figuring out the last conundrum, a key turned in the lock, and the door was opened. Senior Officer Turner stood there. Charlie looked up from his seat by the table, meeting the gaze of the officer.

'Giving an officer lip is not a good idea,' Turner advised, 'but I'm sorry you missed breakfast.'

'I'm sorry I missed lunch and dinner yesterday too.' Giving an officer lip *really* wasn't a good idea, but Charlie figured he didn't have much left to lose.

Turner frowned. 'Pardon?'

Charlie had seen enough liars to know honest confusion when he saw it in a man's eyes. 'I've been locked in here nearly 24 hours solid. No respite, no meals.'

Turner stepped into the cell, kept his voice low. 'Who locked you in, and when?'

'Robbins, around 11:45 yesterday morning.'

Turner was obviously considering the point, but Charlie couldn't figure out what he was thinking. 'The shop's open. Have you got money?'

Charlie nodded. 'Are you and Teddington friends?'

'Yeah. Why?'

Charlie shrugged. 'Just wondered if she's been released from hospital, if they gave her the all-clear?'

Now, Turner's face clouded. 'You haven't heard? Of course not, you've been locked in here.'

Bile rose in Charlie's throat, lead lined his stomach, and it felt like every ounce of energy had drained from his body. 'Heard what?'

'Teddington had a reaction to the painkiller they gave her in the hospital. She had to be intubated. No one's sure what her condition is this morning.'

If Charlie still had a pulse, he wasn't sure blood was getting to his brain. This really didn't make any sense. *Teddington in trouble?* 'But, she was fine last time I saw her.'

'Like I said, unexpected reaction to the painkiller.' There wasn't much else Turner could say. 'Anyway, DCI Piper is here, wants a word with you.'

Like an automaton, Charlie put the book down. Still reeling, he barely noticed the walk to the visiting room; he didn't really know what was going on, until he was sitting facing DCI Piper again.

'You look like you've seen a ghost,' Piper commented.

'Is it true?' Charlie asked. 'Teddington's on a machine to keep her alive?'

Piper took a deep breath and averted his eyes, a sure sign things weren't good.

'Detective Chief Inspector?' Turner called the man's attention. 'Would you object to me locking the two of you in here? There's something I need to do.'

Piper frowned. This wasn't usual protocol, but Charlie hoped he'd agree all the same. He did. Turner left; the door was audibly locked.

'Don't ask,' Piper advised, when Charlie moved to do just that. 'Be assured Mrs Teddington is receiving all necessary care and attention.'

'Seriously?' Charlie was far from impressed. 'You're giving me a catchall phrase that doesn't actually mean anything now?'

Piper's lips compressed.

'Turner suggested there was a reaction to the painkillers they gave her.'

Drawing breath in through his nose, Piper assessed him. Charlie hoped he'd see he wasn't about to let this go without an answer.

'She was given too much morphine. Some damn fool got the dosage wrong.'

'Christ, that could have killed her.' Charlie slumped back in his seat. 'Medical negligence?' Something about the way Piper wouldn't quite meet his eye told him not. 'Piper?' He sat back up again. 'What really happened?'

'A double dose. Thankfully, the nurse who had given the first injection thought she saw an agency nurse come from Teddington's room, and caught the error before it did too much damage.'

Charlie pushed his hair back with one hand. 'Jesus. I wish there was something I could do.'

'Right now, all any of us can do is hope and pray. And concentrate on something else.'

'Are you sure it was just a mistake?'

Piper frowned at him. 'What do you mean?'

He tried to find the words, but there was nothing concrete. 'I don't know. Just with everything else that's going on … what if it wasn't a mistake, but an attack?'

Piper sat a little straighter, his brows down, his lips straight, as he considered the possibility. 'I think you're being paranoid.' He raised a hand to cut off Charlie's objection. 'Think about it. Why would anyone attack her? Where's the motive? Now … about Thomas Walters – Tommy. I believe you were asking questions about him. What answers did you get?'

'Bugger all, Guv,' Charlie slipped into old habits. 'Something's going on, but since getting back I've pretty much been locked in my cell, no contact with the others.'

'Surely you can mix at meal times?'

'You'd think so, wouldn't you?' he watched Piper watching him.

'I came to tell you the investigation didn't reveal any evidence you had anything to do with the shooting, but we're drawing a blank on other avenues. Now, about your parole.'

'What parole?'

'Exactly.'

Now, Charlie was confused. 'What?'

'A hearing has been scheduled, but I'm going to apply to have it held back. This shouldn't go against you in future hearings, but I'm delaying it. I want you in here, and asking questions.'

* * *

When Turner escorted Charlie back to the wing, he didn't escort him to his cell. Instead, Charlie paced through the eerily quiet hall to the shop. He brought fruit, a paper, a drink, and turned back. Cell doors were open, a couple of lags stood in doorways, watching him, but they shifted away when he caught their eyes.

The gardening detail was returning, dirty as usual, but they headed straight for the showers. Their silence was unnerving. Winehouse acknowledged him only with the smallest of nods, before heading directly for the shower block.

Charlie moved across the floor. He would see what Keen had to say, but Keen was heading away from the shower block. Winehouse and Keen acknowledged their passing in silence, and their respective groups moved passively, no exchange of looks, let alone insults. Charlie frowned – this wasn't normal.

His timing, however, was perfect; it put him precisely by Keen, as they ascended the staircase.

'What's going on?' Charlie asked under his breath.

'Truce.'

'What brought that on?'

Keen fixed a hard look on Charlie; for the first time, he saw the darkness under the older man's left orbital. The remains of a black eye. *What happened to Runt?* He hadn't seen Hightower around, and Keen went nowhere without his bodyguard. *How had that happened?*

'Winehouse?'

'Don't be ridiculous.'

'Then, why not work with him?'

'Too late,' Keen offered under his breath. 'Watch your back. Leo catches up with all of us, eventually.'

* * *

Charlie sat in his room, tapping his foot. *Stir crazy.* That was it. Attempts to reintegrate were stymied by increasingly long hours of being locked in his cell. There was only so much a man could read. He got on the bunk and lay back. Closing his eyes, he thought of Teddington, the way she'd felt in his arms, sleeping against him. Images swamped him of her alone and vulnerable in a hospital bed, a machine doing her breathing.

Every part of him screamed for news of her. But how could he ask? Strip away the delusion of intimacy, the Stockholm Syndrome, and they were jailer and prisoner. It wasn't an easy mental adjustment, but one he had to find a way of making.

No good.

With a frustrated groan, he rolled off the bed. The door was open, so he stepped out. Again, no one around. This time, he headed to the ground floor. Baker was in his cell.

'What are you doing?' he hissed wide-eyed, as Charlie walked into the cell.

'I just came to talk,' he said, as he sat on the lower bunk. 'Where's Holden?' he asked after Baker's cellmate.

'He's got some education programme thing.' Baker's eyes kept zipping between Charlie and the door. 'That it? Can you go now?'

Charlie frowned. 'What's going on, Baker?'

Baker shrugged, the nonchalance was too studied. 'Nothing. You know what it's like. People are keeping to themselves, 'cept you, apparently. Everything's running like clockwork.'

'And we're all supposed to act like good little cogs and stay in our cells all day and night?'

'Would it kill ya?' Baker whispered harshly. 'Of everyone in here, that should suit you best. You already spend most of your time in your cell. Normally, you hardly talk to anyone, even me. Can't you go back to that?'

'I might not interact much, but I've a basic human right to do so, if I want. I miss the background hum of humanity that used to be around. The place feels more like a dungeon than a prison, each of us locked up with our own heads. No release, no reprieve. This isn't how it's meant to be.'

Baker's eyes were still constantly on the lookout. 'It is what it is. Go away.'

This wasn't getting him anywhere. 'If you need to tell me anything—'

'I don't.'

Charlie stood. At the door, he paused. Across the way, he saw Brett. The man literally just popped his head from around his cell door, his wide eyes fixed on Charlie, his face paled, and he darted back behind the door again.

'And there's the problem.'

'What?'

Charlie turned back to Baker. 'Brett, how's he been acting lately?'

'Nervous, but when ain't he?'

The medication and socialisation had helped with that. 'Is he eating?'

'I guess.'

'Guess?'

'No more communal eating. Hadn't you noticed all the tables are gone?'

He had noticed, but assumed they'd be brought back out for meal times. As he headed back to his cell, Charlie glanced in at Brett. The man was pacing, head down shoulders hunched, muttering to himself.

Charlie noticed the prison officers were relaxed. If they relaxed too far, they could get complacent. Not immediately, of course, but it would happen.

For a couple of days, he kept his head down. Just watched and waited, observed.

'Officer Robbins?' he called the man's attention, as the officer patrolled the landing.

The big man stood in the door and glared. 'Don't you think you've had enough attention?'

Charlie wasn't about to be beaten down just because a man could overshadow him. 'This isn't about me. It's about Brett.'

'Brett is not your problem.'

'But, he could be yours,' Charlie said. 'He's nervous, acting paranoid, may not be eating. That's exactly how he was before he had to go on suicide watch last year.'

Robbins' eyes were hard; he was considering how to respond. 'I'll look in on him.'

Charlie tried to find out if anything improved, but the days passed without news.

He continued to request work, checked the rota every day, just in case, but his name never appeared. He asked about the mechanics course, only to be told it was cancelled. He read and re-read the books Teddington had left him, and more from the library. He thought about Piper, and the million and one things he hadn't said about the delay for parole. How being in here was safer for him. Charlie was at a loss to understand, but he had to trust Piper. That he still did trust Piper remained a surprise to him.

No matter who he asked, he couldn't get news of Teddington.

'Bell!'

Charlie was surprised by the call for correspondence. Never having received a letter while inside, he didn't know what to expect. Gingerly, he took the envelope and returned to his cell, looking over the letter. It had been opened and vetted, someone else getting to read first what was meant for him. He knew the handwriting.

Containing himself, he returned to his cell, jumping up to the top bunk to read what she had sent. The handwriting was unusual, the name and address written in italics, while the letter inside was much more upright.

Mr Bell,

I hope you're in good health, my own health is much improved, and the doctors assure me of a full recovery. Thank you for your part in tending to that when I was incapable.

I really just wanted you to know that I went back to the cemetery and spoke with the vicar after the unfortunate incident. The boys were given a respectful send off, and have been laid to rest in peace. A headstone will be added in due course, though for the moment, the grave will stay unadorned. I think that best, while any notoriety remains.

After a clear out of my own bookshelves, I came across a number of titles I thought might interest you and have sent them on to the library. They should be waiting for you. The others you can donate to the library once you are done with them. Remember, ladies first.

Yours sincerely,

Teddington.

Charlie wasn't certain what it was about the letter that bothered him so much, the coldness of the tone, or the fact she had cared enough to check on the boys, which was something he hadn't even thought about. She had a wonderful way of making him feel like a heel, even though she didn't mean to.

Chapter 21

The drumming of her own fingers was driving Teddington up the wall, as was her mother's constant fussing.

'Where are you going?'

Teddington steadied herself as she stood. 'I'm going to go for a walk.'

'I'll come with you.'

'No,' Teddington stopped her mother as she moved.

'But—'

'Mum, I'm just going to get some air.'

'You just got out of hospital.'

'Twelve days ago,' she pointed out. 'Look, Mum, I'm sorry, but I'm not a baby, and I want some time alone.' As bad as she felt for dropping her mother, she needed to clear her head. Grabbing her coat and bag, she headed out.

In town, window shopping was far from riveting. The problem was, she needed something to occupy her mind, as well as her time. Reading wasn't doing it. Whenever she opened a book, she started thinking about all the times she'd seen Charlie reading in his cell.

Stop thinking about Charlie! It's not real.

At least today her fifteen minutes of fame seemed over. No stranger came rushing up asking her about her 'ordeal,' and how terrified she must have been. She'd tried to be polite, but her life wasn't public property, and she was finding such interest intrusive. Only … her life wasn't back to normal, like it should be. Still, she could just pop in. Especially since it seemed she was already standing outside the prison.

She headed in via the staff entrance, went directly to the Governor's office, and asked Vera if he was available.

'I am.'

Teddington jumped to see the Guv appear at his office door.

'But, I need to visit the little boys' room first, do go through.'

This was rather a turnaround from the last time she'd been in this office and spoken to the man. Eyebrows raised, she turned to Vera in the Guv's wake. She simply shrugged.

Teddington stepped into the office. A visitor's chair was still waiting, but her restlessness turned against that. Instead, she looked around. The room was largely utilitarian, except for the leather executive chair, but on the one wall was a display of certificates. She went over to read them.

Set before her were the qualifications of Peter Jones, her boss for the last five years, each one in a thin black frame. Certificates from Trent University, another from the University of Kent, one from National Offender Management Service, a diploma in Custodial Care, just to prove he was keeping up to date. Business Management and Psychology … an odd pairing, but – she shrugged – they'd be useful in his current position. There was even a picture of him with the Secretary of State for Justice, a congratulatory moment for the way he had turned around a 'problemed' prison. She didn't remember which prison, so moved up to look.

'Good morning, Mrs Teddington,' he greeted, as he came into the room, closing the door behind him. 'Ah, I see your admiring the article about my work in Featherstone.'

She smiled. 'Yes, Guv.' As she shifted back to the front of the desk, and he moved behind it, she wasn't sure admiring was the word.

'He's been very helpful, you know.'

Teddington looked up as they were both sitting. 'Sorry, who?'

'Anthony,' he indicated the picture, the minister. 'He's been helping with my campaign.'

'Campaign?' Teddington wondered if she was suffering with amnesia suddenly.

'I'm running for election.'

'Oh.' She felt she should say something better than that. 'Didn't know you had political ambitions, sir. Good luck with it.'

His smile was broad. 'Thank you.' Then, he plastered on a more concerned face. 'Now, how are you?'

'Very well, sir, thank you.' She couldn't completely keep the smile from her lips, as she looked at the PlayDoh hair do. Just what a man needed for political photo ops, hair that never moved.

'The shoulder?'

'Sore in the cold, but otherwise fine.'

'Good. Good.' He nodded like the proverbial dog in the back of a car. He put his hands on the desk, his long fingers woven together, a very earnest look on his face. 'To what do I owe the pleasure of this visit?'

Given her career status, she couldn't afford to mess this up. That was why she had kept him informed of every move regarding Oscar's funeral arrangements and her subsequent involvement. With a calming breath, she spoke.

'I want to come back to work,' Teddington said, noting the surprise on the Governor's face. 'Not on the wing, I know I'm not ready for that, but I would like to be back in work. There's a number of systems I need to brush up on, and there's that training day for the new Prism computer programme next week I'd like to attend.'

His face closed slightly, considering her words and looking at his hands. 'That demonstrates an impressive dedication, Mrs Teddington, and God knows we are down on manpower at the moment.'

She could hear the 'but' coming.

'But, I don't want you coming back before you're ready.'

She nodded. 'I understand, but sitting at home isn't doing me any favours. As I said, I know I'm not ready to work on the wing, but I'd have thought that this would prove the perfect opportunity for me to undertake some training, and since it's all arranged, isn't it better I attend the Prism training now, rather than going to the expense of arranging another session in a few weeks' time?' He wasn't the only one who had a business degree, so she knew he couldn't reasonably argue.

He levelled his gaze at her. 'You're putting me in a difficult position.'

His smile was probably meant to be avuncular; Teddington found it creepy.

'I can appreciate the business arguments, and I wouldn't expect anything less from you. However, I have to consider your health—' He stopped her objection with a raised hand. 'I appreciate your eagerness to return, truly I do, but as an employer, I have to be sure I'm not putting you at risk. If you can get a written confirmation that you're fit to return on light duties, then I'll allow it. But, I need that letter. Is that acceptable?'

On a personal level, not really, but she could see the reason from a business standpoint; she just hoped her doctor would agree. 'That would be great. I'll speak with my doctor.'

'Erm …' His hedging stopped her when she moved to stand. 'Was there anything else you wanted while you're here?'

She sat back down, frowning at him. She knew exactly what he was asking, but she had to play dumb. 'Is there something else you think I should want?'

His discomfort became more pronounced.

'If you have something to say, sir, just say it,' she said evenly.

He opened his mouth, then stopped. Then, tried again. 'Bell,' he said. 'I need to know there isn't something between the two of you.'

Teddington did her best not to react. 'I understand the dilemma. But, I can tell you, just as I told the police and psychiatrists, I've been forced to see, nothing questionable happened. I remember being shot, I remember waking up in a dingy room with blacked out windows and being handcuffed to a bed. I know between the two, someone removed the bullet from my shoulder, but I don't remember it. I do remember being blindfolded and taken to a sunless back alley, and then walking up to the police press conference. I even remember the belief I was going to die in hospital. But, at no point was there ever anything between Bell and I, other than general concern for a fellow human being. Despite what the papers say.'

'Then, why did you write to him and send those books?'

She met his look openly. 'Since you read the letter, you know what it was about. I checked the burial of his son and the half-brother, and was sending him books I was otherwise going to throw away. The rate he reads, he'll go through the library before he's out of here.'

'Which brings us to another problem. Why are you persisting with this personal oversight of his welfare?'

Teddington made sure her breathing was steady. 'I'm not overseeing his welfare.' She tried to remain firm, but could feel heat running up her neck. Hopefully, her foundation would keep the blush from her face. 'I checked on the children. There was no-one else to do it. As you know, I lost a child, a daughter, before I started working here. *You* have children.'

There was a happy family picture on his desk.

'Imagine how you'd feel to lose one? Well, that's what I live with every day, and now, Bell has to live with it, too. I have family support. Bell doesn't. There was no one else to arrange the funerals, take care of the details, so I did it. I don't believe that's a crime.'

The Governor looked to the picture of his own two sons. 'No,' he agreed, 'it's not a crime, but it may be a breach of protocol. You are already on a warning.'

'Yes, sir. And you know I don't want to jeopardise my career. Which is why I've kept you in the loop with everything I've done, and why I agreed to see the service psychologist last week, and she gave me a clean bill of health. Well, she suggested I might benefit from some grief counselling, to which I've agreed, but that was all.'

* * *

'Hey, Mum!' Teddington called, as she stepped through the front door. 'I got the shopping you called about!' She was carrying two supermarket bags, which she took directly to the kitchen.

'Thanks, love! We have a visitor, put the kettle on.'

Plonking the bags on the side, Teddington checked the kettle was full and switched it on, as she started putting the shopping away.

She could just about hear there were voices in the front room, but she didn't know who the visitor was – probably just one of her mum's friends from the various social groups she was involved in. She was only halfway through when her mother appeared.

'I'll finish that. He's here to see you,' her mother surprised her by saying, as she took over unloading the second bag. 'You go talk to your caller. He's been waiting ages for you to get back.'

Frowning at her mother, Teddington asked who it was.

'That nice Inspector who was looking for you when you were kidnapped.'

DCI Piper here? *Why?* 'I wasn't kidnapped,' she reminded her mother absently, as she went to the front room. 'Chief Inspector,' she greeted.

'Mrs Teddington.'

'What do you want?' She closed her eyes, took a breath. 'Sorry, that was rude. But, really, what do you want?'

'How do you feel about going back to work with Bell?'

Well, that's direct. She crossed her arms, but the move was overly defensive, so she put her hands in her jeans pockets instead. 'I don't *feel* anything particular about it. I want to get back to work, but the Governor won't allow it without a doctor's fit-to-work note. Even then, it'll be light duty only, off the wings. Besides, Charlie's on the list for a parole hearing – this week, I think. He shouldn't be there when I go back.'

'The hearing's been delayed, indefinitely.'

She shifted, fidgeted. Piper was watching her too closely. She had the feeling he could read her all too easily. 'Oh,' she said. 'Didn't know that. What happened?'

'I did.' His attention shifted to her mother coming in bearing two matching mugs of steaming tea. 'Thank you, Mrs Whittaker.'

Teddington took the mug, finding her hands had gone colder than she had realised. As Piper thanked her mother, Teddington paced to the front window. Through the dazzlingly white nets, she could see the street where she'd done most of her growing up. Looking to her left, she could see the house on the opposite side of the road where Enzo lived. She felt colder knowing he wasn't there yet.

'I'm going over to the Sanchez's to put on their evening meal,' her mother was saying. 'Will you be visiting Enzo today?'

Teddington nodded. 'This evening.'

Her mother turned to Piper. 'Mia and Dino, Enzo's parents, are back from Italy, to be with Enzo. I put a little something in the oven for them while they're at the hospital. It's nice to come home to a cooked meal, don't you think?'

'Indeed.'

'Mum?' Teddington interrupted when she could see her mother was going to continue the conversation. 'You don't want the Sanchez's coming home to a half-cooked meal.'

'No, no,' her mother fussed, busy collecting her stuff, 'quite right.'

When her mother went out of the door, Teddington watched her head across the street, and didn't hold back the sigh of relief. 'I love Mum, but right now, I'm struggling to cope with her incessant chatter.'

'She's a generous woman,' Piper observed quietly.

Teddington started to murmur her agreement, as she went to sip the tea, only the tea halted untouched to lips that hung loose, as her eyes widened and she turned to the DCI, struck by recognition at last. 'You?' She wasn't sure she believed it. 'You were the second man?'

For a moment, he stared directly back. 'Of course.'

Teddington couldn't focus. She leaned on the window sill, placing her tea down on the white sill so her shaking hands didn't spill it. Her whole world was tipping. Corruption in the prison service. A prisoner had saved her – twice. A mother who let her children die. A serving police officer who gave assistance to a man on the run. Where was the nice, ordered world she'd grown up believing in?

'Mrs Teddington?'

She nodded. 'Yeah, sorry, I'm fine.' She picked up her tea and moved over to the sofa. 'Why did you delay Charlie's hearing?'

'Because I need him where he is,' Piper stated. 'So do you.'

'Me?' Teddington frowned up at him. 'What is this about?'

'Thomas Walters.'

Teddington swallowed, becoming engrossed in the swirling mists of her tea. 'Suicide.'

'You don't believe that.'

His certainty unnerved her. 'Says who?'

'The fact that you asked Charlie Bell to investigate.'

She knew she hadn't told anyone else about that. 'Says who?'

'Charlie Bell.' Piper rolled his eyes. 'Look, this will be a lot easier if you just trust me.'

'You were the one who pointed out it's difficult to know who to trust.' She glared up at him, but didn't have the will to fight him. 'But, then again, this Mexican Standoff isn't doing either of us any favours. Let's start over. How about you start with telling me what your relationship with Bell is?'

'I was Charlie's commanding officer for ten years. And a better officer I've rarely met.'

Teddington watched Piper. He meant every word he said, which somehow didn't make her feel any better. She was already doing everything she could to not like Charlie too much.

'What about your relationship with him?'

She huffed and smiled. 'Wow, you're the second man to ask me about that today.'

'Who?'

'The Guv, when I told him I want to go back to work. But, I'll tell you what I didn't tell him, when it comes to Charlie Bell, I just don't bloody know. He's an inmate, I'm an officer.'

'You said that before,' Piper countered. 'Didn't exactly ring true then, either.'

Teddington couldn't answer immediately, but she knew Piper would wait on a response. 'It's an impossible situation. I think, had we met in other circumstances, that Charlie and I would probably, that is, possibly—' she couldn't find the words.

'You fancy him.'

'Are we teenagers?'

Piper laughed, his smile surprisingly becoming. 'You're attracted to him.'

'Of course I'm attracted to him. Six-four, great body, beautiful eyes. He's intelligent, considerate, and he treats me with respect. I'd have to be dead from the brain down not to be attracted to him, but here's the killer – he's a convict, I'm a prison officer. It's probably not real. It's not allowed to be real. It cannot happen.'

'He wants it to,' Piper spoke lightly, and she couldn't detect any note of censure. 'So do you.'

Teddington looked away. 'Wanting and having aren't the same thing.' Which didn't make any of it easier. 'What do you know about the man he killed?'

'Phillip Mansel-Jones? Nasty piece of work. We'd been looking at Mansel-Jones for years, but the guy was good when it came to hiding the evidence. The operation was slick. There was a fall guy at every turn. And with each year, Mansel-Jones got worse. His perversions grew, as did his cruelty. Either we'd get a witness who'd disappear or withdrew testimony, there was always a 'water-tight' alibi. In the end, we were both getting too damn close, almost obsessed with the bastard. It was clear we'd never get anything on him. Then, a body turned up.

'I won't tell you the details; it was horrific. But, from a professional point of view, wonderful. The body yielded DNA evidence – a definitive link to Mansel-Jones. The pathologist got his hands shattered, claimed it was an accident. The evidence disappeared. He never looked me in the eye again. Then, another little girl went missing. It wasn't our case, but I knew what it meant. I went to the Mansel-Jones house in the early hours of a moonless night, though that was more accident than design. Charlie got there before me. He broke in, found the girl, got her out, passed her to me. I was getting her into the car, when I heard the shots.'

Teddington sat, stunned, as the DCI provided her with information that could ruin his career, not to mention, see him in prison as an accessory to murder. There were many ways he could have gained her trust. This struck her as the riskiest.

'I dropped the girl in woods close to her house, watched her run home, saw the joy on her parents' face when they opened the back door, and there she was.'

He took a sip of his tea. 'The girl never said what happened to her. It's been assumed she just got lost in the woods, and the search failed to find her. Charlie, on the other hand, didn't even try to hide, he just went home. Though when the police arrived, he'd obviously taken quite a beating. At his trial, he told the truth, but omitted my presence, never named the girl he'd saved, said he didn't know who she was.'

'I'm amazed he was only given seven years.'

'Extenuating circumstances.'

She frowned the question at him.

'He hadn't just been beaten, he'd been shot, the bullet fired from a gun used in three robberies. A gun that was later found in the sewers a hundred feet from the Mansel-Jones house. Charlie says Mansel-Jones shot first.'

'But, is it true?'

Piper nodded. 'There are other details that didn't come out, but, yes, I believe so. Charlie never had access to a gun. Mansel-Jones did.'

Teddington stared at him. 'How am I supposed to feel about this?'

This time, he shrugged. 'Sometimes, heroes wear black, and good men are guilty. If you figure out how to feel about it, tell me. I haven't worked that one out yet.'

She forced herself to swallow over the lump in her throat. 'It's a screwed up world.'

'Yes, it is.' Piper passed her the manila file that had been resting on the arm of the chair.

In silence, she took it and read with absorbed fascination. The case file of Thomas Walters, including autopsy report. Piper sat in silence as she poured over it, before passing it back. 'Thanks for the nightmares.'

'Still think it's suicide?'

She sighed. 'I never thought it was suicide, but without a murder weapon, what hope is there?'

'What about this mysterious "Leo" everyone refers to?'

She shook her head. 'I don't know. People I've never seen scared of anything, are nervous. He's powerful, but that's all I know. What happens if we don't figure out who he is?'

The tight line of Piper's lips, the darkening of dread in his eyes all made her rather grateful to be sat down. She feared her knees had become gelatinous. 'Tommy's death may not be the last. And it may well not stop at inmates.'

Fear constricted her throat. 'You think my colleagues and I are in danger?'

'Perhaps not your colleagues.'

There was no oxygen left in the room. The world. 'Like, in hospital?'

Then, the left side of his mouth started to tip up. 'Don't worry. That investigation is on-going. Yes, there is a possibility of danger. We know tendrils of this reach beyond the tall walls of Blackmarch Prison. We're less clear on how far, and we don't know the ultimate plan. That's why we need to find out who Leo is.'

She shrugged. 'There are no Leos in the prison. Closest I could find was a Mahatma Lyons in A-wing.'

'What about your partner?'

'Robbins?' she frowned. 'His name's Len. I suppose I could ask him—'

'No,' Piper cut her off. 'Don't bring anyone else into this. You'll have to be careful, keep your eyes and ears open, but don't put yourself at risk.'

'I don't intend to. As far as I'm concerned, I've been at way too much risk these last few weeks as it is, I don't want to go there again. You know, it's not like I haven't been trying to find out what happened, I just can't find any evidence.'

'Try harder.'

Chapter 22

On the third day of asking, Charlie was finally handed the books Teddington had sent. Looking through them he wondered about Teddington's reading habits. Ian Rankin, Michael Crichton, Christopher Brookmyre, Simon Kernick … And Anne Frank.

She'd said 'ladies first,' so she meant to direct him to Anne Frank. He'd checked for messages slipped inside, but if there had been one, it was gone now. It could have been found and removed before he'd received the volume, or it could be something in the volume itself. He'd have to read it.

The reading was a surprisingly harrowing experience. Like most people who studied Modern History at school, Charlie was well aware of what the Nazis had done, what Jews like Anne had had to suffer. But, the mood and the writing from the young girl showed more than literary talent. It was a journey that gave hope, that taught one should never just surrender, but always make the best of a situation. It was a wonderful and enduring message, one Charlie was grateful to Teddington for trying to tell him.

He was still thinking about the book through his evening meal. He missed not being able to sit with the other men. He might not have taken much part in the conversation, but he would hear it, find out what was going on. He wasn't going to make much progress if he couldn't talk to anyone.

As he returned his dinner plate, not a single inmate would meet his eye. They'd cower away, distinct aversion to talking to anyone. The screws would, but he got the distinct impression if he didn't look away quick enough, he was in trouble.

On his way back, he saw Senior Officer Turner entering the wing, he judged his pace to make sure he naturally crossed Turner's path.

'Officer Turner,' he greeted, as they approached one another.

'Bell.'

'Any news of Teddington?'

Turner stopped. 'You got her letter.'

'True, but she didn't say anything about when she'll be back in work.'

Turner took a deep breath, Charlie figured he was about to get told to butt out. 'It's not your place to ask.'

'No, sir.'

He saw the frown flicker over Turner's forehead, as he moved away and headed back to his own cell. Standing just inside the door, he looked around the room. It was neat, minimal, tiny. Boring, restricted, cramped. Airless. This was a cage. This was the point of prison. Locked up away from the world. Away from the people who were worth something.

His eyes slid to the child's pictures on the wall. Though he had torn down the one, the others remained. They provided the only colour to the grey room. Every time he looked at them, he felt the loss of Oscar again, but better that than feeling nothing.

Sighing, he moved over to the chair, which felt way too small, but he was used to it. He picked up the book again, Anne *Frank: The Diary of a Young Girl*, before he reached for Teddington's letter.

It struck him, again, that inside the script was very upright, and, on the outside, slanted. No matter how many times he read the letter, it didn't tell him anything new.

'You've never called me "sir" before. Why start now?'

Charlie was surprised to see Turner in the doorway. He placed the envelope on the table and joined his hands over it. 'Is that a serious question?'

'Yes.' Turner came into the room, closer to Charlie, towering over him.

Charlie shrugged. 'Since I got back, I've noticed changes. "Sir" seems appropriate these days.'

'Want to detail those changes?'

Charlie wondered how much he dared say. 'It's too quiet. The lack of socialisation isn't helping. Particularly for Brett.'

'Brett?'

'Ground floor. Was on suicide watch last year.'

'I know the man, but what makes you think he's having a problem?'

'I told Robbins the other day,' Charlie reported what he had said to Robbins to Turner.

'Hmm,' Turner said. He scowled down at Charlie, then, spun on his heel, pulling the door closed behind him, the key sounding as the door was locked.

Leaving the letter beside the book, Charlie swung up into his bunk. The writing on the outside of the letter was slanted. Towards a stamp that *hadn't been cancelled*.

* * *

For breakfast the next morning, Charlie got a large mug of steaming hot coffee and quickly returned to his cell. It was hot enough to burn his hands, but not hot enough to steam off the stamp. He needed a kettle. Only, he didn't have one. Very few people did.

Keen had a kettle.

As eager as he was to speak with Keen, it was pointless until the man got back from the gym and the shower. To fill the time, he completed the routine he had devised for use in his cell. The exertion didn't stop his mind doing twenty to the dozen. What was the message? How had it taken him so long to figure out where it was, and was there something more he should have done? Had he missed something time-sensitive?

He checked his watch. By now, Keen would be back in his cell. Standing, Charlie grabbed the letter, tucked it into his back pocket, and headed up to the second floor.

Runt stood by the door; he was the only person out of a cell on the second floor. He glowered at Charlie as he approached; a more obvious warning was hard to imagine. Still, he had to speak to Keen and couldn't afford to let something so insignificant as a muscleman with a grudge get in his way.

He moved to within a metre of the man before he spoke, asking to see Keen but keeping his voice low, respectful. It was all bullshit, but it all helped.

'Let him in.'

At Keen's quiet command, Runt stepped aside, and Charlie moved into Keen's relatively palatial room. The old man was sitting quietly, pondering a chess board.

'Don't you need two to play that game?'

'Indeed. That's why I'm awaiting a response from my opponent in B-Wing.'

Charlie wandered briefly who the opponent was, but he didn't know anyone in B-Wing and chess had never been his game. The only point of interest was the idea that cross-wing communication was still possible.

'What game would you like to play, Mr Bell? Twenty questions, perhaps?'

'Actually, I came with only one. Can I use your kettle?'

Keen frowned up at him. 'Only if you're going to make me a coffee.'

Seemed a small enough price to pay. 'Okay.'

'Wait.' Keen's voice stopped him, as he reached out. 'Why should I help you? It seems people who help you get hurt.'

That made Charlie frown. 'What do you mean?'

'Teddington tried to help you, and it nearly killed her.'

'The shooting wasn't down to me.' He was already sick of having to explain that one.

'What about her attempted murder?'

Charlie felt like he'd been punched in the gut. All he could do was stare at Keen. 'What?'

'You didn't really think the overdose of morphine was an accident, did you?'

Dear God … Charlie sank unbidden to sit on the foot of the bed. Accident was exactly what both Turner and Piper had told him it was. His worry had been controlled by the knowledge he dared not show that concern, but when he told Piper, Piper's assurance he was being paranoid had helped. News sent via Towers later had been clear. Administrative error. Towers hadn't been lying to him, but it was possible Piper had lied to Towers. His mind rebelled at the idea. Yet …

'Someone tried to kill her?' *Was it possible that this was what the shooting at the cemetery was about? Was someone trying to kill her, specifically? Nothing, nothing at all to do with him?* Nothing was making sense. 'Why would they?' He couldn't believe *anyone* would want her dead.

'Because they could get to you through her.'

Charlie couldn't assimilate that. Maybe he just didn't want to. He rested his elbows on his knees, his hands hanging loose. 'Who?'

'You're not an idiot, Bell. Who do you think?'

Charlie considered the idea, scraping back his hair before intertwining his fingers, elbows on knees again. He'd been a cop; there were a fair few who'd want him dead, but Mansel-Jones was the most obvious. 'Even if you're right, how would they know I care about her?'

'Every man and his bitch in here knows you want her – it's not a huge leap from want to care,' Keen pointed out. 'Why do you think she was arranged as a present?'

'*You* arranged that?'

'No!'

Keen actually looked offended, but then again, Keen had only permitted him time in the gym after he'd protected Teddington. 'Just what is the relationship between you and Teddington?'

Keen met his regard without expression. 'And before you ask any more stupid questions, Winehouse had nothing to do with it, either.'

'Then, who?' Charlie's frown only increased when Keen didn't answer. 'Something's rotten in the state,' he mused.

'Indeed. Why do you want the kettle?'

Charlie observed the man's bruising was gone, and he got the impression Keen wasn't so much cowed as biding his time. Keen had been in here for a decade; he'd seen people come and go, probably knew a lot more about what was going on than he let on. Keen was on a life sentence, properly institutionalised, and unlikely to even want to get out. Did that mean Charlie could trust him? It certainly meant Keen had known Teddington longer than he had, and she had told him to trust Keen over Winehouse.

'It's not real.'

Keen frowned and glanced at the small electrical item, reaching over to waggle the very solid lead to the electrical socket. 'It is.'

'Not the kettle.' Charlie smiled, half laughing. 'Whatever it was between me and Teddington. It's not real.'

'How do you figure that?'

'I don't,' Charlie admitted. 'She does.'

'Stockholm Syndrome.'

'That was what she called it,' Charlie admitted. 'Me, I don't know what it is. Feels real to me, but there's nothing to it for her. Seems somewhat unfair she's being targeted for something she doesn't have any involvement in.'

'We all chose to cross the line, Charlie, which means we drag anyone we know down with us, no matter how hard we try not to.' Keen narrowed his eyes. 'And you didn't answer my question.'

'It's not the kettle I want,' Charlie told him, coming to an unexpected decision about trust. 'It's the steam.' He twisted and took the envelope from his pocket. When Keen reached out, he placed the paper in the old man's hands.

He watched as Keen unfolded it and turned the letter over in his hands.

'May I?'

Charlie nodded his consent. If there was anything hidden in there, he hadn't seen it.

'It's Teddington's handwriting,' Keen observed before he'd even taken the letter out. The older man clocked the curious look Charlie couldn't keep from his face. 'I've known her a lot longer than you have.'

Only a year, two at most, Charlie figured. That's how long Teddington had been working the Whitewalk, but it *was* longer than Charlie had known her. He watched Keen open the letter, read it.

'The books she sent you,' Keen mused, as he refolded the letter and returned it to the envelope, 'was one Anne Frank's Diary?'

Charlie frowned. 'How did you know?'

Keen stood, carefully moved to the kettle, and switched it on. 'Do you know what to do?'

'You got there a lot quicker than I did.'

'Been around the block a few times more than you.'

They waited in silence, as the kettle boiled. When steam started to show, Keen held the letter in the flow. When it was ready, Keen removed the stamp and handed the envelope back to Charlie. Thanking him, Charlie looked at the letter. There, hidden under the stamp, in tiny capitals, was the message 'MJ ACTIVE WATCH BACK'. A warning. There was little else to say, or do. Charlie returned the letter to his pocket. 'Thanks.'

Keen surprised him, stepping into his way. 'Whatever may, or may not, be real, be careful … for Teddington's sake. She's tough, but she's vulnerable.'

* * *

Try harder.

That phrase damned her for days, still hanging around her head, when she headed back to the prison and handed in the doctor's note clearing her for light duties.

The Governor wasn't around, but Vera took the note and confirmed all details for the upcoming training course.

Teddington wanted to speak to Charlie, but she wasn't sure if her motivation was to solve a murder or just to see him again.

Try harder.

She'd already sent him a message, assuming he'd got it. There wasn't anything else she could do. Yet. She couldn't risk another move until she was back in work. Still, she wasn't ready to leave, so she headed to the staff canteen. No one was there. She made a mug of coffee and slipped onto one of the uncomfortable plastic chairs, staring into the distance, sipping.

Try harder.

Those were the words of an annoying teacher, and Teddington had known plenty of those. She *was* trying – she didn't know what else to do. Since she had time and quiet, she delved into her handbag, pulled out her small pad, and started making notes.

Weapon:
Metal
Hollow
Possibly quite blunt
A lot of force used
Dirty

That was what the pathologist had concluded, but what did it mean in practical terms? 'Quite blunt' made sense; there weren't that many sharps allowed in the prison. And very few 'sharps' opportunities were allowed within the prison environment. There were tools and knives in the workshops and kitchens. But if inmates were in there multi-dutied officers hovered like vultures. The public might not want the gangs inside prisons to 'tool up,' but they'd probably be horrified at the expense that the government had to to go to to avoid that. The officer: prisoner ratio in such situations was so high, days off were often interrupted to cover the number requirements. She'd often welcomed the overtime, but sometimes missed the R&R.

She closed the pad and picked up the Prison Service Instruction she'd noticed earlier. New internal instructions. The PSI had Blackmarch printed all over it. The tone was the Guv's. She wasn't really reading it. Her coffee was hardly touched, when Turner walked in ten minutes later.

'Hiya, doll,' he greeted, as he put a dirty mug in the dishwasher. While Turner's back was to her, she tore the page from the notepad and slipped it into her jacket pocket.

'You just can't keep away, can ya?'

She smiled at him. 'This is what you get for not having a life.'

'So, why are you in?'

'Handing in my fit-to-work note. I've asked to come back on light duties, so you'll have to partner me with someone other than Robbins.' Which was something of a relief.

'I'll see what I can do.'

She offered him a quick smile. 'Did Peggy forgive your birthday pukeathon on the bathmat yet?'

'Just about.' He made another coffee, before coming to sit opposite her. 'Took some grovelling, but I got there. How are you doing?'

'Mostly just bored. How are things in here?'

'Quiet,' Turner grumped. 'You know what the guys were saying that night in the pub, about things being quieter?'

'Yeah?'

'Well … quieter's an understatement.'

'Something wrong with that?'

'If it sends someone like Brett over the edge, yeah. Bell's settled back in, by the way.'

'Good.'

'He's been reading a lot.'

Teddington didn't want to be seen to be eager for the news, but she couldn't avoid the conversation – that would just look odd. 'He always did.'

'True,' Turner allowed.

'Oh, did you hear?' Teddington reached for another conversation. 'Enzo's out of the coma!'

'No, really?' Turner smiled at the news, his tone hopeful.

'Yeah, you know his parents flew back in?'

Turner indicated he did.

'Well, they sit with him all day, and I tend to visit in the evening. Yesterday evening, we were all there, changing over as it were, and Enzo opened his eyes.' She couldn't help smiling.

'That's *great* news. I'll let the rest of the team know. So …' Now Turner was looking at her, all speculation. 'Have you heard the rumours about you?'

Teddington paused, the cooling coffee halfway to her lips. 'Erm, no. And I'm not sure I want to.' But, she could tell she was going to hear them anyway.

'Rumour one, you and Sanchez are, or at least were, getting it on.'

Given what Turner had witnessed in the pub, she could hardly speak against that.

'Rumour two, you and Bell *did* get it on.'

She rolled her eyes at that one. 'Ah well.' She smiled and shrugged. 'If I say nothing, then I'm confirming the rumours. If I deny them, I'm confirming the rumours.'

Turners grin was broad. 'That's usually how it works.'

'Well, it was reported in the papers, so it must be true.'

'Must be.'

She laughed at how a man in his mid-forties could conjure up such a boyish look. 'Ok, well, here's the down low. Enzo and I have been friends for two-thirds of our lives. We're very close. And no, the phrase "kissing cousins" wouldn't be entirely inappropriate, despite the lack of blood relation. Whereas Bell is a good man, but—'

Turner snorted. 'He's a murderer.'

She started to respond, but was cut off.

'Ah, Teddington, I'm glad I've caught you.'

Both Teddington and Turner twisted to see Rebecca Fry walking in, all tweed and twin set again. Somehow, Teddington always got the image of a "before" when she looked at Fry, like one of those terrible seventies shows where the frumpy secretary would suddenly take off her glasses, let down her hair, and instantly turning into a sex siren.

'Do you mind if I join you?'

'Do you mind if I stay?' Turner asked, checking his watch.

Fry ignored him and shoved in at the table.

'I wanted to ask you about Bell.'

Teddington couldn't hold back a smile, as Turner covered his grin with a sip of coffee.

'Popular topic,' Teddington said.

Fry looked momentarily confused, but apparently, decided not to ask. 'Are you aware his parole hearing got cancelled? That DCI Piper has put an indefinite hold on it?'

'No,' Teddington worried herself at how easily she could lie, 'but I'm not surprised. What of it?'

'I want to get a new date set, soon, and I was hoping you could help me with that.'

Now, she frowned. 'How can I help?'

'I need a statement from you that when he abducted you, he treated you well, didn't hurt, harm, or force himself on you. And he readily agreed to give himself up at the earliest opportunity.'

'Firstly, he didn't "abduct" me, anyway. Secondly, I've already made that statement,' Teddington pointed out, 'to the police. To DCI Piper himself, in fact.'

'Then you won't help?'

'I don't think I can actively do any more. See, here's the thing … Regardless of anything I say, I was alone with Bell for two days and two nights and people believe, however wrongly, that we became lovers. My statement to the police made it clear nothing happened, but if I start pushing for his release, people will say it's because I have feelings for the guy.'

'And you don't?'

'No,' Teddington said. 'Well … yes. I do have some feelings about him. I mean, he *did* save my life, after all, got me out of the line of fire, and got me decent medical care, when a delay could have cost me the use of my arm, if not my life. He's been a model prisoner in here, never causing hassle, and rumours are he's actually squashed trouble before it escalated to us getting involved. And he got me and Dyer out of a potentially very damaging situation. If anyone deserves a reprieve for good behaviour, it's Bell—'

She cut off as her mobile rang.

Chapter 23

The hairs on the back of Charlie's neck prickled. It was like watching the first few scenes of a movie; all the tension was building, waiting for the horror to explode.

No one moving around, conversation kept to a muted minimum, and everyone quietly queuing to be served at meal times. It was like someone had taken all the fire out of the inmates. Perhaps they were all being drugged into submission. Charlie didn't like it. He had tried to talk to a number of other inmates, but after that trip to Keen, it seemed every time he opened his mouth, either they would run in fear, or one of the screws would stop him.

Charlie waited in line with the other inmates, the anaesthetised sheep, to get his lunch. Running through various ways of how to get more information on Tommy, nothing stood out as likely to succeed. People shouting shocked him into paying attention. At the head of the line, not far from Charlie, two bodies were scuffling. He was half surprised more people weren't bundling in. Another symptom.

'Cut him! Cut him!'

Instantly, Charlie looked closer. Brett had another inmate – a recent arrival Charlie knew by sight but not name – in a headlock under one arm, and a bloody great kitchen knife in the other. As passive as the wing had become, they were all gathering now, the murmur of surprise giving way to the chant. As the instigator of the chant was two men in front of him, Charlie stepped round and pulled him up short.

'Stop!'

The man he had by the scruff of the neck was a weasel at the best of times. He shut up instantly.

Since Charlie was now as much of a centre of attention as Brett, he called out, 'Everyone move back, give Brett room!'

He was only echoing what Norman and Robbins were already shouting, as they ran down from the upper floors, but now the men obeyed. It struck Charlie as odd to realise there had been no guards on the ground floor at meal time. But, Brett was the immediate problem, so he stepped forward, carefully, slowly, his hands open and wide, showing no hidden weapons.

'Come on, Richie, what's all this about?'

'Keep away!' The voice was high and stressed.

Charlie could see the mania in Brett's eyes. Whatever else he needed to do, he needed to keep Brett from getting any more stressed. 'Okay.' He stopped where he was. 'I won't come any closer, just tell me what this is all—'

'Drop the knife!' Robbins had made it onto the floor, was storming across, his hand reaching for his Taser.

'Keep away!'

As Brett screamed, Charlie stepped in front of Robbins. He hoped to God the man didn't turn the Taser on him – he didn't want to repeat that experience.

'Officer Robbins, please, don't.'

Robbins halted in front of Charlie, a look of pure hate on his face.

'Get out of the way.' It was a cold command. 'This is none of your business.'

'Maybe,' Charlie kept his voice low, so as not to carry as he looked down at the officer. 'But, one of us has had negotiation training, and it clearly wasn't you.'

'Keep him away!' Brett was screaming. 'Keep him away, or I'll do it, I'll slash 'im.'

Charlie listened, but he looked at Robbins. Evidently, the officer wasn't happy about the situation, but to Charlie, it was obvious – all his training, all his instincts were to keep Robbins and everyone else back.

'You,' Robbins grated, 'are not the one with the power.'

'No,' Charlie agreed, 'the man with the knife and the hostage is the one with the power, and right now, that is Richie Brett, and he wants you to back away, so please, back away.'

Behind him, Brett continued to scream for Robbins to back off. With a glare at Charlie, Robbins did just that.

'Keep going.'

Robbins backed up again.

Glad the man was several steps away, Charlie finally turned and faced Brett again. He saw now that Brett's eyes were wide and red-rimmed, his lips badly chapped; the man had been chewing and sucking on them too much.

'Okay, Richie,' Charlie said carefully. 'Officer Robbins has moved back like you wanted. What's all this about?'

'Things are wrong.' Brett focused on Charlie. He spoke in a horse whisper, his eyes moving from side to side as soon as he'd spoken. 'They're coming. They're coming. They're going to kill me.'

'No one's going to kill you,' Charlie assured him. 'We just want to help. I'm not asking you to let your hostage go, but can you loosen your grip a little?'

'I'm in control.' Brett moved back. If anything, his grip tightened.

'Yes,' Charlie agreed, 'yes, you are in control. But, you need to loosen your grip, or your hostage will pass out. Then, he'll fall, and you'll fall, you'll lose control. Just ease your grip a little, okay?'

Brett looked around, made sure no one was near him. 'I'll cut you,' he threatened the crowd, waving the knife around. 'Any of ya comes near me, and I'll cut you.'

'It's okay, Richie,' Charlie told him. 'No one's coming near you. Just tell me why you're doing this. What do you want?'

'Teddington,' Brett said, the knife wobbling as he pointed it in Charlie's direction. 'I want Teddington.'

Know the feeling, Charlie thought. 'She's not here. She's not working at the moment.'

'I want Teddington!' Brett screamed and waved the knife tip way too close to his hostage's face. 'Get her here.'

'Richie, mate,' Charlie spoke, trying to keep the smile on his face, 'Teddington isn't here.'

'Get her here!'

'Alright! Alright. Hold on.' Charlie felt his heart hammering.

The only way to deal with a hostage taker was to at least make them believe they were in control. He walked backwards towards Robbins, making sure he kept Brett in view, and his voice down, he spoke to the man who looked like he'd rather tear his throat out then help him.

'Is there any way to get hold of Teddington?'

'For that scrote?'

'No,' his controlled the volume so Brett couldn't hear, 'for the guy who's got a knife pointing at his eye.' Charlie clenched his fists, kept them tight at his side and tried again, his voice low. 'Look, just at least make it look as if you're going to call her, get her here. I can stall him, and maybe even talk him down, but he has to think we're working with him, not against him.'

Officer Norman came down the stairs. 'I'll see if we can get a call out to her,' he was answering Charlie but making sure his voice carried to Brett. 'But even if I can get through, she'll take at least an hour to get here.'

'Tell her to move faster. I want her here now!' Brett screamed.

Since Norman was already on his way, and Robbins was useless, Charlie moved back towards Brett. 'You heard that, right?' he spoke gently. 'Officer Norman has gone to get that call made. They're going to call Teddington. But, remember, she's still recovering from a gunshot wound. She may not be able to get here very quickly. These things take time.'

'But, she's coming?' Brett said. 'She'll come?'

'We're working on it,' Charlie said, risking moving slightly closer. 'Why do you want Teddington? Isn't there anyone else that can help you?'

'No!' Brett shouted. 'No. Just her. Only Teddington. I want Teddington.'

He was sounding like a child – a spoiled, selfish child – but there was a tone of desperation that worried Charlie. It also worried him there was a lunch service that should be starting but wasn't, and there was a limit to the length of time the action was going to distract the best part of two hundred hungry men from filling their bellies.

Charlie tried not to think of all the bad things that could happen. In the meantime, he had to stall. 'So, you trust Teddington?'

'She's not been replaced.'

That threw Charlie. Technically, she had been replaced; all her shifts were covered. 'Replaced?'

'She's not one of the zombies,' Brett confided. 'Not like these lot. They've all been replaced. The Lion got to them. They're just zombies. Most of them are zombies.'

While Brett's insanity was distinctly to the fore, Charlie kind of knew what he meant. 'Most of them?' he asked. 'So, some of us are still …' He searched for a word, somehow 'normal' just didn't fit. '… Human?' That was questionable, too.

'Some.'

'What about me?' Charlie asked. 'Am I still human? Can you trust me?'

Brett looked at him, his eyes narrowed, and his head tilted. 'You look alright, but stop moving closer. I don't want to talk to you. I want to talk to Teddington.'

'Then, talk to me.'

Surprised by the voice, Charlie twisted and saw Teddington passing through the last gate into the wing. Her voice wasn't the only surprise. He was still more used to her in uniform, but she wasn't in uniform now. By God, no. She wore skin-tight jeans, heeled knee boots, a tailored jacket, and a white top. Her hair was loose, hanging in curls to her waist. She wore make up. She looked good, feminine, attractive. Hell, just plain sexy.

Undoubtedly, he wasn't the only one noticing; his wasn't the only jaw dropping. She must have metal heels, given the way they clicked as she walked across the floor, getting closer, and all-consuming of attention.

She stopped beside Charlie, her attention firmly on Brett. She licked her lips and took a deep breath as she spoke again. 'You said you wanted to talk with me. Well, I'm here. Talk to me.'

Charlie couldn't stop looking at her. He half suspected he was drooling. He had to get over it.

It's not real.

He closed his mouth, swallowed and concentrated back on what was important right now – Brett. Brett was looking at Teddington like he couldn't quite believe what he was seeing.

'Teddington?'

'Yes, it's me. I'm not working at the moment, so I'm not in uniform, and I figured this talk you wanted to have was too important to wait.'

Brett was frowning, he was also swaying back and forth, the knife making a worrying sawing action before the hostage's face. A hostage who was surprisingly quiet, given how terrified he obviously was, tears and snot running from him, dripping on the floor. He'd wet himself, too. 'He said you could be some time. You were only a couple of minutes.'

She shrugged. 'You got lucky. I was on site when Officer Norman called me. I popped in to sort out a few things with the Guv before I come back full time.'

'Will it be soon? Will you be back on the wing? We want you back on the wing.'

Her pause was so long, Charlie found himself turning to look at her. He watched her swallow and lick her lips.

'I'm not sure, Richie. Is that what you wanted to talk about? My return to duty?'

'No.' He frowned. 'Yes.'

'Okay, then let's talk, but let Pearson go.'

Pearson, of course. Matthew Pearson.

Her voice was calm and gentle, reasonable. But, Charlie could see she wasn't as calm as she was trying to make out. Her breathing was deep, she was managing it, but being so close, he could hear her swallow, and more frequently than was her norm. Her left hand was in her jacket pocket. He could hear paper crackle.

'He said you got shot.' Brett waved the knife towards Charlie again. 'But you look alright to me.'

Without a word, Teddington reached to her own jacket fastening. Slipping the two buttons free, she removed the black jacket.

There wasn't a man in the place who didn't react to the sight of bare shoulders, a tightly laced corset … and the things it did to her cleavage. Lust was an audible gasp.

'Oh, for God's sake, boys,' she addressed the wing as a whole. 'Just put it in the spank bank. You ain't never seeing this again.'

What only a few of the men would bother to see, was the remaining bruising and the irreversible scarring of the gun shot. She turned her focus onto Brett, and her hand with the jacket came up. Automatically, Charlie took the jacket, and she stepped forward, careful to move slowly and openly.

'Look. See?' She pointed to the damage on her shoulder. 'I was shot, but I'm recovering.'

Brett peered a little closer, mumbled something.

'Okay, Richie, you have my attention, I'm here. What do you want to talk about?'

'They're changing, all changing.' Brett moved forward, dragging Pearson with him. 'He's changing them, turning this into his hive.'

Her heel clicked as she took the next step, one more, and she stopped. 'Okay, they're changing. Let Matthew go, and you can tell me who's changing, and what they're changing into. And, who's changing them.'

'No.' Richie pulled Pearson back. 'He's staying here. He's my protection.'

'May I move closer, Richie?' she spoke softly as she did so. 'Okay, Richie, who's changing? Tell me who's changing.'

'They all are.' He was moving nervously from foot to foot, his eyes darting around the room, full of terror.

She waited, but Richie didn't elucidate. Another careful step, as she spoke, 'Richie?' Her use of his name brought his attention back to her. 'What are they turning into?'

'Zombies.' He leaned forward, his voice a harsh whisper, as if he was confiding in her.

Charlie heard sniggers in the crowd behind them. He turned his head to shush them, his hard look pinning the perpetrators to silence.

'What about Pearson?' Teddington asked softly. 'Is he a zombie?'

The knife, which had been wavering in the direction of the prison officer moved, pointed back at the sobbing man's face. 'He is. He's just like all the rest.'

'What about me?' she asked. 'I don't think I'm a zombie. Am I?'

He tipped his head to look at her. 'No … no, they haven't turned you. You and Bell got out at the right time, you two haven't turned.'

'Thank you.'

Though he couldn't see her face, Charlie would bet she was smiling at Brett. That winning smile that filled him with joy and never lasted, but he wanted it to. He wanted to make her smile until it never stopped.

'You think zombies are dangerous, right?'

Brett nodded. The maniacal gleam in his eyes had dimmed a little. He was transferring his allegiance from the psychosis to his trust in Teddington.

'And you know I'm not a zombie, right?'

He nodded.

'So, let's do a trade. You let the zombie go, and you use me as a hostage, okay? A straight swap. You'll be safer then, won't you?'

Dear Lord, Charlie couldn't believe what he was hearing. Was she seriously suggesting that she would willingly walk into the arms of danger? And in an oh-so reasonable tone? He couldn't just let her put her life in harm's way. 'Ted—'

The way she waved him off and scowled over her shoulder at him, cut him dead. But, for that brief second, they connected, and unless he was very much mistaken, she glanced meaningfully down at her jacket, which he still held. Her attention switched immediately back to Brett.

'Richie?' she asked. 'How are you feeling?'

'They're trying to turn me,' he said. 'They're trying to make me into one of them.'

'That's not going to happen,' she reassured him. 'I'm not going to let that happen.'

She was close now, an arm's length. If Brett lashed out, she was close enough to get gutted. He hoped the corset was made with steel boning that, at least, might minimise the damage. She raised her hands to waist height, wide and open, non-threatening, welcoming. 'How's your stomach?'

What's Brett's stomach have to do with anything? Charlie realised his heart was beating every bit as fast as if he were still chief negotiator, but instead, he was just plain scared. Given what else Teddington had been through lately, this was the last thing she needed. He couldn't reach for her, so he pulled her jacket tighter, bringing it to his nose, he caught that scent of apples again.

'It's a bit dodgy, actually.'

Charlie wasn't interested in Brett's internal plumbing. He hugged the jacket closer, heard that faint crackle of paper.

'Like you've been sucking on metal?'

Brett frowned. 'Yeah. A bit. Now you mention it.'

'And your head?'

Charlie saw movement to his right. Robbins had shifted – he was glaring at him. Swallowing, Charlie loosened his grip on Teddington's jacket, slipping his hand into the pocket as he did so.

'My head hurts.'

'Like it's in a vice?'

Charlie frowned. Teddington obviously knew something he didn't.

Brett sucked on his top lip, something he always did when nervous.

'You remember these feelings, don't you, Richie? This is what happened last year when you forgot to take your meds. Do you remember that?' Her voice was calm, comforting. 'You forgot to take your meds, and you thought we were all infected? Remember? Did you forget to take your meds again?'

Brett looked uncertain. 'They wouldn't give them to me.'

Teddington reached out, her hand went carefully around the wrist waving the knife around. 'They're horrible zombies, but not me, remember, I'm your friend. I'll get the meds. I'll keep you safe from the zombies.'

And just like that, Brett nodded. He let go of Pearson, who scrambled as far back as the architecture would allow him, and Brett was sobbing onto Teddington's bare shoulder. The knife stayed a while, but as sobs wracked his body, Brett dropped that, too. Charlie was vaguely aware Teddington was still talking to Brett in soothing tones. He sobbed out some more sentences as she ushered him away. Mostly, Charlie was aware of a sense of relief the danger was over, and she was still in one piece.

Chapter 24

As Teddington and Brett departed, Charlie heard all the conversations twittering around him. Not quite normal, but more like it, a cross between the old normal and the new. There was no way the screws could stop the inmates talking about what had happened.

'Don't,' Robbins snarled at Charlie, as he snatched Teddington's jacket, 'ever try to assert your dominance over mine again.'

Dick. Charlie ached to smash Robbins' stupid face to a pulp. 'No, Officer Robbins. May I return to the lunch line now?'

The way the man's eyes narrowed, it was clear he was considering other options.

'Back in line, Bell.'

Charlie looked to the other officer at the command. 'Of course, Officer Norman.' He was well aware of how Robbins eyes bored into his back as he turned and retook his place in the line.

'Jeez,' the inmate in front of him turned and said to Charlie. 'Teddington is one sexy bitch, huh? You shag her while you were out?'

Disgusted by the tone and the fact the other man had his hand down his trousers, Charlie felt his lip curl as he snarled the negative, glad to be so much taller than the norm, so he could stare straight ahead and not have to see what the little pervert was up to. He was worse than Partridge.

'Christ, how'd ya stop yourself? I'd've been on her before she could've said ouch from the gun shot.' There was controlled laughter and mutters of agreement all around. 'It wasn't like she could get away – you were handcuffed together.'

Charlie remembered the feel of her body curled up beside his on that single bed, the press of her butt against his groin. He swallowed, and tried not to think about it. 'Lucky for her, then, it was me she was cuffed to, and not you.'

'How did you get out of the handcuffs?' This time the question came from behind him.

Charlie didn't bother turning to see who'd asked. 'Bolt cutters.'

It was a lie. As the Doc had peeled back Teddington's blood-soaked blouse and bra, he'd taken a pin from her hair and picked the lock, but there were some skills it was best not to reveal to a bunch of convicted criminals. The swell of her pale breast, the colour and pride of her nipple, was an image that haunted his dreams and too many of his waking moments. He pushed them aside, lest he end up as obvious as the man in front of him.

* * *

Talk about zombification, Teddington thought, as she sat through the computer training. She shrugged it off as the predictable result of having been an IT programmer herself before Sasha's death had torn her life apart.

Since she was completing the tasks in a third of the time of everyone else, she spent most of her time either showing Turner how to do what they were being shown, or playing with the reporting facilities. This was supposed to be a copy of the version going live on Monday, with all data entered. She did a search on the name Leo. Since the training version had less restrictions than the live one would, she checked both inmate and officer data. Nothing came up, not that she'd expected it to. Just to be nosy, she viewed the personnel file of Jones, Peter. It was virtually empty. She checked her own. Same lack of data. No point in restricting access to data that wasn't there.

'Wish I could type half as fast as you,' Turner grumbled, as he used two fingers to tap out the data entry he was under instruction to input.

'There are more important skills in the world.'

'Maybe, but that one certainly seems to make things easier.'

'True,' Teddington said and smiled. Playing with the data, Teddington started frowning. Then, she started digging. She entered one more name 'Bell, Lucas Charles,' and what she read didn't make sense.

'Tony?' she called the attention of the trainer who had left them in an exercise. 'Did you say the data in here is the same data that will be going live?'

'Yes, why?'

'Because there are some major errors in it.' She was frowning at the screen. 'Information and reports on inmate behaviour that just isn't correct.'

* * *

Worried about the information she was seeing on the database, Teddington asked to see the Governor, but Vera said he was booked tight over the next few days.

That evening, she went to the hospital to see Sanchez. She was pleased he had been moved out of the high dependency unit and into a general ward, and he was looking much better than he had the previous day. He smiled broadly as she approached.

'Your mum and dad gone early?'

'I don't need babysitting anymore, not sure I needed it before.'

'You were in intensive care,' she mock-scolded him. 'They care. Intensively. They wanted to be with you. So did I. That's why we all spent as much time with you as we could. Besides, there's various medical theories which suggest you could hear every word we were saying, and talking helps. Personally, I would have thought you'd have woken up sooner, just to tell your mother to shut up. That woman always could talk the hind leg off a donkey.'

Sanchez smiled, 'And you got that saying from *your* mother.'

'Oh God!' She put one hand on her heart and the back of the other wrist on her forehead. 'I'm turning into my mother.

Shoot me now.' The amateur dramatics brought a laugh, but as she lowered her hands, her shoulder pulled. She put her left hand up to it. 'Guess I really shouldn't joke about that.'

Sanchez smiled. 'Hell, if we can't joke about getting shot, who can?'

She spent the next hour surprisingly pleasantly with a friend, who wanted no more than to just be a friend. Well, that … and to recover from being shot.

She left the hospital and walked to the bus stop. Taking the 61, she stared out of the window, numbly watching as they drove. There wasn't much to look at, but warm light spilled from the Ink Spot Tavern as they approached. As it was a popular stop, the bus slowed, and as it pulled over, Teddington looked through the windows of the recent extension, into the new restaurant space. She had to blink and concentrate, uncertain she was seeing what she was actually seeing.

Could it be?

She was focusing as the bus started to pull away. Yes it was. Robbins out dining with Rebecca Fry. And that was a more than friendly way to be holding a companion's hand.

Chapter 25

Her throat was dry and her palms sweaty as Teddington got out of her car and looked to the door of Whitewalk. Instead of coming back on light duty, she was coming back to a full shift on the wing. Staff shortages and a limit to overtime had forced the Governor's hand in asking her to come back full duty. She had said she was ready, but now, she wasn't sure.

This first shift was an early. She found the morning too cold to stand outside for long, so she locked the car door and rushed inside, before nerves got the better of her and she ran in the opposite direction.

The elevated heartbeat didn't help as she reached the locker room to stow her bag, nor did the way her hands shook when she tried to open her locker.

'Oh, get over it,' she berated herself under her breath. 'You managed when Richie asked for you – you can manage now.' Determined again, she took a deep breath and headed to work.

The senior officer on the night shift gave the quick handover brief, which was a lot briefer than Teddington remembered them being, since all he had to report was everything was quiet and everyone behaving. She couldn't have hoped for anything better for her first day back, but the butterflies in the stomach felt more like a flock of pterodactyls in attack mode.

She tried to control her breathing, as they moved through to the wing.

'You okay?' Robbins asked, as the last door was closed behind them. 'You're white as a sheet.'

She swallowed and took a deep breath as she turned to him. 'I'm fine. Just out of the habit of getting up this early.' It was good to be in without the inmates around, it gave her the opportunity to take a moment to gather her wits. 'You take the left, and I'll go right.'

'We could unlock together,' he suggested.

She smiled. 'Thanks, but why waste the time?' Instead, she headed off to the right and started unlocking the first door and pushing it back. 'Morning, Phelps, Mercy,' she greeted as she saw the pair.

'Morning, Officer Teddington.'

'Good to have you back.'

The two voices came out to her.

As she moved down the row, opening up, the different greetings were all variations of three themes; those two, and when was she going to wear the corset again. By the time they had moved up to the first landing, she found she was actually smiling. The pterodactyls had evolved into butterflies and even they seem to have settled down. Then, she came to Charlie's cell, and she felt the hesitation, but she forced herself not to show it, as she slid the key in the lock and opened the door. Careful not to look into the cell, she pushed the door open and moved to the next, which she was unlocking when Charlie appeared at his door, frowning at her.

'Isn't this too soon for you to be back?'

She risked a look up as she drew the key from the lock. 'A little, but after Brett, seems like I'm ready for it.'

She opened the door and pushed it wide into the room, before moving on to the next. She couldn't show any preference for Charlie, and she had to do something to quiet the pterodactyls again. She felt sick, and had to make sure she didn't glance up to see Charlie, because the urge to run to him was surprisingly strong.

She met up with Robbins halfway round, and they went directly up to the next floor to repeat the process. Though her heart did a flip when they had to walk past Charlie, she tried desperately not to react. She also wanted to stop and speak to

GB Williams

Keen, but that wasn't possible with Robbins always too close beside her.

In fact, she found he was at her side far too much through the shift. Part of her was grateful, but as time moved on, she just found it increasingly annoying. Eventually, just before lunch, Robbins left her in peace. Careful not to run, she headed up to the second floor and along to Keen's cell.

As usual, Runt was at the door, but as she approached, she could hear muttered voices. It was normal to see Runt block the entrance of any potential attacker, but today, he just stepped aside and indicated she should step straight in. So, she did. She only faltered when she saw Keen's visitor – Charlie Bell.

Oh, great!

'Welcome back, Officer Teddington,' Keen spoke seriously, as Bell passed him a hot cup of frothy coffee. 'Cappuccino?'

She controlled her smile, mostly, as she said, 'Please.' It was Bell who stood by the kettle and mixed up the conveniently prepared sachet, requiring neither milk or barista. At Keen's invitation, she sat in the second chair opposite him, as Charlie made the coffee.

She only realised Charlie had brought his own mug when he started making a third cup. Keen, she knew, only had two cups and saucers. She sipped the offering.

'Urm, still the best coffee in the building.' She looked from the coffee to the older man. 'Since when did you start letting people sit on your bed?' She noticed from the corner of her eye Charlie had frozen an inch from the mattress.

This time, Keen smiled, a rare and precious thing. He shrugged, then scowled at Charlie. 'Oh, sit down, boy. Neither it, nor I, will bite.'

'Well, he might.' She smiled at Bell. 'But only if you ask him nicely.' The uncertain look that engendered almost made her laugh, but she turned back to Keen. 'Things are different.'

'Yep.' He covered his words with the raised cup, which he blew across. 'And you need to be careful.'

She frowned at him. 'Why?'

'Up until now, you've been sacrosanct, but that could all change.'

'Is that a threat?' Charlie asked.

'Not from him,' Teddington assured.

'Down, boy,' Keen jokingly reprimanded the younger man, before turning back to Teddington. 'Charlie here has a theory about what killed Tommy.'

'A bloody great gash in the belly?' Teddington suggested.

Charlie tipped his head, his eyes nearly sparkling with laughter, but the subject was too serious to reach it.

'He was thinking, a pipe,' Keen's voice was kept low, his lips hidden by the cup.

Teddington thought about it. 'Possible,' she mused. 'But, where from?'

'Workshop.' Charlie also kept his voice down, his mouth hidden by resting it on his hand, thumb beneath the chin, forefinger beneath the nose.

She looked to Keen. 'Checked?'

He nodded. 'Walters wasn't my order.'

She conceded with a small blink. 'Nor Winehouse's.'

'No,' Keen allowed. 'Leo's.'

'There isn't one,' she muttered. 'Neither inmate nor staff. Did you speak to Holden?'

'Why?'

'He was supposed to be paroled a month ago. He's still here, and I can't find out why.'

Keen nodded. 'I'll look into it.'

'Partridge is gone, too,' Charlie said. 'He shouldn't be out.'

'Fry pulled some strings,' Teddington said.

'Rumour is, that's not all she pulled.'

Teddington frowned, her memory flashing up the image from the Ink Spot. 'That has to be just a rumour.'

Charlie shrugged.

'Anything else?' She turned to Keen.

Keen shook his head.

Teddington's eyes slipped from Keen to Charlie. She was overly aware Keen's gaze was pinning her, not Charlie. 'Your name's on the work rota for tomorrow. You've got a shift in the garden.'

'Why?'

She shrugged. 'Guess Winehouse needs a strong back.'

'What's this?'

The three of them looked up at the man at the door. Officer Robbins wasn't looking happy. 'Meeting of ex-federation members?'

'What?'

'Best coffee in the house.' Teddington raised her coffee to Robbins, before finishing the brew. She turned to Charlie, where he remained seated. He looked quizzical. 'Didn't you know? You've been talking to ex-Detective Superintendant William Keen of the Metropolitan Police.'

* * *

When Teddington took her lunch break, she ate her sandwiches while looking through the shift rota and workload allocation. It confirmed what she'd thought when she'd seen who she was on shift with that morning. Other than her and Robbins, they shared each shift on the wing with two other pairings, plus additional staff with specific task allocations. While she considered the implications of what she found, she thought about going over and looking through the work rota again, but thankfully, she hadn't moved that way when Robbins came in looking for her.

'What you up to?'

She couldn't tell him. 'I'm thinking about booking some holiday. God knows I could use a break. Just looking for times that have cover. Which it looks like we haven't got for at least two months.'

'If you need time off,' Robbins looked concerned, his hand rose to her arm, rubbing it in an overly familiar way, 'take it on medical. You shouldn't be back yet.'

He was right, but he was also so very wrong. 'Maybe.' She smiled, checked her watch, and sighed. 'God, time to get back to the coal face already.'

As they headed down, she could feel the weight of Robbins' regard on her. Before they got to the wing, he asked what was on her mind.

'Why did you go and see Keen this morning?'

'Coffee,' she explained easily, a carefully crafted look of open curiosity on her face. 'I was desperate for one, and he has the best in the wing. It's better even than the stuff in the canteen.'

If he had the slightest inclination she was lying, it didn't show.

'Put decent stuff in there, and it goes missing all too quick.'

* * *

Early shift ended mid-afternoon, and as eager as Teddington was to get home, she was more eager still to speak to the Governor.

Vera told her she'd have to wait, so she sat. Almost instantly, she was back up.

'Vera?'

The woman looked up at her, all open and friendly.

'What do you think of Rebecca Fry?'

Vera's mouth formed a tight, straight light, her eyes darkened. 'It's not my place to think anything of her.'

'Yeah,' Teddington agreed. 'I don't rate her much either, but I'm hearing some worrying rumours.'

Vera's eyes slipped towards the Guv's office. 'I can't say anything.'

Teddington doubted it. But, Vera was openly uncomfortable, so she sat down and waited. Five minutes later, the Guv called her in, and she told him her concerns that the rota left staff vulnerable if the inmates did kick off.

The Governor smiled and shrugged. 'The population is quiet. The improvements in behaviour just go to show the policies I've put in place are working.'

Policies he'd put in place? Teddington wanted to scream. The PSIs were coming thick and fast; she was struggling to keep up with them all. But, it didn't change the fact he wasn't the one working to those new instructions. She and the other officers were. 'But, sir—'

'I appreciate you're on high alert after everything you've been through.' He stood, making it clear she was to leave. 'But, I believe all will be well.'

Entirely less certain, Teddington let him lead her out of the office. She pulled up short, surprised to see Rebecca Fry in the outer office. Forcing herself to be as natural as possible, she stepped out, nodding to Rebecca before the other woman went in.

At the outer door, Teddington glanced back. The smiles Fry and the Guv were sharing, the way the Guv's hand lingered on the much younger woman's lower back, was just a little over familiar. She glanced to Vera, who was head down, studiously not reading whatever was on her monitor. Cold chills ran down Teddington's spine.

* * *

The following morning, Teddington felt much less nervous than she had the previous day. Her breathing was more regular, and her heart rate normal. Whatever she might think of the Guv's attitude, the quiet on the wing helped. As she paced the landing, she glanced into Charlie's cell. He was sitting, reading, and he didn't look up from the tome.

Good. That's good.

She told herself she was glad. It proved she was right. Whatever had happened between them, it wasn't real.

Liar.

Yes, she acknowledged it was a lie as she moved on, but she was having to lie to herself a lot these days.

At the appointed time, she headed out to gardening detail. She pulled in a lungful of the much-needed fresh air, though there was little to be had, as she worked her way through the necessary checks, counting every implement to be sure all the equipment was present and correct before the men came out. It was.

As she had the job allocation before her, she knew who was to have what. When the inmates filtered in, she handed them the allocated tool and had it signed for. Near the end of the list now, were two more names to check off, the first man stepped forward. She handed over the dibber. She was staring at it, as the man took hold. She felt the frown building on her forehead. Was it possible? Could a dibber do that much damage?

'Officer Teddington?'

The man called her name. She blinked at him. She felt the tug on her arm. She let go.

'You away with the fairies there, ma'am?'

She smiled, 'Apparently.'

As he moved away she looked up, Charlie was already before her.

'A dibber?' he queried, as he took and signed for the spade.

Could it be? It would match all the criteria from the autopsy.

'Ari!'

She was surprised by the harsh whisper of her first name, and she blinked up at Charlie.

'You okay?'

The frown wasn't easing. 'Get to work, Bell.' Her heart sank to watch him go, for all she was glad of it. She was too close to the edge, and sympathy or understanding from him, of all people, might just push her over.

Her stomach in knots and her lungs feeling as constricted as if she still wore that corset, she was finally alone, so she stepped up to the hooks from which the dibbers hung. Three remained there. One at a time, she lifted each from the hook, and took it over to the shed's barred window to inspect it in the light. What she found put a ligature around her neck, and someone was tightening it.

She needed air.

Stepping outside the concrete prefab shed, she closed the door behind her, and took a great lungful of air. It had the opposite effect to the one she expected – she just managed get behind the shed, before she gave up her breakfast.

Still bent double, she leaned with one hand on the shed, letting it take her weight, careless of the jagged stone render, as she struggled to control her breathing and tears in the aftermath of vomiting.

'Here.'

Hating that she knew it was Charlie, she still took the water bottle he held out to her. She straightened, taking a big swig and swilling her mouth, spitting the result to the floor. She rinsed again, before she wiped the sport top and stood up to face him. She missed the three inches her boots had added when they'd been away from the prison.

'Should've run when we had the chance.'

He frowned down at her. 'Now *that* isn't real.' He looked her over, and she was willing to bet she looked awful. 'You shouldn't be back in work yet.'

'No,' she agreed. 'But, you need to get back to it. Go on.' She pushed him lightly on the shoulder when he just stood there. 'Put your back into it.'

She watched him go and wished him back. Drawing in and slowly exhaling a deep breath, she returned to the front of the shed. She was surveying the general activity, making sure everyone was doing what they should. Which was when she noticed Winehouse standing across the way. As she caught his eye, he shifted and moved over to her. Paul followed, but Winehouse told him to wait an oddly far distance away.

'Officer Teddington,' he greeted quietly. 'Feeling any better?'

'Compared to being shot, I'm fine,' she answered. 'Where's your deckchair?'

'The question was an absolute, not comparative,' his voice was low. Teddington wondered just when all these conspiratorial conversations became *de rigueur*. 'I understand the need not to show weakness, but don't take it too far.'

Since she didn't know what to say about that, she let it hang in the air.

'I don't know what happened while you were both out, but looks like you're not the only one still reeling.'

He nodded over towards Charlie, who was digging as if his life depended on it, like he was tunnelling out of there. If he kept turning over huge clods like the one he had on his spade at that moment, he probably could. She forced herself to look away. She didn't need this.

Turning back to Winehouse, she pressed her question again. 'The chair?'

'Missing.' He shrugged as he walked away.

Chapter 26

Charlie dug over the vegetable patch. It had been harvested a couple of days ago, the lettuces making a fresh and tasty addition to their meals at lunchtime. He was worried about Teddington, and ploughed all his frustration into turning over the soil. She shouldn't be back. She wasn't physically ready for that yet, and her mental health was looking even more questionable. She was tense and nervous; even when she'd surprised him by looking comfortable in Keen's cell, she still hadn't been her old self.

Or was it just because he'd seen her vulnerable side now?

He jammed the spade hard into the earth, turning over a huge, heavy clod. He had to get over it and move on. Worst thing was, inside, the work was as heavy going as this digging. Nothing was coming together regarding Tommy. If it was a dibber and not a pipe, that at least made sense of the "dirty" part of her note.

Then, there was Holden. Sean Holden should have been released a month ago, but he was still here. When Charlie had asked him about it, he'd said 'don't ask.' When Charlie had pushed it, all he'd said was he hadn't misbehaved enough. Which made no sense. But, then, so much of what was going on didn't make any sense.

He was still mulling it all over when he felt a tap on his shoulder. He jolted away, surprised by the touch, surprised he had been so concentrated on the manual labour he hadn't noticed anyone approaching.

'Clocking off time,' Winehouse advised him.

Looking around, he saw everyone else was either returning their tools or lining up to return to the wing. He also saw he had less than a half square metre of the plot to finish. He must have worked like a man possessed to have so little left. 'Let me finish this.'

'I would,' Winehouse said, 'but do you think the screws would agree? Now is not the time to be rocking the boat. I'll get you on the list for tomorrow, you can finish it then.'

* * *

Charlie went to the shop after lunch, brought a paper, an envelope and a stamp. He wanted to speak to Teddington, but couldn't seem to catch her eye. She always had a shadow, usually Robbins, but one or other of the screws was constantly close to her. He wasn't sure if they were there for her protection or control. He guessed only she'd know that. Or maybe not.

With nothing better to do, he headed to his cell, he had a letter to compose.

* * *

Not willing to wait for the bus, Teddington drove to the hospital. She tried to avoid taking her car because parking was either difficult or expensive. The hospital having expanded beyond the capacity of its car park, this usually meant waiting for someone to leave, or going into the multi-story built for the nearby business development that only opened to the public after 5 pm. Anything to increase the capitalist buck, apparently.

She got lucky; a car was leaving, and she was able to pull straight in. Seeing Sanchez sitting up and smiling brought a smile to her own face. He was looking so much better. She'd brought him magazines and contraband, which she quickly stowed in his locker, though some chocolates stayed out. She knew she'd really brought them for her, which was why only one box got hidden.

'What's up? Really?' Sanchez asked, after a few minutes of over-bright conversation.

She felt her face fall. 'Oh, God, am I that obvious?'

'We've known one another a long time.' He laid his hand over hers. 'Come on, Ari, spill.'

She bit her lip. 'Swear to me you won't say anything to anyone?'

Sanchez frowned. 'Okay, now I'm worried.'

She shook her head and turned away. 'Forget it. It doesn't matter.'

'Clearly, it does,' he said squeezing her hands, keeping her with him. 'Okay, I swear I won't repeat this to anyone, but you have to tell me what's going on.'

'I'm not sure I can do it anymore. Work, that is. Inside Blackmarch, anyway. I've always loved doing what we do, but now ...' She shook her bowed head. 'I don't know anymore. I go in, and I'm tense. God, I got so scared in the garden today, I actually threw up.'

'Did anyone see you?'

'Charlie Bell came over. He's the only one who commented, but I'd be surprised if the whole detail didn't hear me.' Her face flushed at the memory.

'How is Bell getting works details suddenly? He never used to.'

Her frown this time was curiosity instead of shame. 'I don't know. I hadn't thought to ask. I'll look into it.' She looked around, made sure no one was listening, though she was pretty sure they all had better things to do. Still, she kept her voice down. 'I've done something that's probably really stupid.'

'Go on,' Sanchez encouraged when she didn't.

'I've been looking into Tommy Walters' death. And I asked Charlie Bell to help me.'

Sanchez's face was a picture of surprise. 'Actually, that makes a lot of sense. The police don't seem to be doing much. At least Bell has the right skill set and easy access to any potential witnesses.'

'Well, not really.' Again, she checked over her shoulder, the paranoia getting to her. 'That's the thing. The inmates hardly socialise anymore. I told you about Richie Brett right?'

Sanchez nodded.

'Well, he's not the only one looking strained by the isolation. I mean, I know prisons are punishment, but the way things are at the moment … it must be torture for some of the guys.'

'No one wants to be that isolated.'

Teddington watched the emotions and thoughts cross his face. He was frowning when he turned back to her. 'How are the other female staff doing?'

She shrugged. 'Fine, I guess. I haven't heard any complaints.'

'What about Fry?'

'She is around a lot at the moment.' Teddington thought about it. 'An awful lot.'

'How does she seem?'

When she opened her mouth to speak, Teddington wasn't sure what to say. 'Okay. I haven't really spoken to her. Why do you ask about her in particular?'

'There are rumours.'

'Okay, now, I'm curious. What rumours?'

'The kind of rumours that could ruin her career, but there's no evidence.'

'Of what?'

He flushed red, as he forced himself to say it. 'That she likes it rough.'

Teddington stared at him, slack jawed, then, she felt a smile creeping over her face. 'I don't believe there's actually anything illegal about that.'

'With inmates.'

'Oh! Ah. Well, it's not exactly *illegal*.'

'Partridge was the last I heard claim it, but …'

'Who's going to believe an inmate over a probation officer?'

'Oddly, these days, I'd say pretty much anyone, given all the scandals these last few years. On the other hand, prisoners want out ASAP, so why would they complain?'

Good question, and one she contemplated, as she reached for another chocolate. Only she couldn't find one, she tipped the box, it was empty.

'Good God, did I eat all of them?'

'Yup, but then Malteasers are your favourite and you're stressing out. You shouldn't be back in work yet.'

'I know.' She smiled. 'Seems like pretty much everyone else knows it, too. Except the Guv. After an initial insistence I get certified as being ready to come back to work, once I had it, he couldn't wait to get me off light duties and back on the floor. In fact, I never even *got* a day of light duty.'

He shook his head. 'What else?'

She smiled up at him. 'Wow, you really do know me too well.' She took a big breath before telling him. 'It's just weird in work. Too quiet, like just before the storm, you know?'

He nodded.

'It's odd you should ask about Fry. She's fighting to get Bell out, while everyone else says he's got to stay in after running, even though that wasn't his fault, and he gave himself up voluntarily.'

'Have you asked him about that?'

She shook her head. 'To be honest, I've been avoiding him as much as possible. I don't want to add fuel to the fire, because according to the rumour mill, we became lovers while we were out of circulation.'

'Did you?'

Her breath caught in her throat. 'No! How can you even ask that?'

'Because everyone is going to be asking the same thing. I believe you, some won't. However, if Fry is pushing for his release, see what you can find out about it. Is there anything else I've missed?'

Teddington nodded. 'There is something else. I've seen no records of any fights, but I've seen bruises that don't come about by accident. There are guys there I haven't had a problem with at any point, but now, they can't meet my eye. Others have become oddly cocky. You know that Regis Fortnam?'

'The forger?'

'That's the one. Should have seen the look he gave me the other day. Usually, he's the one who can't meet my eye, but now, he's looking at me like I'm the only glass of water in the desert.' She shook and hung her head. 'It's a switch I can't explain.'

Sanchez laughed. 'I can.'

She looked up and frowned.

'Well, I can explain Regis,' Enzo clarified. 'Before he turned forger, he was quite the artist. Turner popped in a few days ago. He told me he had to confiscate some drawings from Regis. Drawings of you.'

'What?' Teddington wasn't sure what she was hearing, but she could see it amused Sanchez no end.

'Apparently, they were sketches of you when you walked in wearing a corset.'

She could feel her face flaming.

'And then, there were others where you *weren't* wearing a corset.'

Even her cold hands couldn't stop the boiling in her cheeks. Sanchez's laughter wasn't helping.

'It's your own fault for telling them to put it in the spank bank.'

* * *

Two days later, after she'd finished another shift, she was surprised to see Turner in street clothes waiting in the locker room for her.

'You're coming to the pub.'

It wasn't an invitation; it was an order, and it was so unlike Turner she meekly accepted.

Quarter of an hour later, they were sitting in The Lock Up, the pub directly opposite the prison, with three other officers.

'Teddington,' Turner introduced, 'this is Parry from A-Wing, and Wilson and Malkin from B-Wing.'

Though they nodded in greeting, none of them looked happy. Parry was a big roid-enhanced, black man. A-Wing was the secure wing, and all the officers on that detail tended to be big guys because of the risk of attack. She'd met Parry before, but they'd never done any more than nod in passing. Wilson and Malkin were new to her. Wilson was mid-twenties, fit, mean looking but with intelligent eyes; Malkin was older, with more of a world-weary air about him.

'What's going on?' she demanded of Turner.

'That's what we'd all like to know,' Turner told her, 'but it seems we five are the only ones asking. If anyone asks, we're here on union business.'

Teddington felt like the world was tipping around her. Nothing was making sense. 'I'm not in the union.'

'You joined two months ago,' Turner told her, passing her some papers. 'I just haven't got around to taking the dues from your salary.'

Teddington looked at the papers. Membership papers. He'd tried passing these to her before, but she'd never actually taken them. These particular forms had been completed in her name, and dated two months ago. She felt like she'd been pushed into the corner, and her instant reaction was to push back, but she swallowed – she needed this. Turner held out a pen, she took it, and signed, only hesitating when she went to write the date. She needed to put the date the same as Turner had, but that would be lying. Hating herself for the weakness, she wrote a past date.

Turner's brows were raised when she pushed the document back towards him.

'You really hated doing that, didn't you?'

'Yep.'

'You that anti-union?' Wilson asked.

'They mean lying about the date,' Malkin pointed out.

'Well, this is a bloody heavy-handed method for just strong arming me into joining the union, so shall we get to the point?'

Teddington felt the blood wash from her face, as Turner did just that, and she heard from the others the effects being felt on the other wings. If she was worried there were some weak teams being put out in C-Wing, it was nothing to the risks being run in A-Wing. She slumped back as the others talked. Their words were sinking in, and she could see where it was all going.

'Ian Houghton's getting vocal again,' Malkin grumbled.

'Who?'

'Ian Houghton, B-Wing. The Islamist, now calls himself Mohammed Ibrahim.'

'He's always vocal,' Turner pointed out. 'The joy of religious conversion.'

'They want a riot,' Teddington concluded.

'What?' Turner and Wilson asked together, focusing on her.

She saw four faces turned to her. 'Look.' She sat up, and laid it out for them. 'If you sift through all the changes you guys are talking about, what "they" have effectively done *isn't* to decrease tensions – they've put a lid on them and turned the place into a pressure cooker. The restriction of socialisation just leaves the population isolated and disaffected, which is part of the reason half of them are in there in the first place. Eventually, someone's going to snap. We were lucky when Brett went I was in and able to calm him down, or else all those hungry men could well have kicked off, because when one of them goes, they all will.'

Turner was scowling at her. 'Why would they want a riot?'

Teddington didn't have an answer to that.

'Because there's some pay off in it,' Parry added. 'And there's all manner of things which could come out of it.' He frowned. 'There's all manner of things which can happen during one.'

Teddington felt sick.

'We've had one death they brushed off as accidental,' Malkin pointed out. 'It'd be a struggle to cover up another one without a riot.'

'I think,' Turner tried to lighten the atmosphere, 'we might just be taking this a little too far.'

'Really?' Teddington asked darkly. 'Guess you weren't the one that got shot, then.'

'That's it,' Wilson said.

'What's it?'

'She is,' Wilson answered Turner.

'Makes sense.' Parry was nodding.

Teddington felt like she'd just jumped into a plunge pool. 'What makes sense?'

'Everyone thinks the shooting at the funeral was about Bell, but what if it wasn't?' Wilson said. 'What if it was about the prison officers there? A few months ago, Richmond was whining about having no money—'

'That's right,' Malkin added. 'In fact, he mentioned bankruptcy might be a distinct possibility.'

'Then, how the hell did he afford a luxury holiday in Bermuda?'

'Exactly.'

That was the most chilling answer Wilson could have given.

'Then, there's Sanchez,' Wilson continued. 'He was making complaints to the Guv about some of the things going on, even had a row with the DCI that he wasn't doing enough.'

'Piper?' Teddington asked.

'Yeah, that's the one.'

'Well, you have to admit,' Turner put in, 'he's not exactly carrying out an active investigation. Teddington?'

No amount of acting was going to cover up the fact she'd reacted to that statement. 'It's nothing.' That wasn't right. 'Well, okay, it is something, but I can't tell you.' They all reacted to that. 'You'll just have to trust me. Or not,' she added, looking at the doubting looks around her. 'Anyway, to get back to Wilson's point, why would I be "it"? I haven't done anything to put my head above the parapet.'

'You've highlighted issues to the Guv,' Turner pointed out.

'Only in the last week. I hadn't done anything *before* I got shot.'

'Except help Bell,' Malkin pointed out.

'But that puts the focus back on Bell, not me. To divert this, and ease my sense of paranoia, have any of you had a good look at the new computer system?'

'Yes,' Parry didn't sound impressed. 'They've put a load of data in wrong.'

'Typical IT people.'

'No,' Teddington put in, 'and speaking as an ex-IT person, I can assure you, yes, upload errors do happen, but not of the nature of what you can see in the Prism system. If there are transcription errors, they tend to be wholesale, like you'll get all of one record under the wrong unique identifier, and they all realign, and since I can see you lot glazing over at the techie speak, what that would mean is, I'd find something, like, Wilson's details under Williams' name. But, those aren't the kind of errors I found. I don't think it's the extraction and upload that's to blame; I think the records were tampered with before the IT guys got them.'

'Who'd do that?'

She shrugged. 'Dunno. The kind of changes that have happened are small tweaks, easier to do in the original database than on the extraction, because it's harder to be certain you have the right cell to change, on a BIF than an export, but it's possible.'

'What's a BIF?'

She looked at Malkin, struggling to find a non-technical explanation. 'Err, it's a way of doing a mass upload of data.'

'But why would they change data though?'

'To control who gets what privileges?' Parry suggested.

'Who picked Sanchez and Richmond for the funeral duty?' she asked.

Turner couldn't quite meet her eye when he admitted it had been him. 'I thought Robbins would want the overtime, but he didn't. He had something on, so I figured Richmond would probably want the extra money after his holidays, and since Sanchez was off, too, I asked them to do it.'

When she'd made arrangements for the funeral, Teddington hadn't paid any attention to the rota, beyond knowing it was her day off, but that meant there were only three other choices – Robbins, Richmond, and Sanchez. It was them, or someone off another wing.

'Don't look at me like that,' Turner told Malkin. 'With limited staff, there are limited choices.'

'No one's accusing you of anything,' Teddington assured him, though she knew they were getting close to it. Paranoia was working overtime all around, it seemed. 'Besides, maybe this is taking the point *ad nauseam*, but are we really saying every one of our colleagues is somehow corrupt?'

The five of them slumped back from the table, considering the implications.

* * *

Charlie paced. Paced and worried. Passing information on to Piper wasn't easy. Even though he'd addressed the letter to Miss Sheila Collins, Piper's wife, he couldn't be sure that Sheila would pass the letter to Piper, and he was less sure Piper would decipher the code in the innocent-looking letter. It had been nearly a week, and there was no evidence of anything happening, no guarantee Piper had even received the letter.

He also worried about Teddington. She'd been sick in work, and every new shift she looked paler, somehow more haunted. Her eyes were shadowed, and her cheeks hollowing. And she was avoiding him like the plague. At least that made sense, and he was making it easier for her by showing an apparent indifference.

It was late, and he could hear cell doors being closed, locked. Someone would come to his door soon, and he'd be trapped again inside this cage. He stepped closer to the door, looking over the landing, memorising the space he already knew by heart.

When she appeared and reached for the door, Teddington's eyes were lowered.

'Ari?'

She jumped and looked up, surprised to see him standing there.

'Everything alright?'

'Fine.'

He wondered if the Oxford English Dictionary should add a new definition to that word, "*When said by a woman, this means the exact opposite of fine, but the man she's said it to needs to develop telepathy to understand what she really means."*

'No, you're not,' he said. 'You're closer to the edge than Brett was when he snapped.'

For a moment, he wasn't sure if she was going to cry or punch him, then she grabbed the front of his t-shirt and pushed him to his right, backed him up against the wall in the very front corner of the cell behind the door. He tensed in preparation of an assault, but was totally unprepared when she just lay her head on his chest and leaned into him.

The front, right-hand corner of the cell.

The one place she could be sure the internal cameras couldn't see them. She was trembling. He did the only thing he could, put his arms around her, and held her tight.

In that instant, all he could do was enjoy the feel of her, the warmth, the surging need. He kissed the top of her hair and stayed there, that incredible scent of apples so fresh and reassuring. He could, he *would*, stand here all night like this, if she needed him, but he knew they had limited time.

'Ari, what's wrong?'

'Paranoia working overtime,' she told him softly. 'I feel like I'm constantly being watched. Don't know which way to run.' She sniffed. 'Even the most innocuous comment sounds like a veiled threat.'

He squeezed her. Whoever was behind the attacks, she probably was being watched, and the comments weren't so innocuous, but telling her that wouldn't help.

She drew in a deep breath and pulled away from him. He didn't want to let go, but he had to. She wiped her cheeks unnecessarily. She hadn't let a single tear go, but she was getting close. 'If anything happens,' she told him softly, 'trust Turner.'

Then, she was gone, the door was closed and locked. Charlie stayed leaning against the wall, feeling bereft.

If anything happens. What could happen? Altogether, too damn much. He returned to his desk, retrieved the pad. He had to get another letter to Piper.

Chapter 27

At six o'clock, Teddington kicked off her shoes and flopped into the sofa. Her mother would have scolded her, 'flopped on furniture fails faster.' Thankfully, Mum was across the road; the Sanchez's were having a bit of party to celebrate their son's recovery and to catch up with old friends and neighbours, some of whom hadn't been neighbours for years, but everyone knew Mrs Sanchez did the best buffet. With the house to herself, a large glass of wine, and sole possession of the remote control, Teddington was looking forward to a truly relaxing evening.

Three hours later, she was debating whether to go to bed or stay up and open the second bottle when there was a loud rap at the door. She wasn't expecting anyone, didn't want to see anyone, and it was damn late to be calling.

The next set of knocks was even louder and accompanied by the holler of her name. Recognising the slurring tones of Len Robbins, Teddington put down the empty glass and stomped to the door, her mellow mood having dissipated completely.

She tried to compose herself as she went to the door, but she could feel all the tension back in her shoulders and neck. Opening the door, she wasn't at all surprised to smell the alcohol on his breath.

'Swee'pea!' He was leaning against the door jamb but stumbled in, throwing his arms around her, putting her off balance.

Struggling under his weight, Teddington pushed him against the hall wall to close the door and stop all the heat escaping into the cold night. When she turned to look at him, his octopus arms were around her again, and he was muttering less-than-sweet nothings in her ear.

'Robbins, you're pissed. Come on.' She tried to steer him into the living room, grateful he was on the side away from her mother's knickknack cabinet. 'Let's get you inside and get some coffee into you.'

Struggling to control him, she got him to the sofa, watching disapprovingly as he flopped down, instantly berating herself for turning into her mother, as she moved to put the kettle on. She didn't get far when Robbins hand clamped around her wrist, catching her off guard. He pulled her on to his lap, trapping her there with his hold. She thought about squirming, but figured it wouldn't really help.

He looked down at her with red-rimmed eyes, a leery smile, and beer breath. 'Hello.'

'Robbins,' she spoke calmly. 'What do you think you're doing?'

'I got ya.'

And not in a good way, she thought. 'You've also got a wife,' she pointed out. 'How would Rose feel if she saw us like this?'

'Wou'n't care.'

Teddington was well aware Rose had long ago lost patience with the jokes about her being a Red–ish Robbin, but she was pretty sure the woman still cared about her husband. The memory of him with Fry popped into her head and she wondered if Len still cared for Rose.

'I'm sure that's not true.' She patted his arm as best she could, since her own arms were pinned. 'Come on, let me up. I'll make you some coffee, and you can tell me all about it.'

'She kic' me out.'

Apparently, he was going to tell her all about it, anyway. As he spun his tale of woe, Teddington looked around her, occasionally testing the tightness of his hold. It wasn't diminishing any. She didn't like this. It wasn't comfortable, not because of the position, but because it was Robbins. She hadn't felt this uncomfortable with a bullet in her shoulder, a handcuff pulling the same arm, as she'd been slung over a running man's shoulder. She was pretty damn sure Robbins had copped a feel of her arse, too. On and on, Robbins wittered until she just couldn't stand it any longer.

'Robbins.' When he didn't stop, she left gentle behind and barked in his face. 'Robbins!'

He sat back, the moment of surprise sobering him up for at least a second. 'What?'

'Let go of me.'

As if he hadn't noticed he had hold of her, he suddenly let go, and she was half falling, half scrambling to her feet.

'I'll make you some coffee,' she told him over her shoulder, as she headed to the kitchen.

Glad to be free of the man, Teddington waited as the kettle bubbled, wishing he'd never turned up to spoil her evening. The kettle was making nearly-ready sounds when she felt hands sliding around her waist, his head propped on her shoulder, and this time, she was pinned against the work surface.

'Wish my wife would listen to me like you do.'

Teddington bit her lip to avoid being too harsh. 'Why don't you go home and see if she will?' She shifted, and he let her go. 'I'll call you a taxi.' But, she didn't get far, only far enough to have turned around, and he pressed up against her, his body in contact with most of hers. Now, she *really* wasn't comfortable.

'Come on, swee'pea.' He was looking down at her, his head swaying drunkenly. 'You know you wanna.' He dipped his head. She dodged the kiss, but instead, he started to nuzzle her neck. 'I wanna.'

'Yeah, I can tell.' This time, she squeezed her arms up enough to get purchase on his chest and manoeuvred him away. He was so unsteady on his feet, she had to catch him again. 'Great,' she sighed. 'Guess you'd better stay.'

'Now, ya talkin'. Lez go t' bed.'

'Okay.' She guided him out of the kitchen.

'Share your bed.'

'Nope.'

She steered him into the living room again and got him settled on the length of the sofa. His hands were everywhere. He didn't manage to get under her jumper, but he had a good grope all the same. She slapped his hands and shoved him away. They were both going to be sorry about this in the morning.

'Get to sleep.' Teddington dragged the throw from the back of the sofa over him and took his shoes off, before her mother had that to complain about, too. She wouldn't exactly be happy to find a man crashed out on the sofa as it was.

Leaving him there, Teddington switched off the TV and made sure everything was off, then went up to her own room. Her jumper was over her head when hands grabbed her breasts from behind. She squealed, and rushed to divest herself fully of the jumper, but by that time, he had hold of her, and they were falling on the bed. His weight was heavy and unwelcome, his lips were wet and stank, and she had to move quick to avoid them.

'Get off me, Robbins!' She tried to get out from under him.

'Come on, sweetpea, you know you want to.'

'I do not!'

'Sanchez won't be in any condition to do ya for moths.'

The pedant in her wanted to correct him to months, but mostly, she just wanted out from under. 'Get off me, or so help me God, I will hurt you.'

'Tr'it.

He was slurring, but he had sense enough to grab her hands and pin her down. Panic started to well in her head, bile rose in her throat. Her heart was thumping, and she was having trouble breathing. Attempts to pull her hands free of his were futile, her movements just making him groan appreciatively. She stilled, not to waste energy. She had to figure out how to win her way out of this, instead of panicking and losing.

Taking a deep breath, she suddenly realised she wasn't the only one not moving any more. Frowning, she directed her eyes to Robbins. His head was at her shoulder, but he wasn't trying to sucker himself to her anymore. His eyes were closed, his lips were slack, and the snore convinced her of what she should have realised. Carefully withdrawing her hands free of his, she rolled him off her.

Standing by the side of the bed, Teddington realised she was shaking like a leaf. For a second, she thought it was fear, but realised it wasn't. It was relief. He was too big to move, so she grabbed her jumper again and headed for the spare room.

* * *

'I am so, *so* sorry.'

Scowling at her dishevelled colleague, Teddington plonked a strong black coffee on the counter in front of him. She'd phoned Rose this morning to let her know he'd spent the night at her house, and out had poured the whole sorry story. She'd kicked Robbins out, because she'd thought he was having an affair. Teddington chose not to mention the assignation she'd witnessed.

'For some reason,' she told him, 'your wife's willing to forgive whatever transgression precipitated the argument.'

Robbins sipped his coffee and smiled. Teddington thought it an unpleasantly smug expression. 'I'm a lucky man.'

'Not that lucky,' she snapped. 'I'm not so forgiving. What you tried to do—'

'I know, I'm sorry. Sorta.'

Teddington couldn't believe it. Her jaw dropped and her brows rose. 'You're *sorta* sorry?'

'No, no.' Now, he was frowning through the alcoholic mists. 'I am sorry, really sorry, but I only sorta know what I did. I was very drunk.'

'You tried to rape me.' Thank God he'd passed out, because he'd certainly over-powered her easily enough. If he'd been sober, she wouldn't have stood a chance. There again, if he'd been sober, he wouldn't have done it.

He looked appalled and horrified. 'I am really sorry.' He reached for her, but she dodged away.

'Just get out, and be grateful I don't have to see you again for a couple of days.'

* * *

Some days, Piper hated his job. This was one of them.

'It's a setup, boss,' he told the Superintendent. 'This isn't right.'

Superintendent Broughton sat squarely, regarding the DCI with steady ease. 'I know.'

'Then, don't ask me to do this.'

Broughton blinked, but remained still and calm. 'You have to.'

* * *

Charlie was sweating with the exertion of digging another patch. Every muscle was pumped, and he knew afterward, he'd be grateful for the ache. It might even help him sleep. Teddington wasn't on the shift today, and he hoped she took the opportunity to get some rest. He shoved his spade into the dirt one more time and froze when he saw the suited figures moving towards the garden. They were still on the other side of the fence, but he recognised Piper and Carlisle. Like a number of other inmates, he stopped what he was doing and watched as Turner led them into the compound, then let them to the tool shed, where Officer Norman took them inside.

They came out moments later with an evidence bag full of dibbers, then, Piper fixed him with a steely gaze. Charlie felt his stomach tighten. Piper had got his message, but something was wrong. The way he was being watched meant he was about to get dragged into it. Piper and Carlisle were approaching.

'Turn around,' Piper ordered. 'Hands behind your back.'

'Why?'

''Cos you're under arrest, you murdering scumbag,' Carlisle snarled.

'What?!'

'Turn around,' Piper repeated. 'Hands behind your back.'

Charlie didn't have the vaguest idea what was going on, but he'd be stupid to be anything but cooperative. It wasn't like he'd get far if he tried to run. He turned around and felt colder than the cuffs, as Carlisle took great delight in tightening them too far and roughly pulling Charlie where he wanted him to go.

Forcibly shoved into the back of the police car and driven away, Charlie looked back. He'd never expected to be sorry to be driven away from Whitewalk, yet he was.

'What's going on?'

But, he didn't get an answer, so he sat back and waited. The journey to the station was all too familiar to him. He was surprised by the lack of processing when they went in the back, more so, when he realised although it had been said he was under arrest, at no point had he actually *been* arrested. Failure to read him his rights gave him an instant technicality to get off. It surprised him, because Piper was never this lax. Something was wrong.

He heart hammering, he was part guided, part forced along the corridor to interview room one. The door was yanked open by the tight-featured Carlisle. Charlie stepped through and stopped short. *No, it couldn't be.* This made no sense.

'Teddington?'

Teddington was already there. Sitting alone at a table with four chairs, she stared blindly at the scarred surface. At the call of her name, she looked up at him. She looked awful. So far past terrified, she'd hit calm.

'Seems we have the same jeweller.'

The mirthless sentence only made sense when she raised her hands to the surface of the table. She was cuffed, too.

'What the hell is this?' Charlie demanded of Piper, but Carlisle only pushed him forward, made him sit beside Teddington. Then, Carlisle unlocked one cuff, just to re-shackle him, hands forward this time. Charlie looked around the room. Piper and Carlisle were silent, but anger was unmistakeably written on their faces. He turned to Teddington. She was staring morosely at the handcuffs adorning her wrists.

'Ariadne?'

'They've got evidence I killed Tommy.'

Chapter 28

Charlie could only stare at her.

They've got evidence I killed Tommy.

How was he to process that? He had never heard her voice so dull. He had never heard such a load of rubbish either, and he said so, with several expletives. Then he turned to Piper. 'Surely you don't believe this bollocks?'

'It doesn't matter what they *believe*,' Teddington's voice was low, but it cut through his aggression. 'It matters only what they can prove. They have been handed evidence I killed Tommy.'

'The dibber with Tommy's blood on it is covered in her fingerprints,' Carlisle announced.

His head was reeling but he hadn't completely lost it yet. 'You only just picked the dibbers up. You can't know that.'

'We'll know soon enough.'

'This is nuts!' Charlie struggled to believe anything. 'Besides, even if you're right, it's circumstantial, at best. It hardly surprising her prints are on the equipment. She hands them out to the gardening detail and takes them back in,' Charlie reasoned.

'The original work sheets without Tommy's name and several poor quality forgeries *with* Tommy's name on were found, all with her signature.'

'It's a forgery; her signature will be a forgery too.' Charlie sat forward. 'If that's the best you have, I repeat, it's just circumstantial. It won't hold up in court.'

'The forgeries were found in her home, in her bedroom, under her mattress.'

No. No, it didn't make sense. She wasn't a killer. He turned to her. She turned to face him, defeat written on every feature.

'I don't know how the papers got there. I didn't forge them.' She laughed at herself. 'Christ, I never even forged my mum's signature to get out of school. And I didn't kill Tommy, either. But, it doesn't matter. The evidence says I did.'

'If they are nothing to do with you,' Carlisle sneered, 'how did they get into your bed?'

She just looked at him. Neither hate nor fear showed. 'I don't know.'

'Oh, did they just magically appear?'

'I—'

Charlie shut her up with an elbow to the ribs. 'No comment.'

She shook her head and sighed, diverting her eyes back to her cuffs.

'There's no tape, no video,' Charlie noticed now. 'Teddington, did they properly read you your rights? Advise you of your right to a lawyer?'

She was still staring at her cuffs, but she was frowning now, thinking back. 'I don't know.'

'Right, don't say anything.' Charlie turned back to the two serving police officers before him. 'This isn't right. It isn't legal, and neither one of us is saying another word until our lawyer gets here.'

'I don't have a lawyer.'

Charlie rolled his eyes at the admission, gritted his teeth. 'Then, mine can represent us both.'

She shook her head. 'No … No, you need to distance yourself from me as much as possible. Sharing a lawyer will only make things worse.'

'You know,' Piper mused, when they both fell silent, 'she talks a lot of sense.' His attention shifted from Teddington to Charlie. 'You'd do well to listen to her.' Then, he turned to Teddington. 'And you, young lady, could do worse than listen to him.'

She glanced at Piper. Charlie mourned the loss of the fire in her eyes.

'Every shift I work, I listened to the men in my care. I watch what happens to them. I see the changes, changes which are rarely as much about rehabilitation as they should be. I listen, and you know what I've heard? That in a prison population currently standing at nearly four hundred in Whitewalk alone, there are no guilty men.'

* * *

That wasn't true. Charlie knew it wasn't true. He was guilty as sin, as were most of the inmates. One or two convictions were a bit questionable, but nothing more.

'Carlisle,' Piper spoke in the echoing wake of Teddington's statement, 'would you escort Mrs Teddington to a cell. I believe she needs time to cool off.'

Cool off? Charlie frowned at Piper. Teddington couldn't get much cooler. She wasn't kicking off, wasn't getting angry. She wasn't reacting at all. She just meekly stood and allowed Carlisle to take her from the room. Charlie watched her go, and only when the door was closed and he was alone with Piper, did he turn to the more senior officer.

'This is wrong,' he said. 'Teddington wouldn't kill anyone, wouldn't even be a conspirator or an accessory. This has to be a set up.'

Piper just watched him. 'Of course it is.'

Charlie blinked. 'What?'

'Do you think I've lost IQ points, just because you're no longer here? Of course this is a set up. I know it's a set up. Even Broughton knows a set up when he's being forced into one, which is why we've agreed to do this.'

'Do what, exactly?' Charlie frowned.

'The gun that shot Teddington has been matched with one used in a bungled robbery last week. The perpetrator is so scared of reprisals more than this one case has been moved on because of what's been given up, but at the moment, we have to keep these cards up our sleeves. We have to be seen as playing along with the setup, for now. And if only half of what we believe is true, the safest place for Teddington is in here. We'll keep her in the cells overnight – you, too – that, at least, buys us some time.'

'When you say "us," which "us" are you talking about?'

'Broughton and I.'

'Carlisle?'

Piper shook his head.

'You don't trust him?'

'He's too angry,' Piper lamented.

Charlie thought about it. 'He's angry with me because I let him down. I did what he could never do, never understand. But, he's a good man, a little slower than he could be, but he's honest. If he's angry, it'll be because he knows something is going on, and it'll rankle that you haven't brought him in on it.'

Piper didn't comment, which, knowing Piper, meant he wasn't dismissing the idea out of hand, but wasn't ready to agree to it.

Charlie knew better than to push. 'So, what next?'

'You'll both be kept here until the twenty-four hours are up, and we have to release or charge.'

'Tell me the plan is to release.'

'Probably.'

'You're not filling me with confidence.' Charlie glared at his old boss.

'Confidence?' Piper half laughed. 'How confident do you think I feel, when the person I trust most in this station is wearing handcuffs?'

* * *

Charlie felt numb. The walk to the cells was like a nightmare. A perversion of the memory of the many times he had taken this route to the custody cells leading a cuffed suspect. Now, he was the cuffed suspect. The light metal dragged his arms like weighted manacles. His head was full of impossible thoughts, the ridiculous possibility he and Teddington were going to be charged with a crime they did not commit.

'Should have run when we had the chance.'

'Don't be stupid,' Piper answered his witter with a whisper. At the desk, Piper went through the process with the custody sergeant, even telling him which cell Charlie was to be put in.

'But, sir—'

'Cell four,' Piper grated.

'Yes, sir.' The custody sergeant gave Charlie the oddest look as he made the note, while Piper unlocked the cuffs.

The sergeant escorted Charlie to the cell at the furthest end of the corridor. He checked inside, unlocked the door, and waved Charlie through. Charlie stepped in, and stopped at seeing someone already in the room. No wonder the sergeant had objected. The door clanged and locked behind him.

'Teddington?'

She was curled in the corner of the bed, her feet and knees up, hugging herself when there was no one to hug her, the brown of her jumper almost the same shade as the wide material of the skirt. She looked like little more than a bundle of clothes.

'Charlie?' She frowned. 'What are you doing in here?'

'Same as - '

'No.' The frown wasn't lessening. 'I mean, what are you doing in here?' She pointed to the floor. 'I thought there were rules about numbers in a cell, certainly about not putting men and women in together, and that's not to mention as far as the police are concerned, you and I are suspects in the same enquiry. Putting us together like this is a breach of protocol. Possible collusion, or …' her hand waved it away, 'whatever.'

She was right; it was a massive breach of procedure. In fact, virtually everything that had happened this afternoon had been a breach of procedure. Nothing could come of this, because of a huge list of technical failures, Piper had seen to that. It was good for him and Teddington, but it could cost Piper his job. Charlie added another worry to the list.

Charlie was too numb to do anything but look at her. She didn't move, didn't uncurl from her upright, but nonetheless foetal, position. Her chin was now resting on her knee. But, she was looking directly at him.

'I know what they've got on me, what have they got on you?'

'Time of death could be as much as ten hours before Tommy's body was found. Apparently, other than being in my cell during lock up, no one can confirm where I was during that time.'

'Have they asked anyone?'

The astute nature of the question made Charlie smile. 'Probably not,' he allowed, as he moved to the other end of the ledge. He sat facing her, his back against the wall, picking his right leg up to lay it on the mattress, and hooking his left leg over his right foot.

'I've never been in handcuffs before.'

He wasn't sure how to take that. Her tone was controlled.

He couldn't help smiling. 'You have.'

'Okay,' she flicked him a ghost of a smile, 'but not like today. I've never arrested before.'

'I'm not sure you have been now,' he said. 'If it helps, I remember the first time it happened to me. After I did what I did. I walked away and went home. I could have run, but I didn't want to. Killing Mansel-Jones was a snap decision, but I never had any doubt it was the right decision. So, I just went home. I sat down, and I waited.'

'Piper said you'd been beaten when the police arrived.'

Piper wasn't leaving much room for sanitation. 'His boys heard the shots. I'd had to fight my way out, or stay and be killed.'

'His shot, or yours?'

Charlie swallowed. 'Mine. If Mansel-Jones had shot first, I'd be dead.'

'And the uniforms just arrested you calmly?'

'Uniforms?' If Piper was going to reveal all, so would he. 'It was Piper who came for me. Arrested me. Put the cuffs on.'

'Me, too.'

Charlie focused back on her. 'Sorry.'

She shrugged, but finally she uncurled, moving on all fours to crawl over to him. Not sure what she was doing, he opened his arms, as she twisted to lay her head on his shoulder, half leaning into him, half laying on him, with her leg bent over his. Her hand moved to his stomach, stroking as it moved across his waist, and then, she hugged him. He held her close.

'You'll get free of this,' Charlie told her and kissed her apple-scented hair.

'Don't,' she said softly. 'Don't tell me what you can't know. In fact, don't tell me anything.'

So, he didn't. He didn't tell her anything Piper had told him. Which was just as well, since he was under instruction not to.

* * *

The calm didn't last long. Half an hour later, Teddington was pulled out again for questioning. She looked pale and exhausted when she came back, but he had no time to ask how she was, as he was instantly called out.

Again, he sat opposite Piper and Carlisle.

'Where's my lawyer?'

'On his way,' Carlisle grated.

'Then, why are we talking before he gets here?'

'Haven't you got used to being alone in a cell?'

He had, but he'd rather gotten used to being alone in a cell with Ariadne. Evidently, Carlisle was ignorant of the comforts of his current accommodation.

'This is off the record,' Piper said.

Charlie frowned. 'Okay, what's going on?'

'Besides Mansel-Jones, is there anyone who wants to see you dead?'

He couldn't avoid looking to Carlisle at that point.

'Ha, ha,' the younger man deadpanned.

'Actually, I was looking at you to judge how serious the question was,' Charlie explained. He turned to Piper, drew in a breath as he considered his answer. 'Not that I know of. I mean, I was a cop, so I did arrest men, put several in jail, am now serving my own sentence with a few of them. But, other than Rhys Mansel-Jones, no, I'm not aware of any vendettas. I'm not even convinced Mansel-Jones wants me dead. He wants me to suffer, sure, but he did say death was too good for scum like me.'

'Which would explain why they attacked Teddington,' Piper mused.

'Attacked Ari?' Charlie questioned and frowned, pushing down the bile that rose in his throat. 'Who attacked her? When?'

'In the hospital. She was dehydrated and in pain because of the shoulder injury,' Carlisle explained. 'So, they put her on a drip. A bogus nurse went in and put a second dose of morphine in the drip, enough to kill.'

'Oh, that.' Charlie could breathe more easily.

'She told you about it?' Piper was frowning at him.

'That information hasn't been released,' Carlisle said. 'She was under strict instructions not to tell anyone, either.'

'She didn't tell me,' Charlie responded. 'One of the men in jail did.'

'Which one?'

'Keen. William Keen.'

Piper nodded. 'Makes sense.'

Charlie stared at him, as did Carlisle, then, the two looked to each other. This wasn't the first time they had shared common ground over the boss not telling them something. They both knew he'd get around to revealing the information in his own time.

'Turner knew too, sort of. He said she had an allergic reaction to the painkiller.'

Carlisle nodded. 'That's what we told people.'

Piper focused back on Charlie. 'Anything else?'

'Not really.' Charlie shook his head. 'Just that something very odd happened a couple of days ago. Rebecca Fry, the parole officer, had called me in to see her for a second time. The first time was weird, but this time, she said she wanted to explain she was still pushing for my parole, but if I wanted, she could help make my time inside more pleasurable.'

Piper frowned. 'How?'

'Sex!' Charlie thought it was bloody obvious.

'She openly offered you sex?'

'No, that would be career suicide for a parole officer. The first time it was a lot of innuendo, but I did wonder if I was just imagining it. But that time, she took off her cardigan and there were bruises on her arm. Finger mark bruises. Like someone had handled her roughly. The second meeting, she kept talking about when I was alone with Teddington. She asked if I enjoyed taking advantage of a woman in authority. When I said I hadn't taken advantage of anyone, she asked me if I wanted to. I thought she was talking about Teddington, but after I started questioning if she was offering something else. Now I'm pretty sure she was.'

'Are you aware of her making similar offers to any other men?'

Charlie gave him a list of three men he thought might have been involved with Fry.

The knock on the door heralded the arrival of Towers, Charlie's attorney. After that, the interview became very much a matter of record. Charlie gave one succinct description of what he had done the day Tommy died, after which Towers advised him to use 'no comment' a lot.

'Chief Inspector,' Towers said an hour later, 'it's utterly clear you have absolutely no evidence against my client and very little against the woman you allege to be his co-conspirator. At best, it's circumstantial, more likely it's harassment, because they weren't running and hiding, or conspiring, as per your conjecture after the funeral of my client's son. Now, I strongly suggest you let both my clients go.'

'I can't do that,' Piper responded. 'He's a convicted murderer, who has to remain in custody.'

'Mrs Teddington isn't.'

'She also isn't your client.'

Charlie sat back and watched the sparring, not sure which side he should be cheering on.

'Has she a lawyer of her own?'

'One will be appointed as soon as she requests one.'

'Then, I will represent her.'

'You can't,' Carlisle looked pleased to chip in.

'I assure—'

'She's already said she doesn't want you,' Charlie cut Towers off. 'She thinks we'd both be better served by separate lawyers.'

'Only,' Towers considered, 'if she gets a lawyer in the first place.' He turned to Piper. 'I want to see her, discuss her predicament.'

* * *

Charlie lay on the ledge, the thin mattress doing little to support him, stared at the ceiling, and worried about Teddington. She'd looked exhausted when they'd swapped places in and out of the cell, meekly complying with any order given. An hour had passed. Charlie was beat, but sleep was impossible. When Teddington returned, she waited until the door was locked, then she slipped over the top of him to lay at his side, as she had before.

He held her close. Apparently, they both needed a lifebuoy to survive this storm.

Chapter 29

It was Teddington flinching at the sound the door being unlocked that woke Charlie. After three years, he was used to it, and could happily sleep right through. A woman sleeping beside him shifting, however, *that* he wasn't used to. He moved his head and blinked as Teddington pushed herself up on her arms, nearly knocking him off the ledge in her rush to get away from him. He swung his legs over the edge and rubbed sleep from his eyes.

'Christ,' Teddington's groan surprised him. 'It's only five in the morning.'

Charlie was still trying to transition from asleep to awake, thinking it was odd she still had her watch, but it was a minor point in the current litany of oddities. The door opened and Piper appeared. This early was unusual, but Piper doing the collection was even more unusual.

'Follow me.'

Charlie could see Teddington looking to him, her arms crossed protectively over her chest, her lips tight flat, and her eyes wide. He turned back to Piper. 'Both of us?'

He watched Piper's expression tighten. 'Yes, both of you.'

Charlie let Teddington precede him as he moved and stretched to get the knots out of his neck and shoulders from the bad sleeping position. He followed, unsure how to read the look Piper had given him.

They were led back to the same, dimly-lit interview room, and told them to wait. Teddington took the opportunity to do a circuit of the small room, pacing to each corner before turning, her head bowed and her arms crossed.

'Ari?'

'Yeah.' She stared resolutely at the floor.

'You okay?'

'Yeah.'

'Really?'

She nodded. Having completed the circuit, she headed towards the table and took the seat she had used the day before, her arms still crossed, her brow knitted, her bottom lip between her teeth, and her eyes down. He moved over and sat beside her.

'Ari—'

'You really don't know when to shut up do you?' Her tone wasn't harsh.

'So, you are always this grumpy in the morning?' Had he really said that out loud?

Her lip came out from between her teeth. 'Only when I wake up, somehow, locked up.' She drew her lip back between her teeth.

'Don't give up hope.'

She answered that with a grunt, but said nothing else. He'd always thought she was a strong woman, but she didn't appear to be coping now. A lot of people struggled with incarceration, and it was so different from everything she was used – no, hang on – she worked in a prison … he guessed the difference was she *worked* in a prison; she locked the doors and went home. It was a very different prospect to being locked behind those doors and not going out.

The sound of the latch drew Charlie's attention, and he turned to watch, first, Piper and then, Carlisle come in. Carlisle, he knew, wasn't a fan of early mornings, and it showed. The younger man's lips were so compressed there was a white outline, his eyes tight. He was nose breathing and scowling. Charlie recognised anger when he saw it.

They entered in silence and took the seats opposite; Carlisle before Teddington, Piper in front of Charlie. Piper slid a standard buff file onto the table as he sat.

'Why did you lie to me yesterday?' Carlisle demanded of Teddington.

Charlie reared and blinked. Teddington wasn't a liar. *What*, so what did Carlisle have to be so aggressive about?

'Didn't,' she muttered without moving or looking up.

'You told me you'd done research to figure out what had killed Thomas Walters.'

'Yeah.' She was still slumped in the chair, arms crossed and staring at the table top. 'I just didn't tell you what the research involved.'

'What did the research involve?' Charlie asked, worried about Ari's apparent withdrawal.

'Reading the autopsy report,' Carlisle told him grudgingly.

Charlie turned to Teddington. 'How did you get hold of the autopsy report?'

She was frowning and not responding again.

'Ari?'

Piper drew in a breath. 'I gave it to her.' He shifted, tilting his head, frowning at her. 'Mrs Teddington, are you okay?'

She grunted; it was vaguely positive.

Piper turned to Charlie, raising his brow in mute question. All Charlie could do was shrug.

Pushing the point aside, Piper focused on Charlie. 'The evidence that exists points only to you two, and even that's circumstantial. Whoever is doing this is very good at covering tracks.'

'Yep,' Teddington said. 'It's the only answer. We need to trigger a riot.'

For a second, Charlie continued to watch Piper, who looked as surprised by the statement as he was. Carlisle's jaw had dropped.

That was when Teddington finally lifted her head and inspected the surprised faces around her.

'And I thought *Military* Intelligence was the oxymoron,' she muttered, as she unfolded her arms, using them to hold the chair as she sat up. She looked to Charlie, that spark, he was relieved to see, was back in her eye. 'I know you think I was off with the fairies, but I was trying to figure this out.' Now, she turned to Piper.

'Okay, we're all making the assumption Mansel-Jones is not only the ringleader, but also Charlie is the target. But, we've no evidence to substantiate that, so what if both assumptions are wrong?'

The three men shared a look, before directing their attention back to her.

'Okay.' Teddington sat up and splayed her fingers out on the cool surface of the table top. 'Let me go through what I've seen. To start with, things have been getting weird for a while. I'm used to working in a male-dominated area, so guys shutting up the instant I walk in is fairly normal. Generally, I just shrug it off as them talking about sport or shagging, and don't give a toss.'

Charlie straightened. He wasn't used to Teddington talking this way. She seemed to have surprised Piper and Carlisle as well, as they had mimicked his reaction.

'Thing is … the silences have changed. And there were other indicators, don't ask what because I can't actually name them. It was just a sense around the place of …' she shrugged, '"wrongness." If that's even a word.'

'It is,' Piper assured her. When the other three looked at him, he smiled slightly. 'The wife's an editor. She was complaining about it a few months ago.'

'Okay,' Teddington acknowledged, 'not sure which one of us is losing it fastest, but okay. The changes that worry me come from the PSIs that are being implemented thick and fast. There's the restriction of socialisation, and training courses, which have always been a big part of prisoner rehab, are being cancelled. At meal times, instead of the lively interaction there used to be, everyone lines up with muted conversation only …' She frowned as she said it. 'This doesn't actually sound so bad, now I say it out loud.'

'Try living with it,' Charlie grumbled.

She offered a sad smile and placed a hand over the top of his. Then, she continued, fixing her eyes on the two officers.

'Look, Tommy's dead, and frankly, you're making that investigation look like a cover up. Richmond suddenly comes into money, now, he's dead. Enzo tried to protect me, he gets shot. Richie Brett was pushed to a freak out. Everything's being reorganised, and it's obvious some of the shifts are particularly weak. The place is a powder keg just waiting to go up.'

'Are you sure this isn't just a reaction to everything you've been through?'

The scowl Teddington shot at Piper made Charlie glad he hadn't been the one to ask that question.

'If it's a personal reaction, what motivation are you going to ascribe to the others who feel the same way?'

When no answer came back, Teddington went on. 'Now, I've got some questions for you. Stanton, Mohr, Perkins and Finlay. You interviewed them. Who put them up to it?'

Charlie watched Piper's face close up for a moment, but then he saw his Adam's apple bob.

'They referred to Leo.'

'And they looked scared,' Carlisle added.

'And we still don't know who Leo is.' Teddington sighed. 'Or do you?'

Piper didn't answer, but he did ask her so many questions he made Charlie dizzy. Or maybe that was just because Teddington had yet to let go of his hand.

* * *

Charlie flexed his neck, it cracked loudly.

Teddington looked at him, her lip curled. 'Eew.'

She had gone through every piece of evidence they had, and plenty of suppositions, drawing logical conclusions. She was bright, alert, brain in full gear. In short, back to the Ariadne he knew, and – no, he couldn't go there.

Carlisle huffed and slumped. 'Does it matter?'

Teddington glared at Carlisle. His unwelcome comment came after Teddington had reported her concerns about Fry. Then, she turned to Piper. 'Can I smack him one?'

Charlie watched Piper have to school his features to stay serious. 'No.'

'Shame.' She glared at Carlisle. 'Yes, it matters. It was Robbins who had recommended Charlie for early parole and Fry's been pushing it since he got back.'

'Isn't that her job?'

Teddington shot Carlisle an "are you an idiot?" look. Then, she sighed and put her head on the table, lightly bashing her skull. 'What is it with the police? You have all these rules and regulations you have to work to.' She lifted her head, staring at Carlisle. 'The prison and probation services have the same. Fry is bending the rules. Quite possibly breaking them.'

As annoyed as Teddington obviously was, the tight line of Carlisle's jaw showed he was at a matching point. 'But, it doesn't relate to the case at hand, and none of it explains why you're predicting a riot.'

Teddington's eyes tightened, her lips nearly sneered. 'I'm a fan of The Clash.'

'You're not even a fan of the Kaiser Chiefs.'

'What?' she snapped at Piper.

'The Clash *wanted* a riot, a White Riot. It was the Kaiser Chiefs who predicted a riot.'

For a second, Teddington just stared at him. 'Editor wife?'

'Teenage son.'

Charlie reached forward, put his hand on her upper arm, guiding her back. There was all too much fire in her eyes and all for the wrong reasons. But, her eye line didn't waiver. Then, suddenly, she smiled.

'Are you always so pedantic?'

'Details are important,' Piper pointed out.

'Details are our job,' chorused Charlie and Carlisle.

Teddington looked between the two, then, back to Piper. 'I'm guessing you say that a lot.'

Piper's lips twitched into a brief, acknowledging smile.

'As for you,' Teddington growled, turning to Charlie, 'don't you start trying to control me. It's bad enough in work with Rob—' Her eyes went wide, her lips and jaw slackened, she sat back in the creaking chair. '—bins. Oh, no.'

Charlie felt his heart rate ramping up. Something was obviously clicking into place with her. Her eyes were focused elsewhere, whatever she was seeing, she wasn't enjoying the view. 'Ari?'

She swallowed. 'I don't want to believe it.'

'Believe, what?'

'I know how those forgeries got into my room.'

Charlie felt a fire building in his belly, as she told them about Robbins' apparently drunken visit. He hadn't wanted to rip Phillip Mansel-Jones apart the way he wanted to rip into Len Robbins at that moment.

'That,' Carlisle said, 'is, at best, circumstantial. Any half decent lawyer would claim you were just trying to throw suspicion off you. What motive could you possibly prescribe for him to do that?'

'Anger, jealousy, money, self-interest, coercion,' she threw back as easily. 'I can think of any number of reasons why anyone would get involved enough to do it, but Robbins will be the only one who can actually answer that question for him.'

'That's pure conjecture,' Carlisle snarled leaning forward. 'Where's your proof?'

'Where's yours? Lack of evidence isn't evidence of innocence,' Teddington threw back.

Charlie was rather impressed; most people didn't get that.

'You're grabbing for conclusions that aren't there, dragging an innocent man's name through the mud in an attempt to cover your own guilt.'

'I'm not guilty! Robbins is the only one connected to the prison whose been near my house this last month.'

'What about Sanchez?'

'He's still in hospital, you moron.'

Charlie wasn't the only one who struggled to control his amusement, though Carlisle just looked insulted.

'There are plenty of other men to consider before you start looking at the officers.' Carlisle was trying to be reasonable. 'Keen and Winehouse for a start.'

'None of whom have been anywhere near my bedroom,' Teddington insisted. 'And it's not Keen.'

'What makes you so sure?'

She glowered at Carlisle.

'William Keen,' Piper pointed out, 'was a Detective Superintendent in the Met. Everyone thought he was working wonders on his patch, crime rates down, public confidence up. Until they found out he was virtually running a protection racket. He was originally imprisoned in London, but moved down here to be closer to his only family.' Piper frowned. 'A step-sister, if I remember rightly.'

'Half-sister,' Teddington corrected, 'but close enough.'

'How do you know?'

'She is,' Piper pointed out, 'a prison officer. She has access to his file. But, it's still not Keen.'

Charlie felt his eyes narrow rather than consciously narrowing them. Piper had paused before speaking, and the look he exchanged with Teddington had been calculating on his part, wary on hers. There was some connection between Keen and Ariadne he simply wasn't getting, but it looked like Piper was.

'Point is,' Teddington supplied, 'Keen already has all the control he needs at Whitewalk.'

'Whitewalk?' Carlisle asked.

'Blackmarch,' Charlie supplied.

'Prison humour.' Teddington said. 'Not terribly funny, but it sticks.'

'If you're right about all that's gone on, why would you now be in the firing line?'

Teddington shrugged. 'It's been suggested it's because I'm "incorruptible," and quite why I find that so offensive, I do not know. But, I suspect it has something to do with the fact I lied about where I got pictures I gave Charlie. Robbins checked with Turner, and Turner confirmed he saw me speak with a crying kid on the prison steps, but I'm not sure Robbins was convinced.'

'You prepped Turner?' That surprised Charlie.

'No, it actually happened, just not the way I told Robbins. Neither he nor Turner were in a position to know that, though.'

'Still not proof.'

Teddington's eyes switched to Carlisle. It was not a pleasant look. 'That's kind of what I've been saying. There is no proof.'

'So,' Piper broke the cold exchange between Carlisle and Teddington, 'someone takes control at the prison. Tommy's killed to restrict or stop the supply of drugs, and that's being covered up. Only you,' Piper pointed to Teddington, 'wouldn't accept that, and get you,' the finger moved to Charlie, 'to investigate.'

'Allegedly, Robbins puts Charlie up for parole to get him out of the way. Richmond does something to upset the top dogs, so when the opportunity arrives with the funeral, they risk killing not only Richmond, but Sanchez, injuring you, all to make Charlie run, thereby looking guilty. Only, you get Charlie to go back, and now, Fry's trying to countermand my blocking of his parole. So all this is just to get him out of there. Is that what you're saying?'

Charlie watched Teddington; she was squirming.

'Er, possibly.'

'Now you think they want a riot at the prison?'

She swallowed. 'Yeah.'

If he was sitting the other side of the desk, Charlie wasn't sure he'd believe her.

Carlisle made a disbelieving sound. 'Your argument fails quickly.'

Teddington scowled at him. 'Where?'

'When you were made a "present." Why do something that would keep Charlie in prison, if they wanted him out?'

'Maybe they didn't want him out, they just wanted him neutralised. If Charlie had been tempted to do what he could have, he'd have been in solitary, probably for months, so it could have been Leo's way to get him out of the picture quick.'

'Why?'

'You've never worked in a prison,' she told Carlisle. 'You don't know what it's like. It's a delicate balance. Sometimes, we have to look the other way in order to maintain that balance, and it pisses a lot of us off. We're supposed to be helping, rehabilitation and containment, but most of the time, containment is about all we can do. A lot of people think we should do better, me included. But, our hands are tied.

'Liberalism, equality and "fairness,"' she added the air quotes contemptuously, 'are all great concepts, but in some circumstances, they just don't work. Plenty of officers want to be tougher on inmates, control them more tightly. What if that's what this is about? Riots not only make headlines, they can cover up deaths and bring about reforms. It's actually possible this is driven by someone's twisted idea of how to improve things.'

'Is that what you want?' Piper asked.

'Improvement, yes, but this way? Hell no! The job's tough enough as it is. Tighter control would just make it tougher.'

A frown formed on Carlisle's brow. 'Why target you?'

'A female officer at a male prison? Think about it. The Press would have a field day, well they did, or have you forgotten about the headlines when I got shot? Big debates about how far equality in employment should go have already started. I've heard people saying there shouldn't be female officers in male prisons, that it's too much of a risk, too much temptation.'

'You don't agree?'

'No,' Teddington was quite clear. 'I think lack of socialisation with females would do a hell of a lot more damage. Besides, that's only one possibility. Is there any actual evidence Mansel-Jones is in anyway involved in this?'

'No.'

Piper was emphatic, and Charlie wasn't comfortable lying to Teddington, but it wasn't his call.

'Then, the connection could be just a cover, and now Charlie's a high profile prisoner, the women love him - '

Carlisle snorted.

'No, really, they do,' Teddington assured him. 'All incoming mail has to be screened, so we know what's in his fan mail. Including, on one quite hideous occasion, a used thong.'

Charlie blinked. He hadn't received any such thing. 'Wait a second.' He decided not to think about thongs, because it just brought to mind finding Ari wearing one. 'Both Winehouse and Keen told me to look to the top. That would be Peter Jones.'

'Seriously?' Carlisle asked. 'You think a senior man, like Peter Jones, would be involved in something like this? Just coz you fell from grace don't look for it in others.'

That cut. Charlie shifted his attention to Teddington. Her face was clouded, lips compressed. This was how she'd looked earlier; this was her thinking face. He moved his eyes back to Carlisle, trying to defend the indefensible. 'Why not? Lack of evidence isn't proof of innocence.'

'He's not some scrote who came out of nowhere. He's a good man, who knows a lot of powerful people.'

'He'll need to,' Teddington spoke quietly. 'He's going into politics.'

Piper frowned, his habitual straight posture, straightened. 'You're sure?'

* * *

Charlie paced the room and scrubbed his face with both hands. He couldn't believe they were actually going to do this.

'There's still the issue of evidence,' Piper said. 'No offence, but with your interwoven history, neither of you will stand well as eyewitnesses. Whatever you try to convey, a barrister will remind the jury of your time out of jail together. We need something incontrovertible. You'll have to wear wires.'

'No way,' Teddington objected.

Charlie knew the dangers of wearing a wire, especially in a situation where fighting and torn clothing was likely. 'Why not?'

Her skin was pallid, her eyes wide, as he sat down beside her. She passed a fleeting glance over him, before focusing on the table top. 'Because, if I'm caught up in the riot, it's obvious what could happen to me, especially after the pictures Regis has been circulating.'

Charlie wasn't quick enough to control his smile.

'Oh, God, you've seen them.'

It was rather cute how she could still blush. She closed her eyes and covered her bowed head with her hands.

'I haven't,' Carlisle said.

'Apparently,' she muttered looking up, 'Regis did several drawings of me when I walked into the wing to calm Brett down.'

'So?'

'I was wearing knee-high heeled boots over tight jeans and a corset on top.'

'And they let you in?'

'They didn't know about the corset 'til I took my jacket off.'

Carlisle was beginning to get the image.

'Turner apparently confiscated those, and other images, of me and Regis's drawing equipment.'

'Didn't stop him,' Charlie advised.

She looked horrified. 'You mean he's still …?' she shuddered.

Taking a little pity on her, he shook his head. 'I had to threaten to do to him what I did to Mohr, but he stopped.'

'Good.' She nodded, then frowned. 'What did you do with the pictures?'

This time, he didn't even try to stop the grin.

'Uggh.' She looked pained, but turned back to Piper and Carlisle. 'Personal cringing aside, the obvious happens, and a wire's going to be instantly found. And that could get me killed. But it does bring something to mind – Regis is an artist who turned forger. There's a reasonable chance he's the one who forged the worksheets.'

'Possible.' Piper nodded, addressing Teddington. 'When's your next shift?'

'Thursday.' She thought about it. 'I think I'm on mornings.'

Piper questioned with a look.

'Start at seven, finish at three.'

'How long do you think Keen needs to make arrangements?'

'Depends how detailed you want him to get, but anything from a couple of hours up.'

Chapter 30

Teddington didn't want to get out of bed. This wasn't the usual, early morning lethargy; it was unusually strong. Throwing the duvet off her felt like a herculean task, but the force pinning her to the bed didn't lessen. With a groan, she grabbed her dressing gown. She was at the bathroom door when she heard the knock. She rushed bare foot to the door.

'Detective Inspector,' she greeted, pushing unbrushed hair from her eyes.

'Come in.'

The day wasn't bright, and she didn't feel so either. *Oh, the joys of getting up at half-five.*

She pointed Piper to the lounge, and carefully closed the door, not they would wake her mother. Teddington was hiding a yawn, as she followed Piper into the room.

'Are you ready for this?' Piper asked.

'No,' she said, hugging her dressing gown to her. 'The alarm went off ten minutes ago. I just didn't want to get out of bed.'

'We all have mornings like that.' He smiled. 'Here.'

Curious as to what the folded paper bag contained, Teddington took what she was offered and looked inside. She saw tissue paper.

'It's your wire,' Piper explained as she reached in and pushed the tissue aside. 'A 24 hour battery, so more than enough life.'

She looked at the thing and blinked. She blinked again. Nothing had changed. 'It's a bra,' she said and checked the label. 'In my size.' She looked up at Piper. 'How – Oh, I don't want to know.'

Alone in her room, she dressed. She'd brushed her teeth, and her hair, but it was still loose and kept falling over her face. She felt surprisingly vulnerable.

As she pulled on the works shirt, she looked at the bra again. Apparently, there was a microphone hidden under one pretty white flower and the battery under another. Teddington couldn't see the electronics, but she actually liked the design. That it came from Piper was a bit of worry.

'Surely all this is going to pick up is my heartbeat,' she said as she returned to the lounge.

Piper smiled at her.

'I can't say we won't hear it, but software will filter that out at our end.'

She kept her head down and stared at the floor, doing everything she knew to control the fear, but waging a losing battle. Her heart was slamming, her eyes burning with unshed tears. There was a simple fact she couldn't ignore any longer. 'I'm not sure I can do this.' She dare not meet Piper's eye.

Then, she felt the weight of his hand on her shoulder. 'You'll be fine. Charlie will look out for you. Keen will look out for you. By the time my men are pulled in, they will have been briefed to look for you first, too.'

'That's great,' she agreed. 'By the time your guys are pulled in, I'll be dead. Or wishing I was.'

* * *

Teddington stood on landing one, her hands gripping the rail so tight, her knuckles had lost their colour. She'd already spoken to Keen, and he was on the case, making arrangements. Breakfast was being served, and Keen had actually descended to get his own food, which felt odd. Keen didn't usually come down for service; he had runners to go get him everything he needed, but all that had changed under the new regime. *Can we ever get the old regime back? Do we want it?*

At least they'd spoken, and Keen was going to do his bit. He hadn't told her when or where, or who. She didn't want to know, either. That was her condition – she needed to be as surprised as everyone else.

She felt sick.

She pushed herself upright from the banister and turned right, walking the long way around, deliberately avoiding going past Charlie's cell. Each step was calculated. She controlled her breathing and schooled herself not to react when she saw Charlie step up to the door of his cell. The huge man leaned on the frame, his arms crossed, as he watched her.

Unable to stop herself, Teddington looked back at him. There was no expression in his regard, but she felt her stomach twist all the same. What they were doing was dangerous. Her heart fluttered uncomfortably, and the knots in her stomach ratcheted tighter, suggesting retching was in her immediate future. Looking away from Charlie, she could see three of her colleagues; who she couldn't see was Robbins.

Anywhere.

Shivering, she headed towards the laundry room, nodding to a few people in acknowledgement as she passed. It was one of the warmest places in the jail.

Entering the area, she was surprised to see no one there. There was usually someone in there; that was why it was on the rounds at meal times, to make sure anyone in there didn't miss out.

Sighing, she sank down on the bench and closed her eyes. It was no good. She couldn't keep this up. She was going to have to go back on the sick and take up the service's offer of counselling. She needed to get her head right, if she was going to carry on with this job, and she *did* want to carry on with the job.

The pain split across the back of her head, and despite the instant fear forcing her eyes open, the world was swirling and dimming.

She was already falling, when the second blow landed.

* * *

Charlie couldn't settle to read. The sensation of an approaching storm was no longer just in his head, but in the certain knowledge, at some point today, there would be a riot. Putting the book aside, he went to the open door. There were more bodies out than usual. Still, not as many as there should be – as there used to be – but the place didn't seem quite so abandoned. Looking down, he could see Will Norman and Chris Roberts on the main floor, talking to two inmates. He wondered if they were even aware of the other small knots of men moving into position around them. Never more than four per knot, they were, nevertheless, looking increasingly cancerous. He stepped back into his room, a last bit of preparation. Then, to check out the way the landscape was forming, Charlie adjusted the polo neck of his top and stepped out to do a circuit of the landing. He was just passing the stairs, as Robbins came up.

He nodded in acknowledgement and got a sneer for his trouble, as the other man moved to the steps up to the second landing.

'Where's Teddington?'

Robbins turned only briefly, delivered another scowl. 'Working.'

Charlie hadn't been asking him, but apparently, Robbins had better hearing than he'd realised. The voice in Charlie's ear wasn't exactly helpful. 'Still in C-Wing,' the voice said. 'Not getting an audio feed right now.'

'Equipment?' This time he kept his voice as low as possible that the mic would pick up, but no one else.

'No, she's just somewhere quiet.'

Charlie considered that, as he continued to pace. There weren't that many places she could be quiet, without one of the guys talking to her. He looked around the floor, the two landings, and the men lurking. He saw another man appear, this one followed by Fry. There were folders under her arm, and he looked pleased with himself – someone would be getting out soon.

Charlie stopped. The surprising sight of Keen following Robbins did little to ease the tension tightening his shoulders. He returned to the stairs as they were coming down, able to gather nothing from the two blank expressions as they passed him. Given what Keen had to do, this was a worrying development.

The library.

There was no rule about silence in the library, but those who used it generally did keep quiet. In the wake of Keen's departure, Charlie headed down to the ground floor. The tension here was palpable. Hearing his footsteps, Norman turned, as Charlie took the direct line towards the library.

'What are you up to, Bell?'

'Going to the library,' he said easily. 'Where's Teddington? She's usually visible through most of her shift.'

Norman looked uncomfortable. Charlie got the impression of ignorance rather than malice. 'Wherever she is, I'm sure she's doing her job, and she doesn't need your help.'

Charlie shrugged off the comment, and he just hoped the man was right. It didn't take long to establish she wasn't in the library – it wasn't the biggest room ever. But not only was she not there, *no one* was. He paused in the quiet space, and wondered where to look next.

Pain jolted his head forward, felt like it was splitting his skull, though he suspected it was only his scalp that gave way. He staggered forward, then stumbled in trying to turn towards his assailant. Assailants, he noted as he turned, only just raising his arm in time to defend his head from another crashing blow from what looked like a chair leg. A leg wielded by Paul, Winehouse's bodyguard.

Though dizzy, Charlie saw enough to know however good he was at looking after himself, three-to-one weren't good odds with their weaponry. He had to even the playing field a little. The three men surrounded him, and blows started from all angles. With a war cry roar, he butted into Paul and slammed him backwards, smashing him bodily against the book shelves and driving the air from Paul in one sudden grunt. The shelves wobbled but held, as Charlie grabbed the chair leg, his hand wrapping around the squared wood, twisting and yanking it from Paul's grasp.

Fearing attack from behind, Charlie used the momentum of the yank to carry him around, swinging the chair leg against the cheekbone of the nearest of the men – Hart. Blood spurted, as the man was knocked sideways; the contact with bone reverberated through the groaning wood to Charlie's hand. Hart went straight down. *Too scared of the officers not to attack an inmate on order.* But, a glass jaw was no use in a fight.

Repositioning the leg with a mid-length grip, Charlie propelled it blindly backwards, pumping it into Paul's stomach, just as he started to recover. The third attacker, had clearly been hanging back, but was now just spoiling for a fight, going in fast and hard. Rough fists were brought into heavy contact with Charlie's already sore head.

Charlie was faster and stronger; he forced himself to draw up to full height, leaving his chest and neck vulnerable but his seven-inch advantage over his opponent ensured his head was no longer a viable target. As the man concentrated on keeping a boxer's fighting stance, Charlie brought the wood up like a baseball bat. The boxer saw the blow coming and blocked it fast enough, but was utterly unprepared for the kick that blew out his right leading knee. Charlie followed through, smashing the chair leg down over the man's head, the wood shattering at the weakened spot where the hole had been cut to support the cross bar of the frame.

One down, still and quiet, probably out, but Paul and Hart were recovering, stumbling towards him. Hart was closer and the easier target; Charlie grabbed him by the back of his collar, unerringly forcing his knee and Hart's chin into direct and jolting contact. Hart groaned but didn't quit, his arms flailing widely, so Charlie dragged him half to his feet, gritting his teeth against the blows pounding on his side, stomach, and back. Hart had help from Paul, now. He kept moving, Paul's grasp on his shirt slowing him down but failing to prevent him from running Hart into the nearest wall.

Two down.

He turned in time to see Paul's punch coming and ducked out the way. His own fist connected with the bottom of the man's ribs, not placed right to do any damage. They moved around the space, in almost balletic form, both having been trained to fight by years of experience. The Marquess of Queensberry would despair at the wilful disregard of his rules; this fight was dirty and staying that way. Evenly matched, they swapped blow for blow, but Charlie channelled every ounce of disgust for Paul and worry for Teddington into one final mighty blow that connected hard with Paul's jaw. The man went down.

Charlie dragged in a breath, blinking away the blood dripping into his eye from a split brow. He could see Paul was conscious but defeated. He grabbed him by the shirt, rattling Paul's teeth, as he made him focus bleary eyes which were already starting to swell shut.

'Who told you to do this?'

'Fuck you.'

Charlie jabbed a finger into the man's left eye.

Paul screamed, clapping his hand over it. 'Bastard!'

'Who gave the order?'

When he didn't answer, Charlie pressed his fingers between Paul's until he felt eyelid. 'Unless you want this out, tell me what's going on.'

'I was to be paid when I get out.'

'For what?'

'Killing you.'

'Why?'

'Don't care. Just asked if I wanted to do it.'

'Who asked?' Charlie shook the man when he didn't answer. 'Who was paying you, Paul?'

'Fish Hook Freddy,' he growled.

Fish Hook Freddy – a robber he'd put away some years ago and a known associate of Mansel-Jones. Staring down at Paul's bludgeoned and ruined face, Charlie almost took pity on the man.

'Why now?'

Paul raised his hand. An ineffectual barrier, but the sign of surrender Charlie was looking for. 'They said to do it when the riot happened. We just weren't expecting it today. We didn't have the weapons we'd planned on.'

Only now did the background sound of fighting and shouting and alarms properly penetrate Charlie's consciousness.

'When were you told there was to be a riot?'

'Weeks ago.'

So long before their little plan had been hatched. 'Who by?' Charlie could see the man's pupil dilating. He was running out of time, they all were. He shook Paul. 'WHO BY?'

'Leo.' It was a weak response.

'Who is Leo?'

But, it no longer mattered how much he shook Paul, the man was unconscious. Leaving him to slump, Charlie stood up. The library door was open. He could hear the fighting, smell something burning. Teddington was somewhere in this, and he had to protect her. As he moved off, he put his fingertips to his throat, pulling the polo neck up and re-covering the mike. Then dragged out the bottom edge of the shirt to wipe blood off his face.

'You got all that right?'

'Yep,' said the voice in his ear. 'All utterly inadmissible, of course, but we got it.'

Chapter 31

S he was lost in a world of hurt.

She tried moving, but her hands were tied.

Teddington didn't know what annoyed her more. The pain, the restriction, or that she was getting used to both. She opened her eyes. It didn't help much. She couldn't focus, but was glad to have any sight at all, given that she'd been hit at the back of the head – the optical processing area of the brain.

Before trying to move again, she mentally assessed her position. Killer headache, probably concussion, but miraculously still sitting. Hands tied, but not cuffed; no cold metal around her wrists, only bunched cotton, knotted hard enough to keep a press of something cold against the sides of her fists. Her wrists were tied to something roughly the level of her head – her forehead had been resting on her forearm. Other aches she recognised as scrapes and bruises, nothing serious. She still had her clothes, *something to be grateful for*. It meant the wire was still in place. *Please God it's working*. The scrapes and bruising were probably the result of rough handling when being moved from the laundry to here. Wherever here was.

Blinking again, she finally moved her head.

'Oh good, you're back with us.'

She recognised the human shape moving towards her from the voice. 'Winehouse?'

'Yes, sweetie, it's me.'

Teddington felt his hand on her arm and tried to move away, but there was nowhere to go, and he clamped his hands around her, yanking her arm up so that she had to rise to her feet. She felt vulnerable being tied to a three-inch thick iron downpipe, but more so because her back was to the main part of the room, and she was aware of others there – she just couldn't see who. She could barely focus on Winehouse.

'Where the hell are we?' She looked around, but with restricted sight, she couldn't make it out.

'Maintenance Room,' Winehouse provided.

'I don't hear any motors. Must be Room Three.' Because it was largely just dead space, and the one furthest from the open room of the wing. She hoped Piper got the message. 'Out of the way, defensible.' And accessible from more than just C-Wing.

His hands had moved off her arm, and were running over her shoulders, her back. An involuntary shudder rippled through her. His hands moved around her middle, and there was nowhere for her to go as he moved up behind her, pressing his front to her back.

'There are contradictory reports about you, Teddy-bare,' he whispered in her ear, his mouth too close, his breath fetid. 'Some say you're letting Bell fuck you at every turn, others say you're frigid and don't let anyone touch you. Not even the saintly Sanchez.'

They were so close, she couldn't miss he had an erection. Her heart was hammering, fear washed her cold. Her throat was dry. 'I haven't had sex with any man since my divorce,' she admitted. And right now, she was regretting that. She wished she'd had the sense to enjoy her life more. Bell was sexy as all get out, and surprisingly considerate. He'd have been a gentle and, she was sure, a good lover. She should have opened herself to him when she had the chance. Chances were now, she wouldn't live long enough to even see him again.

'Well, you're going to today,' Winehouse promised her. 'There are plenty of men in here waiting to get their share of your cunt.' His hand moved down, grabbing her crotch. 'And I'm going to let them. Payment and favours, you know how this place works.'

'I know how you work,' she threw back at him. 'You're more interested in fucking Bell than I am.'

'Necrophilia isn't my thing.'

Necro – *No!*

She felt her breath catch in her throat. *Charlie dead?* She didn't want to believe it, didn't want to think it.

Then, she didn't have time to think, new hands were on her, shaping and squeezing her bottom. Smaller hands, softer hands. A woman's hands. She jerked away, twisted as best she could to put her back against the wall. Fry looked like a pixelated picture through her hazy vision, but it was no question that it was her.

'Rebecca?'

'Ariadne.'

She felt Fry's hands on her breasts. Teddington tried twisting, but that didn't help. Rebecca moved closer again, and as she pressed her lips against hers, all Teddington could do was clamp her jaw and resist.

'What the hell do you think you're doing?!' Teddington demanded once Fry broke the contact.

'Checking out the competition.'

Teddington held her breath and gritted her teeth, as Fry's fingers dug painfully into her breasts.

'Mine are better.'

Scowling was as much a function of her inability to focus as the loathing she felt. 'Good for you.'

The slap on her thigh had her catching her breath. 'Be superior, bitch. You'll still goin' get gangbanged.'

Teddington shuddered, as Fry licked up her cheek, from chin to ear, where she sucked on her earlobe before whispering, 'I almost envy you all the cock you're going t' get.'

Fry finally moved away.

Sickened at the prospect, Teddington managed to wipe the woman's spit from her jaw against her shoulder as she hoped Piper was listening because she was going to need a rescue, possibly very soon. She blinked again and looked around, her vision was starting to clear.

There were six other people in the room. Malkin was sitting on the floor, looked like his hands and feet were tied, Runt stood over him with something in his hand. She assumed it was a shiv.

She double-checked it was Runt. Knowing he was Keen's man, she could only assume he was here as a double agent, at least she hoped he was. He might just protect her. If he wasn't, she was going to die horribly.

'Why are you doing this?' she demanded of Fry, as the woman draped herself over Winehouse's shoulder.

'For the thrill.'

That was a worryingly simple answer.

'The thrill of what? Pissing me off?'

Fry's laugh really was unpleasant. 'Oh, Ariadne, you really aren't all that important. I enjoy a good fuck, and there's nothing better for that than a desperate man, and there are plenty of those in here.'

All Teddington could do was stare at the woman. 'So, what? The better they do you, the quicker they get out?'

Fry shrugged and smiled. 'The really good ones stay in, but then they tend not to mind.'

Sickened, Teddington turned her head in the other direction and made out Holden standing by Robbins. Holden was a surprise. She hadn't known he'd aligned himself with either side. Robbins was beside another pipe, like her, so she assumed he was tied up too. Nothing was very clear.

Swallowing, she focused, as much as she could, on Winehouse. She hated the way Fry was making her feel, watching the rise and fall of her chest too closely. It made her skin crawl. Teddington knew panic wouldn't help. But, that didn't mean she wasn't feeling it. 'Okay, Winehouse. What's this really all about?'

He didn't move, she wasn't sure he was going to answer at all. 'It's about control, of course,' he told her. 'Everything is always about control.'

'What do you want to control, Winehouse?'

'The prison,' he spoke as if it was the most obvious thing in the world. 'I'm going to be the only one with power in here. I'm going to control who gets what, and when.'

She couldn't believe what she was hearing. 'All this, just to oust Keen?'

Winehouse laughed at that. 'The old man's losing his grip, anyway. He's not got that many years left in him. If a riot proves too much for an old man's heart, then who's going to mourn?'

She knew she would. The idea of losing both Keen and Charlie cut right through her. She had only one hope; the confessions she'd promised Piper. 'So, you've been behind it all, all along. *You* killed Tommy Walters.'

He smiled, at least, she thought it was meant to be a smile. 'Not quite.'

She tried again. 'You ordered the kill?'

'Of course. How else do you think the dibber could be used?' He moved over to stand beside her, bending slightly to put his face a hair's breadth from hers. 'A dibber you so conveniently took back, and put your fingerprints all over.'

'Who actually did it?'

'I did.'

She looked over at Robbins. He seemed to be proud of the admission. That fact he'd actually answered her was problematic. But, he wasn't the one in charge. She needed the organ grinder and turned back to Winehouse.

'I'm not getting out of here, am I?'

He smiled; it was chilling. 'The only thing in your future is a rough gangbang. What makes you think you'll want to survive what some of those men have in store for you?'

Teddington knew she was in trouble, and this wasn't worth the pay off. Especially not if she didn't get it all.

'Did you enjoy letting Bell fuck you?' As he spoke, Winehouse started unbuttoning her blouse.

She decided not to answer.

'You know, I'm not a bad man. Bell's death is your fault.'

She swallowed, as he parted the fabric, revealing the bra Piper had given her. *Please, God, don't let him try to remove that.* Instead, he was pulling the shirt from her trousers.

'How …' She had to lick her lips, before she could finish the question. 'How is that my fault?'

'He was supposed to be an easy parole. I didn't see any reason to kill him. I just wanted him out, off the wing. If he'd taken his present, he'd have been in solitary, but you screwed all that up. It was you who signed his death warrant when you brought him back. Turn to face the wall.'

Terrified of what he would do if she did, as much as she was terrified of what he'd do if she didn't, she turned. When she heard the snick of a blade being drawn open, she couldn't help looking around. He had opened a three-inch penknife.

The cold blade touched the back of her neck, efficiently slicing through the shirt collar. The sawing action pushed the tip repeatedly into her skin. She angled her head forward to avoid the worst, but she could feel she was being cut. Only small nicks, but enough to bleed and sting. And worse was on the way. She felt sick. Once the collar gave, there was a short catch for the shoulder yoke seam, then the material was shredded from her body till the useless sleeves just hung at her wrists. She desperately tried to concentrate.

'Did you enjoy it?'

'Stripping you?' he asked, as his hands went around her waist. She reared, though she had nowhere to go, as he grabbed her crotch again.

'Killing Bell?' she grit her teeth, as he rubbed her. It was quite possibly the least sexy thing she'd ever experienced.

'Paul did it. He's been looking forward to it. In fact,' Winehouse gave a smile that chilled Teddington to the core, 'that's something I *should* thank you for. If you hadn't brought him back, I wouldn't be several thousand richer right now. That'll come in handy when I get out.'

Teddington stared at him. It was a riot. The police should be all over the place by now, Gold Command called in from Headquarters. 'What makes you think you'll ever get out now?'

'Because I'm not the public face of this joyous event. That's Houghton.'

Houghton? Teddington frowned. She didn't know much about him other than he was a convert to Islam that was more vocal than most about prisoners' rights. 'Houghton is in B-Wing.'

Again, with the chilling smile. 'I know. Once things kicked off here, word went through the kitchen, and the other two wings joined in. We've been waiting for this for weeks. Brett was supposed to kick it off, but you and your bloody boyfriend put a stop to that.'

'So, you're going to play on racial stereotypes and religious fervour to cover up the fact that you're a petty thief with power issues.'

The air rushed from her lungs when he punched her full force in the kidney. Through blinding pain, she could feel him reaching for her belt buckle.

'Don't get ahead of yourself,' Runt warned.

'Leo won't like it,' Robbins added.

Teddington peered at him, now able to see he wasn't tied, just lounging against the other pipe, not tied to it, as she was. She hadn't been cold before, but now, she was, frozen by her fear and confusion.

Winehouse wasn't Leo – she was pretty sure of that. He'd been waiting on a call to riot, same as everyone else. Which left Robbins. But, if Robbins was talking about Leo in the third person, then he couldn't be Leo either.

So who was?

* * *

'She's in Maintenance Room Three.'

The voice in Charlie's ear sounded worried. Not a good sign. Steeling himself, Charlie ran out of the library and into the fray, literally having to fight his way across the floor. Someone was throwing burning toilet paper from the upper balconies, other burning items, too. With odd adrenalin-fuelled clarity, he looked up to recognise one burning cover, *The Eyre Affair.* Teddington had given him that. In pointless retribution, he punched the approaching rioter, feeling and hearing the man's nose break. He needed keys to get past the gates to maintenance, and saw a flash of white shirt in a knot of bodies to his left. Officer Roberts.

Roberts was doing his best; his Taser was on the floor, as was a twitching body Charlie couldn't be bothered to identify. But, now, he was caught between three men, one behind holding him, while the others pummelled, punches and kicks landing with devastating effect.

Charlie waded across.

Grabbing the nearest thug by the back of the shirt, he sent him bumping into his mate, so they ricocheted off each other and onto the floor. The second they were out of his way, Charlie stepped forward and landed another direct punch into the face of the guy holding Roberts. Had this been a video game, he'd have gained bonus points for that; though, had this been a video game, he wouldn't feel like he just broke a knuckle.

As Roberts' captor buckled, Charlie grabbed the front of Roberts' shirt and pulled him out of the fight towards the edge of the floor.

'Please don't hurt me.'

Charlie didn't even glance at the sniveller. 'If I wanted you hurt, I'd've left you where you were.' Charlie's long stride took them past most of the fighting to the quiet of the outskirts.

'What do you want?' Roberts was obviously terrified.

'Your keys.'

'Another breakout attempt? Now?' Keen's voice.

Charlie half turned his head. 'Teddington's trapped in Maintenance Room Three. I need his keys to get through the gates.'

'You need more than that,' Roberts told him, his hand shaking, as he unbuckled the keys from his belt and handed them over. 'You'll need the password.'

'Which is?'

'I don't know.'

Charlie shook him.

'I don't know!' The way he was crying suggested he was telling the truth.

'I do.' Keen's hand stilled Charlie's arm, as he reached back to punch Roberts.

Charlie dropped his hold and faced Keen, pulling himself up short when he saw Carlisle a step behind. The DS's hair wasn't styled, he hadn't shaved, and he wore a faded t-shirt over stained jeans and falling-apart track shoes. Nothing like the suit seen here before. Effective anonymity.

Keen took a moment to step back into the main body of the floor. 'Enough!'

His voice echoed like a drill sergeant's, and enough of the men froze, showing the riot was officially over. Keen led the way towards the Maintenance Rooms. Hardly able to believe he was letting the old man go first, Charlie followed in his wake, Carlisle moving up beside him. Some sick corner of his mind pointed out they were in rank order. Shame two of them weren't in the force anymore.

'How did you get in?' he whispered over his shoulder to Carlisle. 'Deal with the Governor?'

'No,' he snapped, and Charlie realised they'd hardly make deals with a suspect. The Governor was, by now, most definitely a suspect. Carlisle went on. 'With Turner. Once he heard Teddington might be in trouble, he was on board.'

'A lot of people around here care what happens to her,' Keen said under his breath, slowing them as they neared the corridor to the Maintenance Rooms.

Charlie nodded. 'She's a good woman.'

Keen peered back at Charlie. 'Yeah, too good for you. Keep your distance.'

* * *

Teddington clenched her teeth. Winehouse had only listened to Runt and Robbins long enough to remove her belt. It was what he did after that that had her gritting her teeth. She'd had no idea how much one inch of plastic could hurt. So far Winehouse had lashed her twice, and she'd managed not to scream, but she couldn't hold in the tears. She let them fall, burn down her cheeks, as the welts burned across her back, and she leaned into the wall.

'Enough.'

The word left her cold. She felt her knees shaking, as she lowered herself to the floor. She knew that voice. There was hush in the room, and she dared to look up and see the Guv pacing over to Winehouse.

'When I said you should have a little fun,' he spoke with quiet calm command, 'I meant rape the bitch, not torture her. This has to look real. Like she was killed in the riot.'

She saw him turn to Fry and sneer. Teddington couldn't quite believe the pleasure on Fry's face when he slapped her. 'Having fun yet?'

'Want more.'

'There are men in the corridor,' he told her quietly. 'They want cunt. You'll do. Strip and get out there.'

Teddington was shocked by what she was hearing. They may have discussed Fry was a bit of a sex maniac, but she hadn't realised just how far into self-degradation the other woman was.

And just like that, Fry stripped naked and walked silently from the room, heading eagerly towards her own gangbanging. Teddington had no idea what kind of psychosis led to that sort of behaviour, but at this point, she didn't care. She twisted on the ground, moving her back against the wall.

Now, Governor Peter Jones came to stand in front of her.

'You'll have to forgive me for not getting up, sir.' She poured all her loathing into that last word.

'And there's your problem, Teddington. Just too damn smug.'

'Too damn smart for you.'

'I'm not the one tied to the ironmongery, about to become a tragic statistic of another terrorist plot.'

* * *

Charlie moved Keen back, positioning himself nearer to the juncture of the corridor. He needed to know what was going on. A-wing was off to the right, through a set of gates. Usually, they were locked, now, they stood open. Five meters to his left was another gate, this was closed and probably locked, but now, he had to keys. Beyond them, according to the voice in his ear, and just out of sight, was the door to MR3. That was where he needed to be.

Between him and MR3 was not just the gate, but two heavy-set thugs with vicious blades. One weapon was a meat cleaver, so the other was probably from the kitchen, too. They lounged until someone approached, then jumped to attention. Charlie didn't want to believe he'd seen who he'd seen, but he wasn't overly surprised.

Pulling back, he leaned against the wall, looked heavenward, and swore.

'Well?' Carlisle kept the harsh demand low.

'Peter Jones.'

'The Governor?' Carlisle needed confirmation. 'The rot really does go all the way to the top.'

'Well, it couldn't stop with Robbins,' Keen muttered, 'but I wasn't sure Jones was smart enough for all this.'

Charlie risked popping his head around the corner again. This time, he watched the men's attention caught by something else, one of them put his hand straight to his crotch. A naked woman walked into view. Charlie was so stunned, it took him a moment to realise it was Rebecca Fry. He could hear other men's voices, as Fry moved towards them. She ran her hand over their groins, whispered something, then the three of them moved out of sight. When the way was clear, Charlie walked up to the gate, which took a moment to unlock. 'We're through,' he whispered. 'Maintenance Room Three ahead.'

'Negative.'

He greeted that command with a restrained expletive.

* * *

'I'm screwed,' Teddington allowed, finding herself surprisingly calm. What was left to fear? Charlie was dead, she would be soon. As far as she could tell, Piper couldn't get here in time. 'All of my rescues are gone. Winehouse is doing this to control a wing. What's your excuse?'

'Reformation.' Jones crouched down before her. 'If you'd been susceptible, you would have been an asset to the team, but you and Malkin over there are going to have to be the sacrificial lambs to the greater good.'

'Are you Leo?' she asked. 'Odd choice for a code name.'

'It's not a code name,' he told her easily. 'It's my name. Leonard Peter Jones.'

She frowned. 'That's not on the records, or your degree certificates.'

He shrugged; it clearly wasn't important to him. 'I didn't like the name in school, so had it removed by deed poll.'

The more she learned about the man, the odder he became. 'What about Bell?' she asked. 'Winehouse said he was dead.'

'He is,' Winehouse was overly happy to tell her.

She didn't dare look at the smug bastard. Accepting she was going to die was somehow easier than accepting Charlie already had. 'What's your cover story there?'

Jones shrugged. 'He's a bent cop. Plenty of people in here want him dead. He's just another insignificant, who'll get lost along the way.'

If Jones thought that, he hadn't understood what he'd read in the papers or in Charlie's fan mail. 'So you just agreed to have him killed, because you could?'

'I'm not the one bank-rolling that.'

'Who is?'

'What's it to you?'

She laughed. 'Nothing, but I'm wondering if it's something to do with Mansel-Jones. You're a Jones,' she said. 'If you'd lie about your first name, why not lie about your surname. Are you really a Mansel-Jones?'

Teddington swallowed as she peered up at the Guv. She had to be careful how she played this. Piper would be listening. With luck, his men were already calming the wings. 'Bell killed a Mansel-Jones. Was he family? Is this some kind of petty revenge?'

'Petty revenge!' Jones spat in her face with the roar. 'Bell appointed himself judge, jury, and executioner.'

'Of a murderous -'

Her words were cut off by his punch. This time, she did yell. Her head snapped back against the wall, her vision swam. She felt her lip split, felt her teeth rattle, tasted her own blood. She wondered if the dentist would see her tomorrow, then laughed hysterically at the ridiculous notion she would get to see tomorrow.

* * *

The voice in Charlie's ear repeated. 'Negative. Do not proceed to MR3. We are moving in at the front of the building, locking this thing down, but you hold back. The Honey,' not the most imaginative code name ever, 'has Papa Bear, and the story is unfolding.'

Listening to orders from someone who wasn't risking his life was never easy for those on the front line, but Charlie knew a confession would go a long way to securing a conviction.

But, it was *Teddington's* life on the line here. Wanting to rush in to save her was one thing, but he had to balance that against the risk of barrelling in like a fool and getting her killed. He bit his lip, and moved back to the adjoining corridor. From there, they could hear the movements of other men, the sounds of sex.

Carlisle stepped around him, eyeing the commotion going on where Fry had been taken, thankfully out of the path to MR3. 'Jesus,' he said, when he moved back. 'Three of them, one of her.'

Then, there was the sound of slapping, and Fry cried out. Charlie moved back to the gate, some masochistic tendency demanding he know what was going on. Fry telling them to stop, begging them to stop, was a waste of breath. She'd sacrificed herself, and now, she was paying the price, as they forced themselves inside her in every way possible. She was screaming, and the pain was real.

'You want some of this?' one of the men looked up and asked him. Thankfully, these men weren't from C-Wing. They didn't know who he was.

A third man Charlie hadn't seen before had moved in to grab Fry's head, gripping her jaw, stopping the screaming, gagging her with his cock.

'No thanks,' Charlie muttered. 'You done with that knife?' He pointed to the carving knife the man was carrying.

For a second the man just looked at it dumb, then handed it over. 'Don't need it for this one.'

Charlie nearly forgot to reach for it, he was so stunned at the agreement, but he stepped through the gate and took the weapon before turning away. With no more guards to stop him, he walked towards Maintenance Room Three, trying to block out the sounds of the desperate struggle behind him.

'There's nothing you could do,' he heard Keen tell Carlisle, stopping him from getting distracted by the rape. When he checked over his shoulder, Charlie saw Carlisle looked as wretched as he felt.

It was true, but that truth didn't lessen the self-loathing of leaving a woman to such a fate.

* * *

Teddington looked up at Jones. If he liked submissive women, maybe that was something that she should think about. 'Why me?' she asked plaintively.

'Why not?' Jones asked. 'You made yourself a target.'

'You sent Robbins to my home that night. To plant those papers?'

'Setting you up was so easy. I know you were taken to the station and held overnight. I can't believe they didn't charge you.'

'Just shows how useless that Piper bloke is,' Robbins said from behind them.

'Who did them?' Teddington asked. 'Who forged it all?'

'Regis.'

She hung her head.

'You should be proud.'

Jones, put his hand beneath her chin, and made her look at him, even as his thumb pressed the split on her lip. Apparently, he liked causing pain. She was thankful he didn't appear to be carrying a weapon.

'You are to be instrumental in the sweeping reforms that will ensure no officer ever again has to be afraid to walk a landing for fear of shiv or anal rape.'

The manic gleam in his eye scared Teddington more than his words.

'I'm going to make this world better. No more over-crowding, no more under staffing. Just a nice, quiet, steady life.'

That would be good, but she didn't believe it possible. 'How?'

'Politics.'

She'd forgotten in all this that he was running for election somewhere.

He pressed one last time on her damaged lip, then stood and puffed up like a peacock. Strutted his stuff. 'It will take time, but I'll introduce a new Private Members Bill. Bring back the death sentence for multiple convictions. That'll reduce prisoner numbers.'

Teddington stared at him. The man was utterly delusional. The British public might be getting more radical, but they weren't *that* radical. *Were they?*

'We, the humble honest tax payer, won't have to continually pay for these institutionalised scumbags to live in luxury.'

Luxury? She swallowed, wondering when Jones had last looked into the cells, when Jones had last walked in the real world, full stop. She kept her voice level. 'This is nuts.'

'We've more of a supportive following than you think. These hard times have made for harder people,' Jones went on. 'Tougher immigration laws are already going through, more will follow, and soon – thanks to your sacrifice – the campaign for the return of the death sentence will start. It'll all be in your honour, and, of course, memory. Ariadne's Law, perhaps? Winehouse, a knife. I want to kill this bitch.'

Chapter 32

'Go!' the voice in his ear virtually screamed. 'Get her out!' Charlie smashed the door in with one good kick. It hadn't been locked, and the movement drew all attention to him, as he strode into the room.

Winehouse was to his right with Runt and Malkin, to his left, Holden and Robbins. And directly in front, Jones rose from where he knelt before Teddington. Holden and Robbins lunged at Charlie, while Jones was hauling Teddington to her feet. Runt raised his arm, and Holden, who'd got closer to Charlie than Robbins, jerked to the ticking sound, howled, and fell to the floor in a twitching, trouser-wetting heap. Charlie was glad the big man was apparently on his side.

Robbins only hesitated long enough to jump over the body, as he leapt towards Charlie, who side-stepped, pulling the blade across Robbins' front. He felt the warmth of another man's blood on his hands, but Robbins was neither down nor out. Carlisle grabbed him, twisting him round. In Charlie's peripheral vision, he saw Keen facing Winehouse; the younger man looked momentarily cocky, then an unexpectedly accurate karate kick chopped him down to size. Runt moved over and stamped on Winehouse's head, before grabbing his hands behind his back and producing a zip tie to bind the hands of the Garden Godfather. Charlie left Carlisle to slug it out with Robbins, and twisted to Jones.

He was faced with Teddington.

Her shirt had been reduced to cuffs hanging at her wrists, which were tied with torn sheeting to the down pipe. Her lip was split. Because of her angle to the pipe, Jones couldn't quite hold her flat in front of him, and the awkward angle displayed welts across her back. Charlie saw the belt on the floor. Red coloured his vision, but now wasn't the time for anger. He had to be calm, and get that damn knife away from her jugular.

'What does it take to get rid of you?' Jones demanded. His left hand was around Teddington's neck holding her up against him, nearly choking her, as his right hand moved down to slice the binding at her wrists.

Charlie knew she was looking at him, her eyes were wide, but he didn't dare meet her gaze - that might just push him places he couldn't afford to go.

'What's the plan, Jones?' he asked, as the Guv finally released the material around Teddington's wrists.

The knife was instantly back at her neck as his left hand moved to span her waist and cleave her back to his chest, the knife biting against the soft, white flesh of her throat. 'I'm going to walk out of here, and you're going to let me.'

Teddington was keeping her eyes down, dealing with this as best she could.

'Not happening,' Charlie snarled.

'Let it happen,' the voice in his ear told him.

Jones laughed, cold and humourless. 'I know you've no hesitation to kill. What makes you sure I'm not the same?'

'Step aside, Bell.'

He couldn't believe he was hearing it, or who from, but now, Teddington looked up at him. Tear tracks marked her cheeks, but her eyes were blazing with anger. If she was at all afraid, it didn't show. All he could do was stare at her.

'Step,' she grated, 'aside.'

'Do it.'

Piper's voice in his ear took him back to past operations.

'I step aside,' Charlie spoke ostensibly to Teddington, but the words were as much for Piper, 'you won't live long after he's out of this room.'

'Step aside!'

He heard the instruction in stereo. Swallowing the lump in his throat, Charlie stepped aside.

He couldn't look at her directly, as Jones stepped forward, which was why he had no idea just what Teddington did to make Jones grunt in surprise and pain. Then, she was stepping backwards, the pair of them falling over Holden's prone body.

The air was forced from Jones' lungs, as Teddington's weight landed squarely on him. Then Teddington was over, straddling Jones, the hand with the knife held away from her. Charlie kicked out, his toe connecting with Jones' hand, the knife went sailing away. Jones tried to scramble out from under her, but Teddington was quicker, her fear and anger overtaking any other consideration, as she took Jones' head in both hands and smashed it repeatedly into the concrete of the floor.

Jones was weaponless, and he flailed at Teddington. A few of his punches would have landed, but Keen was dragging her off. Charlie grabbed one of Jones' arms, Runt was on the other, then, they flipped Jones over. Runt knelt on the struggling man's back, as he produced another zip tie to bind Jones' hands.

Charlie turned to Teddington, but she was hugging and being hugged by Keen.

The noise in the corridor had reduced to a woman sobbing, the men around her spent and quiet.

'They're on their way.'

Charlie turned to Carlisle, not understanding. 'What?'

'C-Wing is quiet. Piper's team are coming in. The prison officers have taken back A-Wing and B is being controlled.'

Carlisle told the room the details Charlie was being fed into his own ear. Charlie wasn't paying attention to either voice. Mostly all he could do was stare at Teddington, wondering why she was so comfortable being held by Keen. The old man's hand was stroking her hair, holding her tight, yet mindful of her injuries.

'Here.' Malkin had taken off his own shirt revealing a white vest. He placed the shirt around Teddington's shoulders.

Charlie moved in closer.

Teddington lifted her head off Keen's shoulder and moved away, struggling to unbutton her ruined cuffs, before wincing as she pulled Malkin's shirt around her. Malkin had moved away, a last moment for revenge as he kicked Jones in the side. The way he groaned suggested the action hurt Malkin as much as Jones.

Teddington glanced up as Charlie moved in closer, she was trying to button the shirt, but her hands were shaking too much to close. Seeing Charlie's confusion, she explained, keeping her voice down. 'Charlie,' she said, as Keen took over buttoning the shirt, 'meet my Uncle Billy,'

Charlie felt his jaw slacken. *How had he missed that?*

Chapter 33

Charlie didn't bother reading the newspaper reports about the riot. Start to finish was less than an hour. Keen had never given up as much control as Jones and Winehouse had believed, and he had pulled the riot back as easily as he had started it.

The whole thing was a mess. No one came out looking good, not the prison, parole, or police services.

Jones had been vilified, but that was nothing less than he deserved. There was to be a full public enquiry.

Fry was being portrayed as a poor, hapless victim. She was still alive, her body was recovering, though it was questionable if her mind would.

Houghton from B-Wing, still calling himself Mohammed, had gained an unwelcome reputation and an increased following. It wasn't going to last; Keen was seeing to that.

That was two months ago. Now, the prison was back to normal; people were circulating again, talking was above a hush, the backchat and the interactions, both good and bad, had returned. The balance of power had settled again. There were new rules, there were new guards on duty, and the population was showing the due respect. As things should be.

Sanchez had returned to work, and Teddington was due to. And, in two hours, Charlie would be gone. He was fully packed, an archive box crammed full of all his stuff. On the top, he placed the books she had sent.

The Sacred Art of Stealing.

If only it was that easy.

* * *

Teddington was watching the monitors. Having been back in work for a month, she'd done what she could to repair the records on Prism, but she wouldn't be trusting anything she read in there for a while.

She knew what today was, but she hadn't said anything to anyone. She was still being watched too closely. Jones might be gone, but the stain on her record wasn't. At least no one had mentioned her relationship to Keen; if they did, one of them would have to move on, and she didn't want that, because as the employee, she was the one who'd failed to report the fact, so she would be the one moved on. Probably to the unemployment line. Where she was now, yes, she had to prove herself all over again, but she wasn't starting from scratch. Added to that, if the acting Governor didn't become the new Governor, then she was going to have to go through the whole process a third time with whoever did fill that post. The future was looking like hard work, she didn't need to make it harder.

It wasn't going to be easy, but she was determined to show she was good at her job, because she was determined to keep her job.

'Okay?'

She looked up at Malkin, who had transferred to monitoring since the riot; a vicious kick to the pelvis hadn't done him any favours. Long term, he'd be fine, but was in no fit state to be on the floor just yet. 'Fine, thanks,' she smiled.

'Aren't you going to see him off?'

She lowered her eyes.

'The Guv's not in,' Malkin pointed out. 'And even if he was, I don't think he'd mind.'

She chewed her lip. She wanted to, but ...

* * *

'Time to go.'

Charlie looked up to see Sanchez in the doorway. He stood, took up the box, and followed the man out. He was processed and told it was hoped he was never seen in HMP Blackmarch again.

'She'll show you out,' Sanchez said casually before he walked away.

Charlie turned and saw Teddington, in uniform, standing behind him.

'This way please, Mr Bell.'

'When did you come back?'

'A month ago,' she said, as she led him out. 'I've been working in the observation room.'

'Avoiding me?'

They were at the door now. 'Yes.' She turned to face him. 'Acting Governor Turner felt it would be best for all concerned, if we were kept apart. Screws and cons, and all that.'

'Then, why are you here now?'

'Acting Governor Turner isn't in.'

She smiled, but it looked kind of sad.

'Besides, I booked you in, remember? Seems somehow right I see you out.'

She opened the door, one step, and he was free. He leaned out, breathing deeply of the clear air. It was the same air he had been breathing for the last three and a half years, yet somehow, on that side of the wall, it felt fresher. He glanced at the pub opposite; strangely, The Lock Up held no appeal.

'Goodbye, Mr Bell.'

What else was there to say? Archive box held before him, he crossed the threshold, then paused. Could he?

'You're not a "con" anymore,' he heard Teddington's voice behind him. 'Aren't you eager to get on with your life as a free man?'

Not without you.

But, that was a ridiculous thought. *Screws and cons, and all that.* Resolutely facing forward, he crossed the small courtyard to leave the enclave of the prison. At that final barrier, he could resist no more and turned back.

Teddington was still there.

She raised her hand, pointed through the exit, and then opened her hand, thumb across the flat of her palm, fingers up and spread.

Go and goodbye, what more was there? Then, she was gone.

Charlie turned, glanced at the pub, then headed out to an uncertain future.

* * *

Teddington closed the door, and allowed herself a small smile. Charlie Bell was a free man. Nothing any boss could slap her wrist for. And, at four o'clock, she'd be seeing him in the pub across the road.

THE END

Author Acknowledgements

Thank you to the army of people that march with the author. The family, friends, writers, readers and critics, that have kept me going through the ups and downs of getting to publication. Special thanks for Tony Fyler and Sam Kruit for being tough critics and pointing out the problems, while encouraging me to carry on. Especially to Sam who pointed out the intricacies of prison officer life, and to the policeman who didn't want to be named, for pulling his hair out on my police procedure and still not slapping me when I deliberately got it wrong (apparently that's assault - lucky for me ☺). A special thanks to all the lovely team at Bloodhound Books, who saved Charlie from being eternally imprisoned on my hard drive.

And thank you to any reader who has got this far. I hope you enjoyed the journey.